Advertising has us chasing cars and clothes, working jobs we hate so we can buy shit we don't need.
—*FIGHT CLUB* MOVIE, SCREENPLAY BY JIM UHLS,
DIRECTED BY DAVID FINCHER,
NOVEL BY CHUCK PALAHNIUK

AT FIRST SIGHT

A Novel of Obsession

STEPHEN J. CANNELL

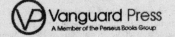

Vanguard Press
A Member of the Perseus Books Group

Copyright © 2008 by Stephen J. Cannell

Hardcover edition first published in 2008 by Vanguard Press, a member of the Perseus Books Group

Mass market edition first published in 2009 by Vanguard Press

"FIGHT CLUB" © 1999 Twentieth Century Fox Film Corporation, Monarchy Enterprises S.a.r.l. and Regency Entertainment (USA), Inc. Written by Jim Uhls. All rights reserved.

Designed by Lisa Kreinbrink
Set in 12-pt Minion

The Library of Congress has catalogued the hardcover edition as follows:

Cannell, Stephen J.
    At first sight : a novel of obsession / Stephen J. Cannell.
        p.   cm.
    ISBN 978-1-59315-482-0 (alk. paper)
    1. Married people—Fiction.   2. Hawaii—Fiction.   3. Adultery—Fiction.
4. Domestic fiction.   5. Psychological fiction.   I. Title.
PS3553.A4995A96   2008
813'.54—dc22

                                                                        2008019464

Mass market ISBN: 978-1-59315-516-2

Vanguard Press books are available at special discounts for bulk purchases in the U.S. by corporations, institutions, and other organizations. For more information, please contact the Special Markets Department at the Perseus Books Group, 2300 Chestnut Street, Suite 200, Philadelphia, PA 19103, or call (800) 810-4145, ext. 5000, or e-mail special.markets@perseusbooks.com.

10   9   8   7   6   5   4   3   2

This one is for my "Hollywood son,"
Mario Van Peebles, friend, workmate, and inspiration.

ACKNOWLEDGMENTS

SEVERAL YEARS AGO, I HAD AN ACTING JOB ON A
Steven Seagal movie that was shooting in Berlin. Long
hours of waiting in dressing rooms during other shoots had
taught me that it is always a good idea to have some fresh
reading material from authors I admire on hand. Since I
was scheduled to be on the film for a month, and since Germany in November can be very wet and bleak, I had a suitcase full of my favorite novelists.

Among them was a book written by Andrew Klavan entitled *Man and Wife*. I thoroughly enjoyed that novel. I
thought it a very unique tale told from a fresh perspective.
I have always felt that Andrew took big chances with his
books, pulling them off beautifully. I began to wonder if I
shouldn't be trying to push a little harder and take more
chances myself. I love writing my Shane Scully mysteries, so
this feeling wasn't because of any loss of excitement with
those books; it was more about trying to pull off something
totally different. I resolved that when I got back to L.A. I

would find time among my other assignments to write my "unique" novel. I already knew what the book should be about because I'd had the initial idea for *At First Sight* three years before. Whenever I tried to explain my vision to those involved with my career, they would beg me not to write it. But then nobody but me could really see what was inside my head. I decided to avoid more discussion and just write it on spec.

The novel poured out. I had a rough draft in around two months.

So here it is. The book nobody wanted me to write.

I hope you like it.

If you don't, send your letters to Andrew Klavan. Even though we've never discussed it, Drew's work inspired this effort.

CHICK

CHAPTER

LET'S START WITH THE ESSENTIALS.

My name is Chick Best. Chick is short for Charles. I'm five-feet ten-inches tall and I weigh one-hundred-eighty-five pounds . . . okay, if you want to be picky, one-ninety-four—but I'm about to lose fifteen. I'm starting the Atkins Diet any day now. I'm fifty-five years old and I live in Los Angeles. My mother was named Celeste, my father was Chick Sr., so that means I was Chick Jr., until Dad checked off the ride on the Hollywood Freeway during my sophomore year in high school. He fell asleep and ran his silver Jag into a bridge abutment. People said he didn't deserve to die . . . but he was drunk, so who else can you blame? Rim shot. Cue the strings. I'll deal with that whole mess later.

That's the birth and genealogy stuff.

I guess I should also give you a quick, personal history. Just the headlines though—I promise not to drag it out.

After Dad died, I lived with my mother and my grandmother. They tried to see me through my wild years, through high school and junior college. For me, this period was pretty much a drug haze—my chocolate-chip period. Instant Zen, the Great White Light, a Sunshine Ticket to oblivion. My excuse is it was the seventies. If you didn't get high, you didn't get laid. I lost my student deferment from City College because I discovered drugs, got wasted, and got an incomplete in Western Civ. Missed the final. Uncle Sam was on me like puke on a wino. The chronology there was unremarkable, but classic: unlucky lottery number, induction, last acid trip, first train trip, Fort Ord, and then six months of pure, ass-kicking misery. I resurfaced half a year later as a buck private and ammo-humper for the good ol' USA with a one-way ticket to Vietnam.

But I never saw combat. In fact, I didn't even see Vietnam. I became a REMF, which in the military stands for Rear Echelon Motherfucker. Here's the quick story on that. My dad had been a talent agent before he kamikazied out on the Hollywood Freeway. He booked comedians you never heard of into clubs you'd never go to. Dad's old partner had a connection to Bob Hope's USO Tour. He pulled a few strings and fixed it so I could stay stateside. I ended up in the chairborne infantry booking USO shows for the armed forces—a post I defended valiantly, holding off talent managers and agents from my fifth-floor office on Wilshire Boulevard in L.A. My joke back then was—I find comics that kill, instead of Commies to kill.

After I got out of the service I spent a kick-ass year on Maui. Sex, drugs, rock 'n' roll. Of course, I've fired up my last blunt. I'm not beaming up on thrusters or bang anymore either. My acid flashbacks are finally history. I'm clean as the Board of Health and am now absolutely against drugs, which I've said at least two thousand times to my sixteen-year-old daughter, Melissa, who listens to these lectures with amused indifference, which is the same expression she wears at traffic court.

In the past two years Melissa has discovered more drugs than Dow Chemical. Every time I do my "Life Is a Choice" speech, she starts rolling her eyes like I'm the biggest excuse for bad behavior since Sigmund Freud.

I should probably add that I'm having a huge problem with Melissa right now. Of course it didn't help that my wife, Evelyn, let it drop last Christmas that I was busted and did six months for dealing Pakalolo in Hawaii after Nam. I'll get back to all this later, but for now, suffice it to say, that after I got out of the Hawaiian prison, I came back to the mainland and started my business career, mostly retail. I got married in 1990 to Evelyn, my current and only wife, and we had our first and only child, Melissa, a year later. For the past twelve years, I've been running my own Internet company in L.A.

That's the quick history . . . short and sweet, like I promised. There's more, but for now, let's move on.

This story begins in January. My wife, my daughter, and I arrived at the Four Seasons on Maui to vacation during the week between Christmas and New Year's. I love that hotel. We go every December. Everybody knows my name there. You walk around and it's, "Hello, Mr. Best," or, "Nice to have you back, Mr. Best." Makes you feel important.

The only thing I don't like about the Four Seasons at New Year's is it's a magnet for A-type personalities. You see them out on the beach doing mortal combat over sun chairs.

They have these cabanas at the pool. Strange as it may seem, there's a sort of pecking order that comes with who gets which one. There are three or four that are on the high ground and command a view of both the beach and the main pool. These have become sought-after sunspots. People scheme and fight for these locations. Personally, I could give less of a shit about being in a cabana. But with my wife, Evelyn, it's a life-or-death situation. She's got to have one. If I fail to secure her favorite, it's some kind of cosmic confirmation of my worthlessness as a provider.

I used to be able to score the right location for a hundred bucks up-front. A little palm grease and a pool boy would set me up for the week. But that was five years ago. Things have changed. Hollywood discovered the hotel. With all the Beverly Hills A-List power players, actors, agents, and directors, you have to grab a flat sword and shed blood to get one of these silly little sun tents. Now on arrival I'm paying five hundred to the pool guy, and that only buys me a place at the starting line for one week. If I can get down there early enough, and edge the competition, it's ours. Great. Except one of us has to get up at four in the morning to beat the rush and secure it.

I've tried to tell Evelyn that it's nuts to make Melissa get up that early and sit in the cabana till we get there, and it's become World War III with the kid every time we ask, but Evelyn loves her power cabana. She preens and struts when we get one. You can see all this in her body language.

As long as we're on my wife's body, let me take a moment to describe it. Evelyn's got a killer shape. I'm not kidding here. It's a Gold's Gym trophy exhibit. Tight ass, cut abs, sculpted delts. We invested thirty Gs last year in some silicone. The results are staggering. From the neck down, my wife looks like Ms. Fitness USA, but in the past decade, her face has become pinched and angry. It almost seems as if her eyes have grown a few millimeters closer together each year. Her mouth is always curved down at the edges, angry and mean like a killer bass about to hit a water bug. Evelyn's face has become a constant mask of disapproval. For a while I wondered if it might be "roid rage." I thought her trainer might be slipping her some gym juice to get all those impressive body cuts. But now, I think she's just naturally pissed off and unhappy.

Why should she be pissed, you might ask? She has everything: a house in Beverly Hills on Elm, in the really exclusive six-hundred block. She has a no-limit Amex Black Card, a Mercedes, a power cabana. She has *moi*. I don't get it either. Okay, she says she's mad because I've changed, and I guess to some extent I have.

The past few years haven't been pretty for me. As I mentioned, I run an Internet company, and if you'll permit a little egotism, it's quite a bit more than just some online flea market. I'm a dot-com wizard. At least that's what *Wired* magazine called me in an article on start-up phenoms that they wrote a few years ago.

My company's called bestmarket.com. A play on my name. What it is is an Internet sales site for CDs and DVDs. Order online and your friendly FedEx man will deliver the movie or music CD of your choice within twenty-four hours. I started this company in 1996 and for the first four or five years had the DVD-CD Internet field pretty much to myself. I was going strong when Amazon, Netflix, and about half a dozen other better-financed companies jumped on my idea. With all the competition, I've been getting pretty badly shredded for the past several years. My bankers have all grown dorsal fins.

The week before we left for Hawaii, I was hanging by a thread. Couldn't borrow any money, couldn't stock enough inventory. I subcontract my product from major studios and record companies. I used to get all my merchandise on consignment deals, but because of my money problems, the entertainment companies I was interfacing with all thought I was on the verge of going broke. They started refusing to let me sell their stuff on consignment, forcing me to buy the product, stock it, then mark it up for my service. Because of the current banking environment, the business was quickly strapped for cash, and soon we didn't have enough of what our online buyers wanted in stock. We ran a survey and found that if our customers couldn't get the titles they requested once or twice, even our preferred shoppers stopped hitting the website. That's my sad story.

So I was bleeding from the ears when we got to Hawaii, but my wife didn't give me a moment's rest. She's become the Queen of American Express. I'm afraid if I ever go to their national headquarters in Fort Lauderdale, there'll be a marble statue of Evelyn out front, abs and delts flexed, Amex Black Card at port arms.

Anyway, that was our happy little family the day we hit the Four Seasons, December 26th, the day this all started.

I had just begun breakfast with Evelyn the morning after we arrived. We were in the open restaurant on the second level of the hotel. The palms swayed in a gentle breeze. Turquoise water glistened, the smell of tropical flowers wafted. You get the idea—Paradise. My wife was wearing a skimpy top with a see-through sarong tied around her butt-floss thong, giving the hotel guests and staff a great look at her buns of steel. Her abs were rippling, advertising hours of physical dedication. As we ate, Evelyn was analyzing the other female guests, criticizing their flabby waistlines.

"Lookit that cow. She should never wear a two-piece. Doesn't she own a mirror?"

I was nodding and trying to stay out of the line of fire. Evelyn's always on me about my body. Okay, I'll admit, I've picked up a pound or two, but I'm killing myself at bestmarket.com, and I'm still losing ground. I eat and drink a little more than I used to—so shoot me.

"You really oughta get into that weight room, Chick. I can have Mickey D set you up with a routine. He could fax it over here and we could get the guy in there to help you through it."

I was back in the squirrel cage running for my life. Mickey D was Mickey DePolina, Evelyn's personal trainer. I loathe Mickey D. Here's the story on that guy: He shows up at our house every day at 5:30 P.M. He used to be Mr. Burbank or Mr. Bell Gardens, I can't remember which—trapezius muscles that slope down his neck like a cobra's hood, abs and shoulders that won't quit, but with the IQ and vocabulary of a tractor salesman.

After he arrives, the two of them wide-arm their way down to the private gym I have in the basement and go at it. I use this term cautiously, because I think he's screwing her. It started while I was out of town doing the road show, trying to raise money to take bestmarket.com public. No proof. I don't have Polaroids or anything, just a guess. So far, I haven't said anything, but if you want the honest truth, I'm close to the end of my rope with this marriage. It was okay when the business was strong. I could hide out down at the office. People were kissing my ass. But now, with the company in shambles and money running low, I'm completely out of ass-kissers and feeling a whole lot less charitable. Why should I put up with this? But for some reason, I do. I keep my mouth shut. I soldier on.

After breakfast I decided to go down to the cabana and relieve my scowling daughter so she could go upstairs and do her morning line of blow. Just kidding.

I found her lying on the chair listening to her music. Another term I use cautiously. She's into some kind of alternative techno-synth that sounds to me like a guy squirming on a vinyl chair making balloon animals. But she's deep into this music, and to further piss me off, has started punching holes in her body. She has ten pierces. Her dedication to her new alternative lifestyle knows no limits. Over the past eighteen months it has become almost impossible to get my daughter through an airport metal detector.

Melissa felt my shadow and looked up, her face wrinkling as if she just smelled something foul.

"Already?" she said. Sarcasm.

"Sorry. Your mother overslept."

"Jesus. I hate Hawaii. I hate this fucking hotel, I hate these phony people, I hate coming down here at 4 fucking A.M. every morning." Melissa, expressing herself. "What's wrong with a regular pool chair, for God's sake? What makes this dumb-ass tent so almighty fucking precious?"

"Your mother likes it . . . and stop swearing."

I should add that Melissa has purple hair. It looks simply hideous. She's got her mother's killer body, but with fewer cuts because Mickey D hasn't been able to convince her to start lifting yet. She's round-faced but mean-looking. Her eyes never smile.

She swung off the chaise longue and gathered up her things.

She looked angry enough to break a window. She's not above something like that, either. When she was ten, the first year we came here, she became enraged because we sent her to her room. She locked the door and threw golf balls at the guests from our seventh-floor balcony. They called us into the manager's office and told us if we didn't control her, we'd have to leave the hotel. Humiliating.

"Where are you going?" My version of parental concern.

"Gonna call Big Mac," she snarled.

A word here about Big Mac. His name is Bud McKenna. He's about six-five, two-sixty, and is the current president of the Devil's Disciples, a Southern California motorcycle gang. This guy is her boyfriend in L.A., and he is way the hell too old for Melissa. He's in his mid-twenties and scares the hell out of me. I think Melissa picked him because she knew I would hate him on sight and wouldn't be able to do a thing about it. He's violent and unpredictable and has tattoos that threaten your life, like B2K, which means "born to kill," or D4H, which is "death for hire." The guy's a homicidal nutcase—an animal.

I believe that, like most of these bikers, he's in the crystal meth business. I can't prove it, but he is always taking her for rides on his Harley up Angeles Crest Highway. It's been in the papers that the sheriff was trying to catch a bunch of crystal cookers brewing blue meth and chicken powder in their double-wides parked up in the mountains. It didn't take Stephen Hawking to see the connection. I'd been watching Melissa, trying to spot any personality changes, which might occur if she switches from pot and coke to crystal meth. But since she only has two moods anyway—pissed-off and about-to-be-furious, it's hard to tell. Being the father of a sixteen-year-old is no damn fun.

Melissa turned a few heads as she did her purple-haired stripper walk around the pool and disappeared into the lobby.

After she was gone, I lay down on the cabana pool chair and tried to shake off my daily bout with lethargy. Over the past year lethargy has become a regular part of my mornings, right along with acid reflux and deep depression.

I looked out across the pool, and that's when I saw *her*. That's when this whole thing started. Her vibe shot across the expanse of pool decking and grass and grabbed me so hard that my body shook. I let out a lungful of air and made a gushing sigh. My stomach flopped and my fingers and toes started curling. It was that powerful, that visceral.

I know . . . I know. I can hear what you're thinking. You're thinking, bullshit. But unless you've actually experienced it, you couldn't possibly understand what I'm talking about.

When I saw her, even from twenty or thirty yards away—when I felt that metaphysical projection lodge in my heart like one of Cupid's arrows—I knew I would never be the same.

In that second, with that brief glance, my whole life changed at first sight.

CHAPTER

2

PART OF ME STILL REJECTS THIS AS IMPOSSIBLE. But the proof of these feelings is right here, in these words I'm writing. Because, as you will see if you keep reading, the downstream events which followed this seminal moment ruined everything.

To begin with, she was beautiful. Not a gym-trained beauty, like my wife, but soft and subtle. There was something warm and forgiving in the vibe she sent me. She wasn't wearing a dental-floss thong, like Evelyn always did. This was a modest two-piece swimsuit. But her flawless skin and sun-kissed complexion were sexier to me, by far, than anything Evelyn had accomplished with hours of grunt work under Mickey D's supervision, pounding out reps in our basement.

She was just coming out of the pool, shiny black hair wet and pasted back against her head, her natural beauty radiant, without benefit of makeup or jewelry. Long legs . . .

slender arms, and a mouth that . . . well, it defied description. Okay . . . I'll use my feeble skills and try. Happiness lurked in both corners. Full lips, but no collagen, no artificial enhancements, just slightly pouty but without a trace of petulance. How's that? Her eyes were blue . . . not just the blue of azure skies or clear crystal lakes, but the intense blue that bespeaks intellectual honesty and purity of soul—that kind of blue.

I can already hear you laughing, because you're right—how could I know of her intellectual honesty? I hadn't even said one word to her yet. But trust me here, some things defy the norm. Some things are transcendental. I just knew.

I sat in my wife's power cabana while she was in the gym pumping up, getting ready for her first grand entrance—her first cartilage-popping pool strut—and watched this remarkable creature. I fantasized what it would be like to possess such a beauty. But you must understand that it wasn't lust alone that fueled these thoughts. Okay, there was some lust, I'll admit; but what I was experiencing was . . . well, it was also deeply spiritual. There was a communion of souls here, a connection deeper than anything I had ever felt before, and, I remind you again, this was with somebody I had yet to speak to. But I knew when I did speak to her she would be everything I'd hoped for, and more. Don't ask me how I knew this. I can't tell you. I just knew.

For at least two hours, I sat and watched, trying not to be obvious about it. She caught me once, and I looked away, my ears turning red. My face felt thick, as if it belonged to someone else. I got up, walked to the pool concession, holding my stomach in like a fucking idiot, and bought a pair of large sunglasses. I went back the long way around to my power cabana. I put the glasses on a little crooked, so I could pretend to read my book, but I was really just looking at her.

Then I had a very uncharacteristic moment—a very un-Chick-like thought. I wondered if she knew that only very important people got issued these high-ground cabanas. No kidding, that's what I thought. I was that fucked up.

About ten o'clock, disaster struck.

A man came down from the hotel and sat in the pool chair next to her. Husband? Boyfriend? I didn't know. She wasn't wearing a wedding ring. I'd already checked that. But he had one, so he was married. But who was he? Her secret lover? No. She wouldn't date another woman's husband. She was too well-adjusted, too pure. I already knew this about her. I know, I know, this sounds like a verse in a Barry Manilow song or the flap copy on a Danielle Steel novel. Silly. But I knew. I could feel it.

I watched in dismay and anger as they held hands and kissed. They swam in the pool together; they laughed at each other's jokes. I forced myself to stop looking at her for a minute and take inventory of this asshole who had joined her.

The problem here was the guy was gorgeous, younger and much better looking than me . . . fit, but not gym-fit. He had an athlete's build, teeth square and straight as a row of tombstones—shiny and white as a porcelain toilet—curly copper hair and a strong hero's jaw. I hated him. I wanted to vomit.

Then Evelyn saved me from further tragic comparison as she plopped down next to me. I'd missed her grand entrance, but she didn't mention it because she was already angry about the cabana.

"This isn't the one," she growled. "The best cabana is that one over there." She pointed with a muscular arm at another tent that maybe, if you had a calibrated altimeter and a topographical survey map, you could prove was a foot or two higher than the one we were in. I'm not kidding. These are the things Evelyn worries about.

"Honey, Melissa couldn't . . . "

"Don't gimme any more Melissa b.s. That girl just sleeps and eats. You ask her to do one damn thing, it's worse than a root canal. She wants to be paid for sitting down here. Ridiculous. After all we do for her we're supposed to pay her for helping us out? She knows which cabana I want. This is just her bitchy way of getting back at me. How many times have I discussed it?"

It went on like that for almost ten minutes. I had learned years ago not to fight with Evelyn because she is an emotional terrorist. You take her on, she escalates the battle way past ground you're prepared to defend. She's capable of throwing an ashtray or a drink in public. I hate public confrontations. Public anger conveys weakness. My father raised me to show no weakness—no vulnerability. Good advice until you get sloshed and pile your fucking Jag into a bridge abutment. In case you're some kind of amateur psychologist, I'll cop to it now. I've got some major abandonment issues over Dad's death, but we'll get to that later.

"Y'know, I've been thinking . . . " I said. "Maybe I will ask Mickey D to fax over a workout routine." Me, searching for a safer topic.

That shut her up. "Really? You'll start weight training?"

"Yeah, I think I should tighten up this stomach a little, work on the old pecs, whatever . . . "

"No kidding?" I really had Evelyn's attention now. She stared at me hard, studying me, using the look she wore when picking out diamonds. "You're serious? You're not kidding?"

"As serious as Robert Schuller interviewing Pat Robertson on the *Hour of Power*," I quipped halfheartedly.

So I spent the afternoon in the gym with Mickey D's workout regimen and a twenty-year-old kid named Brian. Sit-ups, flies, dead lifts—two hours of torture. Two hours spent getting the old bod tuned up and ready for what would come next.

You see, I already knew I had to meet her.

CHAPTER

3

THE NEXT DAY STARTED OUT DISASTROUSLY. TO begin with, I'd overdone it in the workout center. My body felt like I had gone ten rounds with Mike Tyson, taking every shot to the solar plexus. Getting out of bed was like peeling a stuck bandage off a dry scab.

The hot shower didn't even begin to hit it. I was in agony. I canceled Brian—told him I'd be back tomorrow. Then I waved off breakfast with Evelyn and went down to face Melissa.

She was asleep in the right cabana, the higher one. It sat on the top of a landscaped berm, which was fashioned like a huge pork chop and wrapped around one end of the pool. The berm was wide at the end where we were, but it stretched back toward the hotel along a narrowing ridge. Before waking Melissa, I looked at the loser tent we had occupied the day before. No doubt about it, this was high ground—a lofty

Olympian peak. I surveyed our old digs, where a fat woman and a man with the worst toupee in Hawaii lay, thinking they had scored the best location. But they were losers—hotel indigents. We had the primo spot. I had climbed one or two perilous feet to reach this glittering social peak. Evelyn and I had finally become pool-area royalty. Valhalla.

Melissa opened her eyes and looked at me. "Happy?" More sarcasm.

"Delirious," I said.

She grabbed her stuff and got up. That was it for this morning's discourse. Melissa was out of patience. She had a meager supply. But who can blame her? It was nuts getting up at 4 A.M. just to snag one of these dumb things.

I watched her rolling, sexy walk; watched the lechers by the pool sneaking looks at my barely pubescent daughter. As far as I was concerned, they were all candidates for the Mann Act.

I waited until Melissa was gone. Then I sat and scanned the area, looking for my goddess, holding my breath, so that when I spotted her I wouldn't lose it, gasping and sighing like a busted windbag, making the same hopeless gushing sound I'd made when I spotted her yesterday.

And that was the second disaster.

She wasn't there.

I left my stuff in the chair, then got up and walked all over the grounds. I asked one of the pool boys if the ladies' room was empty: a tough question for a mid-fifties guy to ask, but I cleaned up the moment by adding that I was looking for my wife.

He smiled and said, "Yes, Mr. Best, it's empty."

I looked around. I waited. Then fear overtook me. What if my goddess and Mr. Tidy Bowl had left? What if their vacation was over? What if I'd never see her again?

When I got back to the tent, my stuff had been moved and there was a thirty-five-year-old, wide-shouldered asshole wearing a CSI: Miami baseball cap occupying my cabana. His skinny, big-breasted squeeze was sprawled in the pool chair beside him.

"This is my spot," I told the guy. He was big—huge actually. I'm beginning to suspect that a lot of guests at this hotel must be on steroids. Maybe Brian gives shots. This guy had shredded arms and a rippling six-pack. I haven't got the time to work up a set of abs like that. I've got a business to run. His face was crafty but pockmarked. He and Evelyn would look perfect together on a Gold's Gym poster—"The Anabolic Workout." He glared at me with mean, dangerous eyes.

"It isn't your cabana," he said. "It's mine."

"My stuff was in it. I had my book, my sunglasses . . . my radio. It was all on the towel right here."

The guy smiled a lazy, sweet smile. "I think you're mistaken."

"My daughter got up at 4 A.M. to secure this cabana. I just came down."

"Nobody was here when I sat down. I think that's your stuff over there." He pointed to my things piled on a nearby table, while his wife, or secretary, or whoever the lounging cupcake in the string bikini was, just stared, holding her hand up to shade her eyes, squinting at me like I was dirt that blew in under the door.

"Look, this is my cabana," I said, turning up the volume, putting a little more bass into the mix.

"Don't make this into something you can't deal with," the muscle-head in my pool chair said softly.

"Are you threatening me? Is this a threat? Are you suggesting violence?" I was outraged.

"Get the fuck away from me," the man said, softly. Only now, he sat up. Shit, a monster!

So, there you have the gist of it. Me, standing there with a body that already felt like the home stretch at Hollywood Park, him looking like Bluto in a TV-show ball cap. Normally I don't back down, but this morning, with everything else, I just decided to let him have the cabana . . . but not before giving this bastard a good parting shot.

"You haven't heard the last of this," I whimpered. Shit. More and more, I was beginning to act and sound like a total pussy.

Next I had to take on Evelyn. I caught her as she came out of the hotel and tried to convince her that we should go into Lahaina and shop, but she wanted sun. Then I said, "Let's rent a catamaran." Anything to keep her from seeing I'd lost her power position by the pool.

But no, she wanted the cabana. Then, shrewdness born from years of pool-chair infighting crossed her narrow features. "Who's guarding our place?" she wisely asked.

"Uh, well . . . I lost the cabana," I finally admitted.

I won't go into a play-by-play of what happened next, but let me say here that it wasn't pretty, and it did absolutely nothing for my self-esteem.

We ended up playing golf. Evelyn was pissed, but her anger gave her an extra twenty yards off the tee. She beat me easily.

The only great thing that happened on the golf course occurred when we got back to the caddy shack to turn in our shoes, rented cart, and golf clubs. Actually, it was more than just great—it was miraculous. Because, you see, she was standing there—my dream woman and the curly-haired, athletic asshole with the perfect teeth. They were also returning their rented equipment.

"Great course," I said to her as she was passing to leave.

"What?" she said, turning. *God, up close she was even more breathtaking.*

"Great golf course," I repeated.

"Yes, it is." She turned and left with the handsome man.

Our initial contact—our first conversation. Okay, okay . . . I know . . . not much, I agree. But at least we had exchanged words. I would give you some kind of glowing description of her tonal quality if I could, but to be perfectly frank, I was so shaken, and she had said so little, I didn't even remember what her voice sounded like. I was that gone . . . that out of it . . . that completely in love.

CHAPTER 4

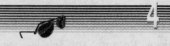

I CAME UP WITH MY PLAN — DEVIOUS, BUT CLEVER.

It was pretty obvious to me that I would never get anywhere just sidling up to her with some dumb opening line about the weather, or how great the hotel was. My approach demanded subtlety.

I may not be a dot-com wizard anymore, but I still remember how to secure an important account.

Rule number one in the sales manual: If you can't get to the client, get to the client's spouse.

I made my move.

The next morning he was standing at the bar getting drinks, his brown, muscled shoulders massive . . . his coppery hair in sun-lightened ringlets. He smelled of aftershave. Minty. I choked down my envy and moved up next to him.

"That's a great course, that Blue Course," I said. Before you ask, let me explain. There are three world-class golf courses at the Four Seasons Resort: the Blue, Gold, and Emerald. We'd all been on the Blue Course yesterday afternoon.

"Yeah, sure is," he said, then turned to the bartender. "Give me an extra cherry in the Mai Tai. My wife loves maraschinos."

My heart clutched. *His wife* . . . This unworthy asshole was actually married to her. I was immediately in free fall. My vision blurred and dizziness descended, covering me like emotional Saran Wrap.

I can just hear you saying, "Give it a rest, Chick. Back up. What on earth do you think you're doing?" And you're right, of course. It was insane. But I had already lost control. I was already on the road to self-destruction.

"The Blue Course is a little easy, though," I continued through my psychic pain. "I'm thinking of trying the Gold tomorrow." The Gold Course was acknowledged as the toughest of the three.

He turned and smiled at me. The guy had a killer smile—perfect ivory—a fucking box of Chicklets. "I played the Gold two days ago," he said. "The Gold's the best course, but the fairways are narrow. My wife shanks every other shot, so she prefers the Blue. Otherwise I'd spend all my time in the brush looking for her ball."

"That was her you were playing with yesterday?" I asked, desperately hoping that they weren't married . . . that my goddess was just a friend. His wife's sister . . . anything.

"Yeah, that was her," he said, crushing that slim hope like a bug on a windshield. "She's just learning. I'm trying to give her lessons but I think tomorrow we'll sign her up with a pro."

So it was true. They were hitched. I remember my body feeling numb with this confirmation, my mind pinwheeling with disappointment and distress. But I held on, dangling from a psychic rope stretched over an emotional cavern of deep despair.

"My wife is a great golfer," I finally managed. "She played on her college golf team. I can't come close to beating her."

"Sounds like we're at opposite ends of the wife-golf-conundrum," he smiled. "Well, gotta get these back before they melt."

"I'm Chick," I blurted.

"Chandler," he said, holding out a pinky finger for me to shake. The rest of his fingers were engaged in holding the two drinks: the Mai Tai for my goddess, and some sort of white foamy calorie-busting gunk for him—a Piña Colada or something.

So we shook pinkies and off he went. I followed him until I could see that they were sunning down by the beach. Then I went back to the power cabana. We had retaken Pork Chop Hill. We were back on top. I'd been contemplating setting up better fortifications. A machine-gun nest and some razor wire. But now I didn't care and just flopped down next to Evelyn.

"I wish we could go topless here," Evelyn said unexpectedly. She has protruding nipples that look like pencil erasers.

She knows they drive men wild, and she loves to show them. She's always pestering me to go to nude beaches, an activity that doesn't suit my new executive spread. Of course, if she took off her top at this hotel, the staff would swoop down on her and run her off the grounds in a towel trolley. But still, the idea of stripping down to her thong appealed to her, and she was still thinking about it as I brooded in my chair. How she got this way is still a mystery to me. When we first got married, she didn't act like this. Of course, that was before Mickey D and the *Buns of Steel* cassette. But still . . .

"We should go to the beach," I said.

"I'm not going to the fucking beach. The beach is Skid Row. All those morons who get stuck in the hotel's back rooms use the beach. We're in the best cabana. We're fine where we are.".

"I'd like to do some body surfing." I think I was whining. I hope I wasn't, but lately I've been turning into such a wuss, it's hard for me to tell. I hate myself for some of this stuff, but let's not go into that now . . . let's get past it.

"I don't see why we can't try the beach just once."

"I don't want to be seen down there. Besides, it's all sandy. I don't want to ruin my tan. The sand sticks to my suntan oil. I hate the fucking beach."

So for the moment, I was trapped in our power cabana, frustrated as the towel boy in a room full of virgins.

"I think I'll give it a shot anyway," I finally said ten minutes later.

"Do what you want." She seemed disinterested in whatever I was going to do because she was checking out another woman with a pretty good body. Competition. This woman had abs almost as good as hers. "That bitch is on steroids. She's way too muscular. Looks like shit," Evelyn said, as I stood and looked down at my own wife's super-enhanced pecs and abs, all oiled and rippling.

Sometimes, I just don't get it. Sometimes, I'm completely at a loss about what's going on in her head. More and more, I find myself thinking about divorce.

The beach was beautiful. A light breeze rippled the water. Up by the pool the air was as still as Texas hair. I had one of the beach boys get me a chair and I dragged it to a spot where I could watch my goddess and Chandler, who I knew had to be using some kind of lightener to get that color on his copper curls.

Then one of those fortuitous things occurred that you pray for but in real life almost never seem to happen. It started when Chandler went up to get the two of them another drink, and my goddess decided to go swimming. She was out past the rocks, snorkeling, so I decided to go in and get as close as I could. I was treading water, my abs and shoulders still stiff from my workout with Brian, and then, when I was about ten to fifteen yards away from her, somebody on the beach yelled, "Shark!"

Okay, I've been coming to this hotel for years and have never seen a shark fin in the water, not once. Some dolphins two years ago, gray whales occasionally, but not one damn shark. But, somebody on the shore yelled it, and everybody in the water went totally nuts, including my goddess.

"Oh, no! Where?" I heard her shriek.

Normally if I heard somebody yell "Shark" I'd be climbing over little kids to get out of the water. But this was an opportunity sent by God. This was destiny. So I made my way closer to her. "It's okay," I panted.

"Shark," she said in desperation, her eyeballs white with fear. "Somebody yelled 'Shark.'" She started to swim to shore, but was panicking, beating the water with her arms and legs . . . thrashing, getting nowhere fast.

Time for Chick Cousteau, the old shark expert, to take over. By the way, just so there is no misunderstanding here, I know next to nothing about sharks. "Don't thrash. You'll look like a wounded seal. Slow, even strokes." I'd heard that on the Discovery Channel and those three sentences maxed out my knowledge of water predators.

"I'm . . . I'm scared to death of . . . "

"It's okay. You go first. I'll stay back. I'll watch out for him." What bullshit.

Of course, if I'd seen the damn thing, I probably would have coronaried and there would be no need for him to kill me, because I'd already be dead, floating in the surf—bloated shark chow. But I was deep into it now, doing my "Wild Kingdom" thing. I took up rear guard, swimming behind her.

"He's not here. I'm right behind you. It's okay," I shouted, trying to reassure her with hollow encouragements.

She was still panicked but was finally drawing closer to shore. "It's okay, you're safe. Nothing's behind us," I said bravely, thinking that at any moment, a Tiger or a Great White was going to tear off my leg, or worse still, my whole reproductive package.

And then we were onshore, dragging ourselves out of the surf and back to safety. All along the strand, terrified swimmers were now standing on the beach, shading their eyes, looking for a shark fin. Nobody could see one—but let's not get stuck on whether or not there was a shark. It's not important. As far as she was concerned, I had saved her.

Big decision now: Should I hang around, accept her praise, make a pest of myself as I tried to weasel my way into her life, looking like just another horny asshole, or should I treat this magnificent water rescue as if it were just a minor part of my heroic existence? Option number two was obviously my best choice.

"God, I was so panicked," she said. "You risked your life to save me. How can I thank you?"

"No problem," I replied in my deepest voice. "Glad I was around to help out." Then I turned away and strode purposefully toward my beach chair. This was no easy feat in the deep sand, because Brian had trashed my abs. They were killing me and I was out of breath, attempting to hold in my aching gut while rolling my shoulders—the old jock walk from high school. I trudged my heroic, shark-fighter ass up the beach, sprawled on my lounge chair, closed my eyes, and waited.

Ten minutes passed.

"Hey, thanks." Chandler loomed over me. I looked up. He was holding out his whole hand this time. "Paige told me what you did . . ."

Paige . . . my goddess was named Paige. There was perfection in those five letters. I had saved somebody named Paige

*from a desperate shark attack, an atrocious mauling in the jaws
of death.*

It turned out later that nobody had actually seen a shark.
The guy on the beach who had yelled admitted that he'd only
thought he'd seen one. But, nonetheless, there *could* have
been one, and I did offer myself as a human sacrifice to protect her, so come on, fair's fair.

"Will you join us? Can we buy you a drink?" Chandler
asked.

"Yeah, sure, why not?" Forced casualness. But as I walked
over to their sun chairs, my heart was pounding like a blown
engine with a bad cam.

"I'm Chandler Ellis. I think I mentioned, this is my wife,
Paige."

Paige Ellis. Her name was music. I shook her hand . . .
It was cool and soft, delicate and perfect as a bird's wing.

Then it got very tricky.

My job was to try and focus on Chandler, not Paige. No
mean accomplishment. I couldn't gawk at this guy's lovely
wife as every fiber of my being longed to. Instead, I acted polite but indifferent as she retold the story of my water rescue,
my heroic act of sacrifice. I did a relatively effective "Aw
shucks"—even had a beach full of sand to dig my big toe
into. As she told the story, she embellished it slightly. "Chick
could have been killed," she gushed. "He swam directly behind me so the shark couldn't get to me."

"I don't think there was really a shark, Paige," I demurred,
modestly.

"But we didn't know that, silly," she persisted, laughing, showing even, perfect teeth. "At the time, we both thought it was there."

"I agree," Chandler said. "To do that for a complete stranger—to risk yourself like that—was pretty damn heroic."

Of course I didn't tell him I was hopelessly in love with his wife. Instead, I engaged him in conversation, almost completely ignoring Paige, who sat with her gorgeous legs tucked under her, listening and sipping a second Mai Tai—two cherries, of course.

Chandler Ellis was named Chandler because he was the nephew of the late Otis Chandler. Otis was a big deal in L.A. The Chandler family owned the *Los Angeles Times* before they sold it to the Tribune for about a gazillion dollars. Chandler's aunt had founded the Dorothy Chandler Pavilion, the main theater in L.A. The Ellises were all involved in managing the family fortune, except, that is, for Chandler.

Chandler had left the corporation behind to live in Charlotte, North Carolina, on a fat trust fund. He had a master's degree in special ed and taught learning disabled children. The more I heard about this guy, the more I hated him. Among his growing list of uncommon assets: He was charming, handsome, filthy rich, and, now it appears, loaded with the milk of human kindness. The next thing was probably going to be an organ donation to a dying orphan. Some things are so saccharine they defy the palate. Chandler Ellis had me in glucose overload.

But I choked all this down. I learned that Paige was a marathon runner and had competed in Boston last year. She was also a developing artist—landscapes and still lifes. But for now, that was just a sideline until her paintings started selling. In the meantime, like Chandler, she also taught school. Kindergarten. Drawing with finger-paints, cut-out pictures from construction paper ... the whole plastic-flower-frog-terrarium-hamster-cage curriculum.

Paige and Chandler were both devoted to teaching and to each other. They had only been married a year and were desperately in love. That much was obvious to anybody who looked, and I was most certainly looking. She held his hand when he talked and looked at him with something close to hero worship, even though, I remind you, I was the one who had dangled my balls for a shark's meal.

He explained to me how the learning disabled children he taught could lead normal lives if he could just give them the tools they needed to survive. He said we had to support them and nourish their inner concept of well-being. Precious shit like that.

Then we finally got around to the old dot-com wizard. Selling Bruckheimer movies and Britney Spears CDs over the Internet seemed like pretty shallow fare by comparison.

I worried my way through the afternoon, hoping Evelyn wouldn't become curious and wander down in her thong to see what had happened to me. But she was obviously way too involved in the Ab Wars up by the pool.

Chandler and I set up a golf game together for the next day—just him and me.

"I'm glad to finally get to play with somebody who can keep the ball on the fairway," he joked, grinning lovingly at his wife.

"Oh, Chandler, stop it, I'm not that bad," she said, slapping him playfully on the arm as she held his hand.

This was some steep mountain I was about to climb.

DURING OUR GOLF GAME, I LEARNED THAT CHAN-dler Ellis had been the walk-on quarterback for the Georgetown University football team in the late nineties. He'd set a passing record for Division I-AA colleges, which was still standing. Just one more on a growing list of things I despised about him.

Naturally, he creamed me at golf.

But one good thing came of it. He suggested we get the girls together and all go out to dinner. By "the girls," he meant Evelyn, Melissa, and Paige.

No fucking way Melissa was gonna get included. The last thing I needed was my angry sixteen-year-old sitting there, reflecting light from studs punched through every corner of her face. Melissa would go out of her way to humiliate us. She would use abusive language, or talk about Big Mac, tell everybody what a great lay he is. Believe me, I've been sucked into these things before. She's impossible.

She wouldn't want to go anyway. She was much happier sitting in the room, talking to McKenna on the hotel phone, eating up my shriveling bank reserves at four dollars a minute on a trans-Pac line.

Besides, it was going to be hard enough just to get Evelyn to agree. Evelyn had a very select group of friends, and they all came with rich older husbands and Gold's Gym memberships.

But I had a plan to make it happen. We had just come up from the pool when I told her about my golf game with Chandler and his invitation for us to all go to dinner.

"Why the fuck would I want to go out with them?" she said, starting this discussion with enough attitude to open at the Apollo Theater.

"It's okay with me," I said. "I didn't want to go, either."

That slowed her down. If I didn't want to go, then maybe she ought to. That was the dynamic our marriage had taken.

"Who are these people again?" she asked.

We were in our suite on the eighth floor of the hotel. The eighth floor is the Club Floor. You need a special key to get up there in the elevator. Evelyn loved that, loved having that special key. It validated her.

The Club Floor cost a few hundred extra a day. *Did I mention I was on the verge of a fucking bankruptcy?* Naturally, with bankers circling me like hungry coyotes, money should be of no consequence. Our top-floor room was one of the best at the Four Seasons, up front, overlooking the ocean. Great views, great size, great sitting room where Melissa bitched and moaned because she had to sleep on the pull-out sofa. I'd been told by my wife that the room was a bargain at twenty-seven hundred a night. Can you believe this?

Anyway, after I mentioned the dinner invitation, Evelyn started pacing and thinking. She was naked, just out of the shower. Her slick, still damp, sun-reddened body the picture of glowing health. My body still felt like it had gone through a meat tenderizer.

"Chandler and Paige Ellis ... " she said reflectively. "They're not part of *the* Ellis family, are they? The Chandlers and Ellises? That bunch?"

I should pause here to tell you that Evelyn studied the society pages like a cloistered monk reading scripture.

I knew that the Ellis name probably wouldn't fly past unnoticed. "Ellises? Who are the Ellises?" Me, acting dumb.

"Who are the Ellises? Well, if they're the same Ellises, they're the other half of the Otis Chandler family, the cousins. If this guy's first name is Chandler, it's probably the same family." She was pacing around, then spun suddenly, walked out onto the balcony, and looked down at the grounds, chewing on her cuticle, thinking.

I probably don't need to remind you that she was absolutely buck-ass naked and was now in full view of everyone down by the pool. Seconds later, I heard somebody whistle and some guy started shouting at her.

Finally, after giving them a good show, she turned and walked slowly back into the room.

"I'm going to check with Lea in the Club Lounge and see if she knows who they are."

Well, of course they were *the* Ellises and so Evelyn went from hating the idea of going out to dinner with them to hating her entire hernia-busting closet full of clothes, which I'd lugged in and out of two airports all the way from L.A. She said she needed new gear for the dinner, so, armed with the Amex Black Card, she was off to the Wailea Center, where I probably don't have to tell you, the designer shops are a tad pricey.

That night, the four of us, sans Melissa, had dinner at Correlli's, an Italian restaurant up the coast from the hotel. The restaurant opened onto a beautiful beach. A light wind flickered candles in hurricane lamps. There were pictures of thirties-style gangsters on the walls, along with shots of every cheese-ball celebrity who had ever wandered in there by mistake.

Of course, because of their social clout, there was a picture of Chandler and Paige from last year—the honeymoon shot. The maitre d', a guy who looked like his name should have been Guido but turned out to be Max, asked them both to sign it. They did, and he rehung it in a place of prominence, up front.

Then a strange thing happened. My wife and the Ellises seemed to hit it off. I'm always surprised when this occurs because, in my mind, Evelyn's flaws so outweigh her good points that I tend to focus exclusively on them.

But on a good day, when she's trying to be nice, Evelyn can be quite charming, and like I said, from the neck down, you can't find a more toney-looking woman. This evening, in preparation for our dinner with the Ellises, she had dressed way down. Gone was the push-up water bra, the Lycra pantsuit, and crop-top, navel-baring ensemble. Her show-stopping cleavage was modestly out of view. In its place, new duds: a tasteful, silk Perry Ellis blouse; tailored Dior slacks; jeweled Manolo Blahnik sandals. Grand total: $1,793, plus tax. But at least the outfit wasn't one of her tit-baring, all-hanging-out-and-in-your-face specials like the ones she usually wears.

Evelyn and Paige chatted about Paige's art and the children she and Chandler were planning to eventually have. It came out that Paige's wedding and engagement rings were being resized because they had almost come off in the water two days ago, clearing up that mystery.

"It's amazing. She takes off her rings and all of a sudden, every unattached Romeo on the beach thinks it's his cue to turn into a complete ass," Chandler said, shaking his head.

"Unbelievable," I agreed, sheepishly.

Evelyn and I both told lies about Melissa . . . said she was planning on college in two years. But after looking at her last two report cards, the only way I could see her getting into a university was if the Devil's Disciples opened a pharmaceutical college to teach better chemistry to that bunch of stringy-haired crystal cookers who kept blowing up their mobile homes in the Angeles Crest mountains.

Chandler and I talked about L.D. kids, something I had to struggle to stay focused on. I was still trying to keep from gawking at Paige.

Of course she recounted the story of my heroic shark rescue. "You never told me about that," Evelyn smiled, acting amused and pleased, when I knew she was pissed to the core that I'd kept it from her.

"It was nothing, really." As this ridiculous cliché popped out of my mouth, Evelyn rolled her eyes, a look that said I was gonna catch hell over this later.

A little further into the evening, I hit them with my next clever plan. I'd been working on it all afternoon.

"You know what might be kinda fun?" I said, softly, dangling it like fresh bait over a still pond.

"What?" they all asked, thinking I had a great idea for where to go for a nightcap. But my idea was far more complex than that, more devious and infinitely subtler. "I was thinking it might be fun to get a few of Paige's paintings and see if we could sell them on bestmarket.com, maybe raise her artistic visibility with an Internet marketing campaign."

"Really?" Paige said, leaning forward. "I'm not sure I'm ready."

"Honey, I've been saying for years you should have your own art show," Chandler chimed in. "If we could afford it, I'd pay for it myself."

At first I was thinking, Who the fuck is he kidding? This guy's family builds music centers, owns media companies, and he can't rent a one-room studio for an art show? But it came out a few minutes later that he'd turned his entire trust fund over to an L.D. Foundation he had formed and now managed, for almost no salary, drawing off most of the funds for brain research. I'm telling you, there were times with this guy Chandler where my gag reflex was on overload.

"We could sell Paige's art on the Internet," I continued. "I get millions of hits a day. We could build a website, call it the Art Paige, spelled like your name, scan a few of your paintings on there, and set up an online auction."

"We could even say the money was going to go for Chandler's L.D. Foundation," Paige suggested, sparking immediately to my idea.

"Right. Maybe bestmarket.com could match anything we raised," I enthused. Of course, if it was over a few thousand, we'd have to take out an IOU on my car to cover it.

I glanced over and caught a dark look passing across Evelyn's face. She doesn't like giving away any of my money. She'd rather spend it herself. I was going to have to be more careful, lest my clandestine motives unexpectedly porpoise into full view.

"Anyway, it might be kind of fun to see what happens," I concluded.

"I could help Paige design the web page," my wife unexpectedly offered, leaning forward and smiling. "I have my master's degree in marketing from Stanford."

She did, too, but it had never been worth much to us, because even though Evelyn had a master's in marketing, she had a doctorate in shopping, so we were destined to lose fiscal ground annually.

"It's worth a try," I said.

"We don't want to take advantage," Chandler cautioned.

"He's right. I mean, you're so busy," Paige added. "We don't want to be a burden."

"Nonsense," I thundered extravagantly.

"It'll be fun," Evelyn shrieked and clapped.

"Well, okay . . . why not?" Paige said, and she reached out and took Evelyn's hand.

Chandler took mine and I took Evelyn's. Of course, Chandler and Paige were already holding hands. They always held hands, so now we had a ring of clasped hands, all of us smiling.

"To new friendships," I said, and we all reached for our wineglasses.

"New friendships," they caroled.

Okay, okay, not exactly the Peace Conference at Malta, I admit, but not bad, all things considered. I had managed to go from a leering pool-cabana stalker to a "new friend," and it had taken me all of two and a half days. Better still, I had involved Evelyn in the plan so she wouldn't be a liability, and we could all interact as couples, which I have come to learn is the best way to do it. I've sold half a dozen accounts this way. When you include wives, it gets everybody's guard down.

We left Correlli's and all walked along the beach back to the hotel. The moon was full and the water lapped over our toes. We carried our shoes, with Paige and Chandler walking ahead of us, arm in arm. Evelyn and I held hands in a decent imitation of marital bliss, although, to be honest, her hand was no delicate bird's wing. It was hard as a blacksmith's anvil, cold and damp. She applied no pressure. I've held dead trout that communicated more emotion.

When we arrived at the Four Seasons, Evelyn and I said good night and left Chandler and Paige on the beach.

I was feeling pretty good about all of this until I looked back and saw them standing in the sand, lit by a three-quarter moon, kissing each other, locked in a passionate embrace.

That night in our bedroom, I did something I hadn't done in months. I made love to Evelyn, all the time pretending I was having sex with Paige. My fevered imagination transformed Evelyn's muscled body into Paige's soft goddess proportions. I got so sexed up I had a diamond-cutter erection. You could have bludgeoned a baby seal to death with that hard-on. When she was close to climax, I thought I heard Evelyn grunt, "More, Mickey, more!" which sort of ruined it.

When it was over, we lay in an exhausted embrace.

"What got into you?" Evelyn asked. "Man, you were pneumatic."

"Did you just call me Mickey?" I asked, my voice flat with suspicion.

"Honestly, Chick, where do you come up with this shit?" Then she got out of bed to go to the bathroom and left me there. It pissed me off, but I didn't dwell on it, because I was more resolved than ever to get out of the marriage. One way or the other, I was determined to move on, to become Paige Ellis's lover.

How I was going to accomplish this still hadn't become clear. When it finally did, it took on a shape more devastating than I could have ever imagined.

CHAPTER 6

THE REST OF THE WEEK WE ALL HUNG OUT TO-
gether. Evelyn and I shared our power cabana with the Ellises.
There were four chairs in there anyway, and after Melissa se-
cured it each morning she disappeared. She told me she'd
rather be staked out over an anthill than sit with us. My daughter, exercising her uncommon gift for colorful metaphor.

Evelyn actually got Paige into the workout room and
started her on a light aerobic routine, using knowledge
gained over years of Mickey D's training and my money to
fashion a new body for a woman who could already stop
traffic wearing a trench coat.

I let it happen, though, because I didn't think in four
days Evelyn would be able to turn Paige's softness into the
kind of anatomical gristle that she had struggled so hard to
achieve for herself.

Now, just so you won't think that I was going over the falls in a barrel here, let me tell you that I really, really tried to put the brakes on my emotions, to rein myself in.

I kept saying what I'm sure you're saying: This is crazy. The woman adores her husband. You're much older, half as good looking. Your father didn't build downtown neighborhoods from Hispanic slums into architecturally renowned music centers, or city newspapers into global media empires. Your dad built opening-act comedians playing rathole dives like the Comedy Cabana into cheesy middle acts at transvestite clubs like the Cross Walk in North Hollywood. While Chandler Ellis was winning football games at Andover prep and then Georgetown, you were fighting for rectal purity in the Hawaiian state prison or throwing up in a Cost Plus wastebasket at rehab.

On every scale, the Chick Bests of the world didn't measure up against the Chandler Ellises.

I said all these things to myself.

I even locked myself behind the frosted, etched glass door in our bathroom, sat on the shitter, and wrote all of it down on a piece of hotel stationery.

Then I did something even more proactive: I started looking for flaws in Paige Ellis. I collected them, diving deep for each one like a bum in a supermarket Dumpster. I even cataloged her few physical imperfections.

For instance, she had a kind of goofy laugh, something between a squeal and a giggle. Of course, on further introspection, I found it irresistible.

She had a birthmark on her left calf that was almost the size of a quarter. The more I looked at that birthmark, the more I loved it.

She had an odd habit of constantly jiggling her foot when she was seated. I asked her about it, putting on my most friendly "you can tell the doctor" expression. She explained that she had suffered from Attention Deficit Disorder as a child. It's what first drew her to Chandler. They had that interest in common. She understood learning disabilities firsthand. She said that even though she had more or less grown out of it, she still found it difficult to sit completely still . . . hence the little foot jiggle. Adorable.

I found every one of these imperfections delightful.

After a week of constantly being with our new friends, Paige and Chandler, we had a farewell dinner at the hotel and promised to stay in touch. We all kissed each other goodbye. Our first kiss—only a cheek peck. But I swear, I almost fainted from ecstasy.

We exchanged digits and addresses, and under most circumstances, that would have been the end of it. We would have never seen each other again, except I was more hopelessly in love with her now than I had been in the beginning. I'm not just talking infatuation here, either. I'm talking deep, soul-defining devotion.

I was dreaming about her now almost every night, and every time I looked at Evelyn, I was shocked that I'd ended up with such coarseness when there were creatures like Paige in the breeding pool. I told myself if I'd married someone like Paige, Melissa wouldn't be as angry as she is, frowning with a face that had more holes than a pool-hall dartboard.

Of course, Melissa used our infatuation with the Ellises to get lost. During the week, I saw her now and again, usually at our changing-of-the-guard ceremony under the poolside cabana each morning. She had taken up with a huge Hawaiian guy. A primo-warrior. Big, with lots of island tattoos. I cornered her once and asked her what was going on with him.

"Bite me," was her cute reply.

What do you do with kids when they won't listen to a thing you say, or care at all about any of the things you think are important?

We left Hawaii on January 8th and flew back to L.A. I reentered my nightmarish business fiasco. I was standing on the bridge of my fast-sinking *Titanic,* driving a leaking dotcom straight to the bottom of a sea of bullshit.

The first couple of months back at work, I noticed that most of my executives were making new resumes and taking long lunches. Who could blame them?

A few weeks later, I took a walk through our warehouse. There had been a time, a few years ago, when I would walk through this acre-sized building and swell with pride, looking at shelves crammed full of studio movie DVDs and recording company CDs. I had been like a rancher surveying my livestock. Pallets piled high with American pop culture whizzed past on forklifts on their way to the loading dock, where twenty FedEx vans were parked, doors open, engines idling. Now, as I walked around the place, my own footsteps echoed in the emptiness. We had some old movies nobody wanted, a few Eagles CDs, some Steely Dan—all stuff that wasn't on the current hot list. As I said, none of the studios would trust us with product anymore, so we were imploding, crashing from the inside.

Then, as if watching years of my life dissolve like an Alka-Seltzer tablet wasn't a big enough load to carry, Melissa picked this exact time to get arrested.

We were called by the narc squad in the middle of the night and had to drive down to Juvenile Hall to talk to a vice detective. It seems she'd been caught in a Valley drug raid, arrested in a house full of crystal meth. She'd been sound asleep when the cops kicked in the door. The house was, of course, rented by Big Mac, but Melissa was the only one being held.

The way it was explained to us was our sixteen-year-old daughter was claiming that the forty or more bags of "Go Fast" the cops had recovered in Big Mac's house were hers alone . . . that Big Mac had nothing to do with it, didn't even know she'd hid it there.

It was pretty damned clear to everyone that Melissa was taking the rap for McKenna, but they weren't even holding him.

"That's nuts," I told the cops. "This guy is the president of the Devil's Disciples. They sell meth. That's their main business. It's obviously his stash."

"Yeah, that's what we think, too," the ropy black detective with prematurely gray hair said. "But what're we gonna do? He's saying he never saw it. She's saying it's hers."

"Can't you see she's trying to take the blame for him? She claims she loves him," I said, thinking these cops can't possibly be this blind. They can't let this tattooed asshole with a shaved head get away with this. "He probably threatened her to get her to say that," I reasoned. "It's duress or something."

"If you can get her to change her story, we'll work with it," he said.

So Evelyn and I went back into the holding cell where they had her and sat on metal chairs, talking through the bars. The place smelled of vomit and disinfectant. I had a flashback from my short jail term in Hawaii. I won't bore you with that misadventure here, except to say that I know my daughter had no idea what she was signing up for.

"Honey, you've gotta tell the truth," Evelyn said. She never calls Melissa honey, and I could see the metal in our daughter's face shifting light as she frowned.

"Melissa, believe me, you don't wanna go to jail on this drug bust," I said.

"You oughta know, right, Dad?" she shot back.

"Melissa, don't do this. You're going to ruin your life," I pleaded.

"Would you two mind getting out of here? I can't listen to any more of this shit. You both ruined my life years ago."

An hour later, Evelyn and I were back in our three-million-dollar French Regency Beverly Hills home on Elm. We were in our overdecorated foyer fighting about what to do about Melissa. As always, we ended up with recriminations.

"It's because she hates you," Evelyn said. "You're such a hypocrite, telling her you never used drugs, then she finds out you did half a year in Hawaii for dealing hash." Forgetting to mention that she was the one who'd busted me to Melissa.

"She's punishing both of us for her feelings of emotional abandonment," I said, bringing two semesters of junior college abnormal psychology into play. "You haven't done a good job of raising her. You made a lot of mistakes."

"*You've* made the mistakes, buddy," Evelyn snapped. "I've always been there for her. I've been busting my ass!" I wondered if getting butt-fucked by Mickey D could technically be described as busting ass. Maybe.

We argued for almost an hour, did a nice two-out-of-three falls, while Melissa sat it out in a detention cell in Sylmar Juvie.

The next morning, I hired the best lawyer that money I didn't have could buy. He was a balding, skeletal guy with a Talmudic beard named Jube Shiver. I got him from one of my dot-com account managers whose younger sister had a drug history.

"Can you get her out?" I asked our new liar for hire, worried about what might happen to her in jail . . . visions of lesbian rape hovering at the edge of my every thought.

"I'll have her out by noon," he said with the confidence of a gunfighter cracking the knuckles on his shooting hand. "But the bigger problem is, what happens when this comes to trial. Her association with this biker isn't going to be helpful."

"But the biker is the one who got her into this. All that crystal isn't hers—it's his. She's taking the blame for him. Aren't you listening to me?"

"She *confessed*," Jube Shiver said, dismissing my argument with a wave of a freckled hand, leaning back in an office littered with B'nai B'rith awards and team pictures of the North Hollywood Little League Pirates. He steepled his fingers under his Talmudic beard, which was graying theatrically at the edges, and studied me like I had just tracked dog shit into his office. I was beginning to take an intense dislike to our new Jewish attorney.

"I know she confessed. That's because he threatened her," I said. "It's under duress."

"It's not duress unless the police force it. Let *me* lawyer the case. You just give me her personal background, answer my questions when I ask, and sign the checks."

He lost the whole Talmudic thing with that one sentence. Then he made some notes and nodded as I told him everything I thought would be helpful. I left out the bad stuff like all the cocaine we'd found in her purse and under her jewelry box; all the money and the portable electronic equipment she'd stolen from us and fenced to feed her habit.

I drove off an hour later with dark visions of Melissa heading to The Big House.

When I got back to the office, there was a message from my CFO. I went down the hall to see him. He told me he'd scared up an angel in New York who wanted to meet with me in the Big Apple tomorrow. This angel was a Wall Street arbitrageur who was interested in buying out my interest in our sinking dot-com.

"I've got this problem right now with Melissa," I told him.

My CFO, whose name is Martin Worth, frowned and shook his head. There were endless plays on both our names at the company. My favorite being—"At Best, he's Worthless." Shit like that.

"This may be our last shot," Martin said stoically.

Why did it always come down to these "no-choice" kinds of choices?

Melissa, or the business?

Nothing simple . . . nothing easy.

Melissa . . . or years of my life down the drain with nothing to show for it?

So of course I went to New York. I had no choice.

Biggest mistake of my life.

CHAPTER

I TOOK THE RED-EYE.

The weather in New York was dismal. A bone-chilling sleet washed the city, falling from a gunmetal sky.

My Jamaican taxi driver couldn't speak American English. He spoke some kind of indecipherable island patois where every sentence either began or ended with "mon." This angry asshole sat in the front seat of his paint-chipped yellow cab, looking back at me through dirty braids, his Rasta beads clicking ominously every time he moved his head. He made me repeat the address three times, laying the groundwork for getting lost later—conning me, trying to drive up the fare. I hate all these immigrants. I'm tired of my tax dollars going to support a bunch of lazy border jumpers.

"Huh? Whatchu tellin', mon?" he asked.

"Financial District, downtown." I handed him the slip of paper with the address on it. We were outside the American Airlines terminal at JFK.

"Huh? What be dat district, mon? Where dat be at?" Who did he think he was kidding? He drives a cab in New York and can't find the Financial District? Then he got on the radio and pretended to get instructions from a dispatcher with a Middle Eastern accent. Urban terrorists, both of them.

I hate New York. I don't get the vibe here. Since September 11th, it's gotten even worse. They all act as if the Big Apple is the new center of the moral universe. Of course, I'm from Southern California and the only things that got knocked down in L.A. on 9/11 were some IRA accounts, so I'm probably the wrong guy to listen to.

My Jamaican cabbie managed to find the address in downtown Manhattan after giving me a fucking tour of Brooklyn and the Lower East Side. The cab fare was a mind-boggling $85.50. See what I'm saying? Thieves, all of them.

The man I was going to see was named Walter Lily. The Lily Fund basically bought assets low and sold high, which was another way of saying they acquired sick companies. Walter Lily had a reputation on Wall Street as a "grave dancer," a man who profited from other men's misfortunes. But I was more or less down to my last few lifelines, so I had no choice. I had to pursue it.

The Lily Building was one of those New York addresses that looks like it was squeezed in as an afterthought, probably when some holdout finally sold his hotdog stand and made his postage stamp of ground available to the hovering killers in the New York real-estate cabal. The building sat on only about an eighth of a city block. The architecture was expensive, turn-of-the-century stone and brick to the second floor, where more cost-effective steel and glass took over and went up for fifty stories. Like nobody on the streets would ever look up and spot it.

I rode the elevator to the top floor. My heart was pounding, and my hands sweating. I clutched the handle of my briefcase, which was full of carefully fabricated numbers and spreadsheets that my CFO, Martin Worth, had supplied.

I was meeting with Mr. Lily himself. He had insisted that I come alone. His appointment secretary explained that he liked his meetings one-on-one. I was told he had allowed fifteen minutes for our little chat.

How the last twelve years of my life could come down to a fifteen-minute chat still baffled me. But I had shot through all of the more probable suitors, swinging from the heels, trying to hammer one out of the park, missing the ball each time, going down in a whirl of air and curses.

As I exited the elevator and felt it wheeze closed behind me, I found myself standing in a very ordinary entryway.

A young, overweight girl was seated behind a marble desk reading *Vanity Fair*. Above her head was some kind of brass logo that resembled a lily, and under that, appropriately enough:

THE LILY FUND

I crossed to her. "I'm Charles Best," I said, handing her my card. "I have an eleven o'clock appointment with Mr. Lily."

She took my card and frowned at it as if it contained the results of her last Pap smear. She wrinkled her brow; she pursed her lips; she dangled it in two fingers like a cat turd fished from her litter box. Then she set it down on her desk and frowned at it.

I should say here that the card cost me a bloody fortune. In the middle it says BESTMARKET.COM in raised gold letters. Our logo, which is a unicorn, is embossed on the top left corner of the card. Why a unicorn? I don't know . . . I really don't. Somebody else picked it. But it seemed kind of show businessy, so I agreed. At the bottom, my name was also in embossed letters.

CHARLES "CHICK" BEST
CHIEF EXECUTIVE OFFICER

She picked up the phone and spoke softly to somebody inside, then looked up at me. "You can wait over there." She pointed to a worn leather sofa and went immediately back to her magazine.

I walked over and sat. I put my briefcase in front of me and picked up that morning's *Wall Street Journal.* I tried to read an article about the mortgage meltdown, but I couldn't make my mind stay focused. My heart was pounding, my senses quivering. I was trying to calm myself down, trying to get my hands to stop shaking.

I kept thinking my entire future was coming down to a meeting with a guy who had been alternately called a grave dancer or the Great White of Wall Street. He was what was commonly referred to as garbitrageur, a derogatory blend of the two words "garbage" and "arbitrageur." I knew he would try to lowball me. That's why I had the doctored spreadsheets Martin Worth had pencil-whipped, putting the best possible face on a large array of unexploded financial grenades.

It was eleven-twenty before I was finally shown into Lily's office.

As bleak and foreboding as the waiting area was, the inner sanctum was just the opposite. Money and wealth reeked off polished wood walls and ornate Louie XV furniture. Louis XV is my least favorite style ever since I noticed that all of the pictures of Liberace I'd ever seen had him sitting in rooms full of that kind of French furniture.

But it was everywhere in the Lily Fund offices: pushed up against the polished oak walls, decorating every available open space. Gold-leaf lion-claw legs stood on carpet that was some kind of expensive custom weave, stretched to fit under the heavy wood moldings.

I was shepherded by a sallow young man in a gray suit, past offices full of people who were so busy making money for my host, they didn't even look up to see who Mr. Lily's next victim was.

I was shown into his outer office. A woman who was in her mid-fifties paused and glanced up. A corporate diva, she studied me fiercely over half-glasses.

"Mr. Best?" she asked, coldly.

"Yes, ma'am. I'm the best Best there is!" giving her one of my cute openers. Then I smiled, flashing my full sixteen, the old Chick Best ivory personality blitz.

She didn't waver under its effect. Total points won: zip. "Go in," she instructed coolly.

The shepherd in the gray suit opened the office door and guided me into Mr. Walter Lily's inner sanctum, then positioned himself right inside the door. I was feeling like a condemned man about to hear a life-altering sentence.

The office surprised me. I don't know what I'd been expecting, but it wasn't what I found.

To begin with, despite the pricey Louis XV furnishings, Lily's workspace was unusually small and cluttered. There were books and financial statements stacked everywhere. One small window looked out on the back wall of a large building. No effort was wasted on frills in this room.

My office, by comparison, was huge and full of expensive gee-gaws. I had a two-hundred-thousand-dollar sound system you could operate with a laser remote, a door that electronically opened and closed from a button under my desk, and a hidden bar that rotated out of one wall.

I instantly saw the dichotomy. I was going broke in my huge tricked-out office, while Lily was making billions in a closet that wasn't big enough to store my sports equipment.

How did I get so fucked up?

Sitting behind a desk piled with spreadsheets was the tiniest little man I'd ever seen. He was bald, and as I came through the door, he had his arms out, his palms flat on his blotter. My initial impression was of a large head suspended on spider legs. Then he rose to his full five-foot-two-inch height and came around the desk to meet me. He had a skinny build and hair tufting out of his ears. A gnome. I'm not going to waste a lot more time describing him or our short visit—our chat—because it was the most ludicrous business meeting I had ever attended.

"Mr. Best?" Walter Lily asked. His voice was high, a squeak actually.

"Yes sir, the best Best there is!" I flashed my grill and got no more out of him with this line than I had with his cold-ass secretary.

"I understand you're interested in selling your company."

"Well, sir, I'd certainly consider it, but only if I got a blowout bid. We're not exactly pursuing a sale right now, because we're quite excited about where we're heading and our new quarter spreadsheets are showing renewed long-term profit and capital return. However, that said, under the right circumstances I might consider taking on the right strategic partner if appropriate terms could be negotiated."

I know, I know. You're thinking, what a load of bullshit. But this is the way you negotiate in business. You don't sell because you're strapped for cash; you take on a strategic partner. You don't roll over and expose your soft underbelly to the Great White of Wall Street; you pretend you don't need him.

The little man wearing Sears Roebuck trousers stood for a long moment before he pulled a slip of paper out of his shirt pocket and handed it to me.

"What's this?" I said, smiling.

"My offer. Not a penny more or less," the midget intoned, looking and sounding like a tiny Shylock, or a badly turned-out Ebenezer Scrooge.

Now, let me say right here, this is not the way business is done. My company, while currently experiencing hard times, was once the third-largest Internet site on the Web.

I admit, we made no profit, but that was a calculated strategy. We used every cent, plus all we could borrow, to expand. Product was flying out the door. Millions and millions of website hits a month. We lost money, but we built volume and name value. Name value equates to dollar value. This is a business truth. A brand name can be sold. If you owned the name "Kleenex" for instance, you would have something you could sell for a fortune. I'm not saying bestmarket.com was as well known as Kleenex, or that it was a brand name by which all Internet entertainment sales were referred to, but I am saying that people knew who we were, and in the intensely competitive world of Web commerce, this is a very valuable asset. Millions of people hit our site just because they knew it was there.

I looked at the slip of paper and I couldn't believe what was written there. Two million dollars.

"Two million dollars for what?" I asked, dumbfounded. I was personally on the line for big long-term leases: the warehouse and our six-story L.A. office building. Walter Lily had to know all that if he'd done his due diligence, which I was sure he had. The two million dollars wouldn't even cover my litigation costs when I terminated all the long-term contracts with my employees, or handle the breach-of-contract problems I was sure to face.

The only thing that was keeping my creditors from swarming me was the knowledge that I had nothing but a thinly capitalized company. If they put me into Chapter 11, they'd get ten cents on the dollar for what we owed them, so they were carrying us, hoping we'd work our way out of debt. But Lily knew this. He knew if I tried to walk away from these contractual obligations, I'd be in court forever.

This little asshole was trying to steal my company for nothing. He had the cash and personal assets to restart the operation, reinstate my studio and record-company deals. He'd make my fortune instead of me.

Ten years ago, in the good old dot-com wizard days, we'd had a paper value of six hundred million dollars, as estimated in *Forbes* magazine. Admittedly, we'd slipped some, but this offer was nuts.

"T . . . two million?" I said, stuttering my disbelief.

"Yes." He looked at me like a malicious child who had just pulled the wings off a moth and was watching it flop around helplessly on a windowsill.

"But, sir, . . . the liquidated break-up value is at least seven," I said, retreating immediately to my absolute bottom-line number. I snapped open my briefcase and went for the doctored spreadsheets.

"Don't bother with any of those," he said as I pulled them out. "That's the offer. This time next month, you won't get a dollar from me or anyone else."

"I can't sell for two million. The name alone is worth four times that much."

"Goodbye, then," he said. The little bandit turned and walked out of his office, leaving me standing there with the narrow-shouldered shepherd in the gray suit.

"Is he kidding?" I said.

"I'll show you out," the man said.

It appeared I'd come three thousand miles just to let a dwarf in shiny pants shit on me.

CHAPTER

8

SECONDS LATER I WAS BACK ON THE STREET, SLEET
washing my head, running down my back.

I still had options. The Brooklyn Bridge was only a few
miles away. I could give these Wall Street assholes a great
headline. I should've cabbed over there and jumped. If I had,
I'd be way ahead of where I am now. But that isn't what I
did. Instead, I did something much worse.

Somehow, I found my way to the Hertz Rent a Car in
downtown Manhattan. Somehow, I managed to rent a blue
Ford Taurus. Somehow, I got out of New York City. I didn't
really know where I was going. The windshield wipers
clicked and clacked. I was out of options. My tortured
thoughts circled the edge of this new business dilemma like
a hungry wolf at the edge of a campfire. I drove for hours
and hours, not even knowing where I was going . . . not caring. I vaguely remember Arlington, then Myrtle Beach. I

drove without stopping, except for gas. My mind was chewing on all the terrible consequences of my life, starting with my father's death . . .

Okay. As long as I brought it up, let's get on that broken-down mule for a minute. When I was a child, my father always seemed to me like somebody who had all the answers. He wasn't some big-time show-biz powerhouse, I admit, but he was funny and smart. He could make you laugh, make you believe. An agent.

He loved Hollywood Park . . . loved the ponies.

He was always taking me to the track. Money was power, he told me. And he bet heavily, trying to become more powerful. He let me pick horses and taught me how to read the racing sheet. I learned to handicap by going to the track with him at dawn, studying workout times and injury reports just like all the other six-thirty railbirds. Once, when I was ten, I got a four-horse parlay, won three hundred dollars. I started carrying wads of money around. I was only in fifth grade, but I learned that my father was right. Money was power, even in elementary school.

Mom didn't get it. She was always bitching about Dad losing the egg money, because lots of times he did. She didn't understand that money won was twice as valuable as money earned.

But Dad understood that, and so did I.

Ever since childhood, I've been a regular at the Jockey Club. When I was in the chips a few years back, a lot of my dot-com bonus cash went right through the pari-mutuel window. Call it a learned behavior, a conditioned response.

Dad was Chick Sr. I was Chick Jr. We lived in a parallel universe. The rest of the world ran in the next lane over. He got to drink and screw the B-girls at the Paddock Bar. I went to elementary school and flashed my track cash. Got my first piece of ass in eighth grade when I bought the girl a fifty-dollar ring and got laid in return. I was fourteen. Talk about a defining moment.

Then came the night when dear old Dad ruined it. The night he got drunk and put the silver Jag into the bridge abutment. They had to cut him out of the car. He came out in four pieces.

Since I didn't get my mother's vibe at all, I had focused everything on Dad. I wanted to be like him even though I'm not sure I even knew who he was. He was a big, happy guy in a checkered coat who taught me that people will respect you if you've got cash in your wallet and bullshit on your lips. Mostly what I liked about him was he paid attention to me. I thought it was about me back then, but as I grew older and gained insight into what motivates people, I realized it wasn't about me at all. It was about him. I was the only person in his life who gave a shit what *he* thought.

We buried him at Forest Lawn and I remember thinking back then that it was pretty much over the day they closed his casket. You see, my one goal in life had been to please him, to one day make him proud of me. And then, before I could do it, he took off for the big paddock in the sky. I was only fifteen when he died.

I was left to be raised by women—my mother and grandmother. What a hen party that was. They clucked and prodded, complained and bitched. My grades were never good enough, my hair never short enough, my girlfriends never refined enough. Then, under all this criticism, I sort of started to veer toward drugs and sleazy women, just like Dad. I went into the army, where I heroically defended my post on Wilshire Boulevard, winning the war of one-liners. Afterward, it was a decade-long party that ended with six months in the Hawaii State Prison.

Through all of this, I slowly began to form a different opinion of my father. More and more, I've come to realize that Dad was just a loser with a great line of b.s. A guy who nobody listened to except sleazy women and a son who had nobody else. So, the hero of my youth slowly became an emotional stone around my neck. As an adult, I came to hate what he stood for and prayed I wouldn't end up the same way. I actually threw away my two checkered sport coats the day this realization finally dawned.

I grew up with no real male role models—nobody to try to be like. So whom did I eventually choose? Pop culture assholes. The celebrities in *People* magazine. First, it was drug-culture rock bands, then investment sleaze balls like Ivan Boesky and John Delorean. I lusted after all the things that the product machines on Madison Avenue told me were cool. I didn't like who I was, so I bought everything these false prophets and culture hucksters told me would validate me. I blew money on exotic cars, dressed out of *GQ*, put almost a quarter of a million dollars into the sound system in an office so large you could use it to play half-court basketball. I married a woman other people wanted to fuck. She gave great blow jobs but had thoughts so thin they disappeared completely in a flurry of demands, complaints, and recriminations.

The age-old loser questions started waking me up at night.

How did I get here?

What do I really want?

Why am I so damn unhappy?

And then the big, scary ones: Am I turning into my father? Is that why nobody takes me seriously?

These were the things I was thinking as I pushed the little blue Taurus south out of the sleet of New York City, onto the cracked, dry roads of Virginia, heading nowhere special, not knowing where I was going until I got there.

I drove all afternoon, into the night, my mind elsewhere, yearning for something I was unable to even describe.

You'll never guess where I ended up. Or, maybe you already have.

I ended up in front of Paige Ellis's house on a residential street in Charlotte, North Carolina.

It was 10 P.M. on the night my whole life changed.

CHAPTER

THE HOUSE WAS SMALL, WITH A TINY FRONT LAWN.
It was not the kind of place you'd expect to find the scion of
the Chandler media fortune, certainly not a house I would
choose if I had his money. I was parked a little way up the
street. The address, written down so carefully in Hawaii, was
open now on my lap. The letters, in her delicate hand, were
wavering under my blurring vision.

2367 LIPTON ROAD, CHARLOTTE,
NORTH CAROLINA

I looked at the house and I remember saying out loud,
"Chick, this is nuts." Of course it was way beyond nuts. This
was real, hardcore, front-of-the-line stalker nonsense.

I had driven more than six hundred miles to park outside
another man's house, so I could look into his lighted living

room, hoping to catch a glimpse of his wife as she passed by the window. Unacceptable.

It was as if just letting the vision of her find its way into my brain might salve the pain of these past few days—of Melissa in jail, my sorry business going bankrupt, and the dwarf in the shiny pants with the hair growing out of his ears.

I watched. I waited. What was I doing? I swear, at that moment I didn't have a clue. I wanted to start up the blue Taurus and leave, but I couldn't move my hand to the ignition key. Every time I tried, I hit some sort of powerful force field. My fingers hovered inches away, unable to make contact and close the distance, which would have saved me.

I don't know how long I sat there. My thoughts were becoming pretty jumbled . . . pretty abstract. I thought about my dad, my wife. The first time I saw Evelyn at Mike Donovan's pool party. I thought she was beautiful then, never seeing the woman she would become. Not seeing the anger or the self-hatred that now drove her to pump iron obsessively for hours in our basement gym. I thought about Paige and Chandler Ellis and this little house so far away from L.A. I thought about the insanity of this trip down here, not knowing until I pulled the address out of my pocket what I was really doing, but then knowing in a flash that it had been my plan to come here all along.

That realization, that truth, hit me harder than any of the events of the past month. I knew this was insane, and still I couldn't leave. I couldn't put the little car in gear and save myself, because, you see, I knew that no matter what happened to me, whether I stayed or left, I would never again be the same Chick Best. Somehow, I knew right then that my coming here had changed who I was forever.

I didn't need some Beverly Hills therapist to explain that, either. The trip here had convinced me I had lost control. My love for Paige Ellis had morphed into an uncontrollable obsession.

That's when the door opened and Chandler Ellis walked out of his house. At first I thought he was going to the mailbox. But instead, he walked to the green Suburban parked in the driveway, got in, started the vehicle, and backed out.

I ducked down as his headlights swept over my car. Then I sat up, and without knowing what the hell I was doing, I started the Taurus.

I followed him.

Why did I follow him? I've asked myself that question at least a thousand times since all this happened. I wanted to see Paige. I came all this way to maybe find a way to talk to her. So why was I following Chandler? I didn't know. I couldn't answer that, except to say some psychic force had taken control and was driving me.

At any rate, my mind reeled with questions. What was Chandler doing, leaving his house at eleven in the evening? Where was he going? Did he have a girlfriend stashed across town? Was he cheating on Paige? Was he so stupid that he didn't know he was married to the most desirable woman on earth? What would happen if I caught him with another woman in some cheap motel someplace? What if I found him screwing his brains out? How would I deal with it?

These were some of my fantasies as I followed him. Of course, the answer to that last one was I'd have to tell her. I couldn't let somebody as sweet and trusting as Paige live unknowingly with a sleazy adulterer. Well, I couldn't, could I?

I was thinking I should try to buy a camera and get some pictures—evidence. And then Chandler pulled the Suburban into a shopping center. It was now almost eleven-fifteen and most of the stores were closed, but the Safeway and a Walgreens were still open. Both were throwing neon light deep into the late-night deserted parking lot.

I pulled around to the side to stay out of sight. For some reason, Chandler didn't park out front, but drove through the parking lot and finally pulled the Suburban around to the same side of the store where I was and parked. I was only ten or fifteen yards away, still in the driving lane. My mind whirled. What should I do? Should I wait? Should I leave?

Without looking at my car, Chandler walked into the drugstore. I stared dumbly at his Suburban. Then I put my rented Taurus in Park with the engine still running. I tried to come to grips with all this.

"Chick, get the fuck out of here," I said out loud to myself. But I remind you, I was not in control, unable to change the course of these events. I was lost, as if some unknown power was setting up this maze and forcing me to run through it. So then who was in control here? Who was making up the rules of this game? Not me—at least that's what I told myself.

And then, for a fleeting moment, sanity returned. I knew I had to get the hell outta there. I knew I had to get away before he saw me.

My willpower surged.

I grabbed the gearshift to put the car in Drive, but as this first sane thought in hours hit me, everything changed. It happened so fast I didn't even see it coming.

I still don't quite understand it. I mean, I know the physics. The chronology. It's the psychology that baffles me.

At the very instant I gained control of myself and reached for the shift knob, Chandler came out the back door of the drugstore carrying a small bag from the pharmacy. He saw my headlights, saw that I had sort of blocked his exit. He started to come toward me, waving for me to back up. In a few seconds he would see me. How could I explain my appearance here to him?

What would I say if he recognized me? "Hey Chandler, whatta you doing here? Small world, right?" He would never go for that. Some coincidences defy explanation and I knew this was one of them. There was no way I could explain this. No way. Or at least that's what I was convinced of at that moment.

He was still walking toward me, gesturing, so I slammed the rental into Reverse and hit the gas.

But I was in the wrong gear and the car lunged forward, not backward. It struck Chandler hard, knocking him down. The front headlight broke and the car shuddered from the impact. Before I could take my foot off the gas, I ran right over him. I heard him scream. I felt the wheels roll over his chest; bouncing the Taurus like a speed bump.

I slammed on the brakes, opened the door, jumped out, and ran around to see. He was lying under the car just in front of the rear tires. Only his head protruded from underneath. He was barely breathing. Blood had already started coming out of his mouth. The bag of medicine he'd been carrying was strewn on the pavement. I remember looking down. I read the label:

PAIGE ELLIS:
DARVOCET for pain.
One tablet every four hours.

Funny, how in a time of extreme crisis, something unimportant and stupid like that registers.

"Help me!" he croaked, his eyes bright but desperate.

Then he recognized me.

A strange look of clarity passed across his face. "Chick?" he whispered.

I couldn't answer. I couldn't speak. And then he started to choke on his own blood. It was oozing out of his mouth, oozing around my feet. I jumped back to keep it off my hand-sewn Spanish loafers.

"Chick . . . help . . ." It was such a low whisper—a moan actually—that I couldn't even be sure he'd said those exact words.

I ran back to the driver's side, jumped into the car, and—God help me—I put it in Drive and inched forward to run over him again, parking the rear wheel on his chest for almost a full minute before pulling off.

Then I got out, ran around the car, and looked down at him again. His eyes were open, but they were no longer bright. They were lifeless—shiny, but vacant. Dark and cold as an empty house.

I'd never seen a dead man before, but it was obvious to me that's what he was.

My survival instincts took over. I looked around the empty parking lot for a witness.

Nobody. At least I didn't see anyone.

I climbed into the car and squealed out of the lot.

"Oh, shit. Oh, shit, oh shit," I moaned, my thoughts a blur as they kaleidoscoped across the event.

I drove for a mile, then pulled over, leaned out, and threw up into the street. I couldn't even begin to get my mind around it.

I didn't know how all this had happened or why. Didn't have a clue.

Had I driven all the way down here just to kill Chandler Ellis, never admitting to myself that was what I was going to do until I did it? Is that why I followed Chandler instead of staying out in front of their house to watch Paige through the window? Did I plan to murder him all along? Did I hit Drive instead of Reverse by mistake, or did I do it on purpose?

You see now why I'm writing all this down. You see why I'm so confused.

I didn't have a clue. I still don't.

But read on. It only gets worse.

CHAPTER

WHEN I WAS SEVEN, MY GRANDMOTHER USED TO drag me to church every Sunday, and after the service she'd make me sit through Sunday school. Even then biblical stories seemed a bit like comic books in their simplicity. I was always bored out of my gourd. Complete waste of time. Almost none of it stuck, but I do remember a few odd religious facts. For instance, Proverbs 27:4 teaches that "Wrath is cruel and anger is outrageous, but who can stand before envy?" Damn good question, especially in light of what just happened.

I had envied Chandler Ellis, envied him for his looks and his money and for the fact that he seemed to reject all of the meaningless things that in my conscious mind I knew were unimportant, but that seemed to dominate me viscerally. I had spent my life lusting after nonsense. Power symbols like a large house in the status-heavy six hundred block of Elm, or important friends, expensive cars, designer clothes, and gaudy accessories. I had a wife with a killer body, who, I admit, I had long ago tired of making love to, but who still turned heads. It was enough for me that other men lusted for her. She was a sexual benchmark attesting to my powers in the bedroom. Being married to a body like that gave me status on the West L.A. cock exchange—identified me as a world-class swordsman. But all these symbols of success, power, and sexual prowess still failed to satisfy me or give me a moment of inner peace.

I wanted to be envied for my status symbols, and sometimes, I was. But even when I saw envy in the eyes of others, it wasn't enough. It felt empty because there were always guys like Chandler Ellis, who had more and seemed to care about it less. I envied him because he seemed to fit so tightly inside his skin, comfortable and full of grace, while I wore my hide like one of my dad's garish sport coats.

But most of all, I envied his relationship with his wife. I envied the way Paige looked at him when she held his hand. Envied that look of love and adoring devotion that she focused on him every time he spoke. So what happened may not be entirely my fault, at least not if you believe the Bible. Maybe I really couldn't help myself, because as Proverbs clearly states, "Who can stand before envy?"

I no longer envied Chandler Ellis. Instead, I'd killed him. Turned him into Charlotte, North Carolina's latest hit-and-run statistic. And I'd accomplished this in a split second without even knowing I was doing it. Then I ran over him a second time, making sure the job was finished, destroying any chance I had of deluding myself later that I had done it by mistake.

But hold it. Let's throw a flag at that for a minute. Maybe there *is* another side to all of this. Maybe there's a sliver of emotional salvation hiding in this human tragedy.

Let's accept, for the moment, the pure insanity of driving six hundred miles to get here just so I could look at another man's wife through his living-room window. Maybe once I'd followed Chandler to that drugstore and he'd started toward me in the parking lot, I'd had no other course of action. Up till then, I had used bad judgment, but had committed no crime. Once he advanced on me, waving his arms in a threatening way, maybe then I had simply panicked, reacted . . . hit the wrong gear by mistake and run him down. After all, it *was* a rental car. I *was* unfamiliar with the gearbox. Maybe I had acted out of pure self-preservation. Maybe I had accidentally hit him, then realized that there was no explanation for my being in Charlotte. Knowing I would be an immediate suspect in a vehicular assault, maybe then and only then had certain brain synapses, bred into me by thousands of years of natural selection and *Homo sapiens* survival instincts, kicked in. I had done the only thing left to do under the circumstances. Back up, park on his chest, and finish the job, ending any chance for *his* survival. Kill or be killed. Law of the jungle, primal and pure.

On the surface, I liked this second scenario a hell of a lot better than the first, but I didn't trust it. I knew it was bullshit—a cheap rationalization for murder. But in those first moments of fear and confusion after I left the parking lot, I clung to that rationale like a man clinging to the side of a life raft. I was in a swirl of white water, wallowing and swallowing, adrift in a confusing storm of emotions.

The first hour after I ran Chandler Ellis down was pretty much time lost. The best way to describe it is to say it was reminiscent of one of my old interplanetary drug hazes back when I was ghost-busting on acid. I was in a daze, my reality strobing and morphing into shapes, sounds, and colors I didn't recognize at the time or remember well later. All the while, I was driving the damn Taurus. Miraculously, I didn't hit anybody else. My mind was elsewhere, skipping over facts, landing on half-truths, bouncing and flying like a flat stone hurled against the tide.

And then I found myself sitting in the car parked next to a shimmering lake. I didn't know its name, or the time, or even where the fuck I was . . . somewhere near the Township of Salisbury, still in North Carolina, I think. A full moon lit the water. My head was throbbing; my neck and shoulders ached from having clutched the wheel in a vice grip for almost two hours. My whirling mind began to slow and I grabbed for it, trying to regain control, but only managed to hold my turbulent thoughts for a second before they snapped loose, spinning off wildly again. Like sparks flying off a miller's wheel, tiny particles of reason finally floated down and landed around me.

Had anybody seen me do it? Somebody in the market? A drunk lying in the shadows? But before I could focus on these questions, my thoughts were spinning again, catapulting over broken memories and the verses of old songs, which I chanted mindlessly as I sat there.

Then another grab for sanity. The car. Was Chandler's blood on the car? As that lucid, worthwhile question lingered, I suddenly heard myself chanting, "Oh God, oh God, oh God," as if the Supreme Deity would have anything to do with me now.

Once more I grabbed. This time I managed to hold my tortured thoughts.

I locked onto something important. Tire treads.

I remembered a documentary I saw on A&E dealing with the new forensic science being employed by police departments. Investigators could trace a car using tire tracks. They could make random pattern matches. Isolate something called "unique identifiers." They could graph the imperfections in the tire tread and scan them into a computer. If they found the car, they could match the tire tread to the unique identifiers found at the crime scene.

There was also something called "paint fragment analysis." Tiny paint particles, so small you couldn't see them, could be left on skin or clothes. They could retrieve dust-sized samples from Chandler's body and tell what color and make of car the paint came from. I was starting to panic again.

I got out of the car and walked around to the front. It was a mess. A broken headlight and frame. A caved-in right front fender. Some of the blue paint was scratched and scuffed. There was blood. Chandler's blood. Not much, but

some. It had seeped into the broken headlight. Shit. I had to
do something about this.

I sat on the hard ground and leaned up against the car
to think about it, trying to sort out my options. Without
warning, I began to cry. Deep, soul-wrenching sobs choked
my throat and constricted my breathing. It wasn't so much
that I was feeling sorry for myself. Although, truth be told,
there was some of that. It was more as if I was saying goodbye to the last remnants of who I thought I was.

No longer could I accept myself as someone who had
been put upon by life. No longer could I blame my emotional shortcomings on my dead father's fucked-up value
system, or on my mother or grandma. In truth, they had all
helped to form who I was, shallow and transparent as that
man had become. But none of that mattered anymore. I now
knew I was no longer struggling against the events of an unfair childhood. I was no longer a victim of my father's death,
or my mother's low-income circumstances. I couldn't think
of myself as someone put upon by the choices and actions
of others. Chick Best, the victim, was gone.

This new Chick had just committed murder. He had killed
another man. This new Chick was an aggressor. A perpetrator.
This new Chick had taken a human life, parked on a man's
chest and waited for him to die. I'm telling you, it was an impossible idea to come to grips with.

Being a victim is so much more satisfying. In failure, as
a victim your excuse is built in. *It's not my fault. I had no ad-
vantages growing up. My father was a cheap, slick asshole.*
When a victim succeeds, he has heroically overcome adver-

sity, risen above cultural and sociological disadvantages to win bravely in the face of all odds.

However, there is no heroic rationale for murder. Murder is pure aggression. Murderers are unredeemable psychotics. So I sat and cried for the loss of the man I had been. I cried until my throat was dry and my eyes were swollen. When I was cried out, I sat in silence, my mind aching, but no longer spinning.

I knew that I had a lot of things to do, and I had to do them quickly. First I had to repair this fucking car. I couldn't destroy it or ditch it, because the Hertz Rent a Car in New York City would want to know where it was. If a blue Taurus went missing from Hertz and the police got blue Taurus paint off Chandler's body, a ten-minute computer run would find me and I would end up hosting a shower party in the North Carolina State Prison.

I had to repair the car so no one would notice. I knelt down and studied the right front fender. It was bent. No large paint chips seemed to have been knocked loose, but the rim was scratched and the paint underneath scraped, so that would need to be straightened and repainted. I had driven over Chandler's chest with the right-side tires. Can skin and clothes be used to match treads? Did I leave tread marks on Chandler or on the pavement? I wasn't sure, but to be safe, I needed new rubber.

How long before Chandler Ellis's death would become front-page news? With luck, it wouldn't make the papers until tomorrow evening. Of course, because he was related to the *L.A. Times* Chandlers, the electronic media would jump all over it, pending notification of kin. That meant it could make the TV news by sometime tomorrow, maybe sooner. So there wasn't much time, and I had a lot to do.

I looked at my watch. It was still only 1:35 A.M. It seemed like a lifetime had passed since I'd hit Chandler, but in reality it had only been a little over two hours. I opened my wallet and counted my cash. Eighteen hundred dollars. I always carry a lot of cash when I travel because I sometimes incur personal expenses that I don't want showing up on my Amex card. Don't ask, because I'm not going to explain that further.

I got back in the Taurus and drove all night, heading north. I stopped at a self-serve car wash in Richmond around 5:30 A.M. and scrubbed the front end of the car until I was pretty sure there was no blood left. I bought some dark glasses and a ball cap at a drugstore. The tire store I eventually picked was in Newport News, Virginia. It was in a grungy neighborhood full of low-end businesses where it looked to me like cash would talk. It was seven in the morning when I parked out front of Dale's Tire Town and shut off the engine. Dale hadn't worked too hard for his slogan. In red script it read: DALE'S Where the Rubber Meets the Road. *Pu-leeze.*

At nine-fifteen, a man who turned out to be Dale himself drove in and opened up. I waited until a few employees arrived, and then, wearing the sunglasses and ball cap, pulled up to one of the tire bays and got out. Dale was a speed-thin southerner with a skinny neck that looked like it was made up of gristle and rubber bands.

"Cha' need?" he slurred at me through tobacco-stained teeth the same color and texture as a grape-stake fence.

"New tires," I said, forcing a smile through my own too-dry pearlies.

Dale squatted down and looked at the rear tires on the Taurus, then he got up and checked the front pair. He rubbed his chin like he was preparing to shave. Of course there was still over a half-inch of good rubber all around, and that turned out to be what was bothering him.

"Zis a feckin' joke? You one a them TV consumer guys with a hidden camera, tryin' ta see if I'll sell ya tires ya don't need?"

"No . . . no. I, uh . . . I don't like the way these tires are riding. I'm gonna throw 'em in the trunk and put 'em on my wife's car." Even to me, this sounded more like an excuse than an explanation. Or was it just my guilty conscience revving?

An hour later, I paid for four new Firestones. They were identical to the ones Dale had just taken off the car, minus the unique identifiers that could be used to match the tread marks on Chandler's chest and send me to prison. Dale threw the old set into the trunk. They didn't all fit, so the last one we rolled onto the floor behind the front seat. I muttered some nonsense about my wife's car, paid with cash, and left.

As I pulled out I glanced in the mirror and saw Dale watching, shaking his head slowly. *This bubba's definitely gonna remember me,* I thought.

"Yessir, Officer. Yankee in a suit. Guy came in here, swapped a perfectly good set of Stonies for a set of new ones. Didn't make no damn sense 'tall."

When you watch this stuff on TV or in the movies, it seems pretty simple. It's another thing altogether when you're actually trying to cover up a murder yourself. Everything you say or do has repercussions. Trying to wipe a trail clean is no simple task. A tiny mistake is like a pebble thrown into a still lake; the circles of ripples roll out, but it's still pretty easy to judge where the stone originally landed.

I parked by a body of water about ten miles away, went through the bushes, and found a good place to ditch the tires. I rolled them into a lake I didn't know the name of and watched while they sank.

As I was doing this, I started to rehearse the story I was planning to tell at the auto body shop. I needed to find somebody who could fix this car immediately—somebody who had the right Taurus parts in stock—the headlight frame, the glass lens, and the correct color of paint so the rental agency wouldn't spot the damage. I couldn't be hanging around in a broken-up blue Taurus while the cops two hundred miles away were finding pieces of Taurus blue paint on Chandler's body. They'd put out a TV story and a four-state bulletin and I'd be toast. I needed to get this done fast and get outta here before the police lab found anything. I needed to fly under the radar.

I drove north again. The further away from Charlotte the better. I had already decided that Newark, New Jersey, would be the best place. It was close to New York, where I would fly out. Big city, lots of auto repair shops. This time, I figured the bigger the auto body shop the better. The more work they got, the less likely they were to remember my little headlight and fender repair job.

As I drove north on the interstate, I kept my mind off Chandler Ellis—the sound his body made thumping under my wheels, the sound of his whispery voice.

"Chick, help me."

Instead of focusing on that I went over my new story . . . Driving at night . . . Hit an animal . . . Damn thing ran across the road. Deer. *Are there deer in Virginia? Had to be, they're everywhere* . . . Hit the deer, it veered and ran on. Never saw if it was hurt . . . Stopped, tried to find it. Walked around looking—following the trail of blood, so I could try to help it, but—

No. Too much. Don't overdo it. Make it boring, so they'll forget it. Just hit the deer. It kept going. I kept going . . . like that.

I picked an auto repair shop called Top Hat Auto Repair. A cartoon of a man wearing a tuxedo and top hat, holding a wrench and screwdriver, graced the chain-link fence out front. Underneath it advertised: Body Repair—Parts Center.

This time I bought a pair of drugstore reading glasses to go with my ball cap and went inside without my suit coat.

The estimator checked out the damage while I mumbled my deer story. He didn't seem to be listening or to care. His uniform identified him as Lou, but everybody called him "Wheezy." "Hey, Wheezy, we got the new parts sheets in from Holbrook Supply yet?" "Hey, Wheezy, you gotta phone call on six." Wheezy seemed to be the guy everyone asked questions of—a manager-type who still wasn't quite managerial enough to keep from wearing his name over his pocket.

After checking the damage, he rocked back on his heels and looked at me. "Cost you around a thousand dollars and 'cause we're busy, gonna take about two t' four days."

"Two to four days? See . . . the thing there is, I'm due in Montreal in ten hours, and I was wondering if there was any way you could get on it right now?"

He shook his head. "No way. If you can't wait, best thing is get it done once you get home," he said.

"Except, it's my son's wedding," I replied. Desperation and panic seeped into my routine like flop sweat on a bad comedian. "We're using this car for the wedding," I continued implausibly. "I sort of don't want to have to pull up in front of the church with a bashed-in fender."

"Rent something else," he said.

I looked shocked. "What makes you think it's a rental?" I was going for indignation but only achieved petulance. He pointed to the windshield. There, pasted on the back of the rearview mirror, was a Hertz decal. Great . . . I might as well have left my confession pinned to the front seat.

"Look, Lou. Wheezy. I'm sticking with this car. There's gotta be a number that gets it done this morning."

I peeled two hundred dollars off a roll of fifties and put them into his hand, thinking, even as I did it, *This is stupid, Chick. No way is this guy going to forget you now.* But I was desperate. I couldn't be trying to fix this car once it was on the news.

"How long you got?" Lou asked, putting the cash in his pocket.

"I really need to get moving. Why don't we start by you telling me how long it'll take?"

Lou looked at the front end again. "Well, providing we got all the parts and paint, we gotta hammer this out and Bondo it. I'll hafta use fast-dry body filler, then I gotta paint the fender, put it in the paint oven for at least an hour or two to dry—still gonna be a little tacky. Then I gotta reattach the new headlight rim and lens. Two o'clock at the earliest, maybe three."

I nodded my head. I didn't trust my voice to speak. I was starting to shake.

Of course, Chandler's death made the late morning news. I sat in the waiting room at Top Hat on a cracked leather sofa, trying to read tire literature as the 11:00 news, with Ken and Barbie, came on. This pair of vinyl cupcakes had too-sprayed hair and too-white teeth. Their padded shoulders were almost touching as they told the viewers that Chandler Ellis, nephew of the late Otis Chandler, of the Los Angeles Chandler publishing family, was found dead in a su-permarket parking lot, the victim of a hit-and-run.

They put up a press picture of Chandler in his football uniform from Georgetown University, right arm cocked back, helmetless and handsome, ready to rifle a pass to a streaking wide out.

His copper ringlets and hero looks made his death all the more distressing to Barbie, although she didn't put it in quite those words. "Chandler Ellis, who was graced with looks, ath-letic skill, money, and social prominence, forsook a modeling career after college to work with learning disabled children.

He also headed the Ellis Learning Foundation, which sponsors research into all forms of learning problems in children. He will be missed," was the way she phrased it, but you could tell that, given the chance, she would've boned the handsome bastard in a heartbeat. I sat numbly, pretending to read an old *Motor Trend* magazine.

The repair work took until four o'clock, but Lou had rushed it, as promised, and the paint and Bondo were both a little tacky when I got the car back.

"Hertz will never know you bent it," Lou grinned.

I paid the bill with cash and drove out, leaving Top Hat Auto Repair in my good-as-new Taurus with the traitorous, Hertz-stickered rearview mirror. Obviously, I was not born for a life of crime.

The rest was relatively easy. I returned the car to Hertz in Manhattan and put the charge on my credit card. The girl walked around the car looking for dings. Nobody touched the almost-dry paint. Nobody noticed the repair job.

I left New York on an eight o'clock flight to Los Angeles. All the way there, my stomach churned. Something told me I was never going to get away with this.

But throughout it all, one thought kept popping up. I'd knock it angrily back down, but unexpectedly it would bounce up again like one of those blow-up clowns with a weight on the bottom—grinning, red-nosed, and ridiculous. One positive thought in this ocean of negativity.

Want to hear it? Get ready, because it really sucks. What I kept thinking was:

At least Paige Ellis is a widow.

CHICK & PAIGE

CHAPTER 11

OF COURSE PAIGE DIDN'T KNOW THAT RIGHT AWAY.
After Chandler left for the drugstore, she sat in the front room of the wood-sided house on Lipton Road and tried to work on a seascape she was painting, but the pain from an extruded disc in her back, which sometimes kicked up after long runs, was killing her. She was getting ready for the Boston Marathon, pushing her distances out, and was experiencing more pain than usual. She wondered how she could have let her medication run out in the midst of her marathon training. Luckily, she reached Dr. Baker before he went to bed. When her back flared up, he normally prescribed Percocet, but that drug was a federally controlled medication, and because she had let it lapse, he said he couldn't prescribe it again without an office visit. As a temporary substitute he prescribed Darvocet. Not as potent, he'd told her, but it should do the job until he could see her. The

doctor phoned in the prescription to Walgreens, and Chandler had rushed out to get it. But that was almost two hours ago. Now she was worried. It wasn't like Chandler to leave and not come back without calling.

The room was getting cold, so she went into the bedroom to put on a sweater, her lower back throbbing painfully with each step. Her MRI showed a slight extrusion at the S-7 vertebra. Dr. Baker had advised her against long-distance running, but when pressed, he admitted that the damage was already done, and said that in due time the disk extrusion would be absorbed. If she could withstand the pain, it probably wouldn't get worse. She decided to keep training and treat it with painkillers. She loved the feeling she got when she was pushing it. Five or six miles out, her endorphins kicked in, her spirit soared, and her body never felt more precious to her. So she kept early-morning runs in her schedule and endured the discomfort.

She returned to her easel and worked for a few minutes longer on the painting, which depicted the sandy Maui beach where she and Chandler had walked each evening at sunset. Several photos she had taken were clipped to the side of her easel. The two distant cone-shaped mountains of Molokai rose majestically from the turquoise- and orange-tinted ocean. Chandler joked that her painting looked like Madonna's leather concert bra.

Hawaii had been a time of immeasurable love. Except for a few dinners with the Bests, she and Chan had been mostly alone. They had walked the beaches holding hands. They would talk until midnight, lying on the beach chairs on the balcony of their room, listening to the distant surf and the sound of palm fronds rattling in the breeze. Then they would strip out of their clothes and screw like bunnies, laughing and holding each other for hours until she would finally suggest they go to bed, knowing they wouldn't.

"Eat me," Chandler would tease.

"You first," she'd giggle, and then, likely as not, they would start all over again. Hawaii had been the happiest time of her life.

Paige loved having sex with Chandler. He was an emotional but tender lover, willing to take her to undreamed-of heights, then hold her up there letting her ride the edge of ecstasy just short of orgasm. She couldn't seem to get enough of him and saw no reason to stop trying.

It was after twelve when she decided to call the drugstore to see what had happened to Chandler. Maybe he'd had car trouble. His cell was in the charger on the desk. Nobody picked up the phone at the drugstore. The answering machine finally clicked on with a message about store hours. They had closed at midnight.

Now she was really worried. Where was he?

A few more restless tries at getting the burnt sienna right on the underneath tips of the billowing clouds at sunset. She was tense and was botching it, layering it on too heavily. She set her paints aside and closed the tops on her oils, then spent another forty minutes pacing.

When the phone finally rang, she jumped at it, snatching it up so fast that she fumbled it out of its cradle.

"Hey, babe, where the hell are you?" she almost shouted.

A slow, drawling voice said, "This is Robert Butler. I'm parked outside your house calling on a cell phone. Is this Mrs. Ellis?"

"Yes . . . Robert who?"

"I'd like to see you if I might," the voice continued softly.

"See me?"

"Yes ma'am. It's a police matter. If I might, I'll go on up to the front door and ring. See you in a second."

"Police? What police?" she said, but he had already hung up.

Dread and fear now choked her.

She rushed to the door and fumbled for the latch chain with numb fingers, swinging it open to face a thin, middle-aged man with narrow shoulders. He was wearing khaki pants and a wrinkled blue blazer. His salt-and-pepper hair was cut into an old-fashioned, fifties-style flattop, which framed a sun-creased, friendly face. He was holding a badge in one hand and a Bible in the other.

"What is it?" she said, her voice shaking with anxiety.

"Could we step inside?" he inquired gently.

"What do you want?" she implored, taking a step backward as he followed her in and closed the door.

"I regret to inform you, ma'am, that your husband was run over by a car in the Walgreens drugstore parking lot. They didn't stick around to report the accident so it's a hit-and-run." He said it fast—gave her the bad news in two sentences, as if practice making these kind of calls had taught him not to draw it out.

The words staggered her. This narrow-shouldered, plain-looking man had just hit her with a sentence more powerful than a fist. Her knees went weak and she found herself reaching for a chair.

"That's absurd," she heard herself say.

"The paramedics who picked him up listed him as 'death imminent.' That's the classification they use until the docs at County Hospital can make it official."

"He's dead?" she said dumbly, feeling the blood draining out of her head. She suddenly felt sticky and wet, white with fear. Her voice was disembodied, and although vaguely familiar, seemed shrill.

"Yes ma'am, I'm terribly sorry. He was dead at the scene. But like I said, the doctors at the hospital have to be the ones to pronounce him."

She felt an agonizing sense of grief sweep over her. Suddenly, her legs buckled and she sank to her knees, falling forward, banging her head on the carpet.

Detective Butler rushed to catch her, but he was a split second late and she went down anyway. He helped her to her feet, then led her to the sofa in the living room.

"Where's the kitchen, ma'am?" he asked.

She didn't answer. She had her head in her hands and could hear herself moaning—long, wailing, groaning sounds that she didn't even recognize as her own until she realized they stopped each time she took a breath.

Robert Butler turned away and went toward the back of the house. She heard water running, but all she kept thinking was, *death imminent*? A two-word phrase so immense she was still unable to comprehend it.

Seconds later, Bob Butler was back at her side, handing her a glass of water. She took it and looked at it, not sure what he wanted her to do.

"Drink," he said softly, and she obediently sipped the water, her hands trembling before her eyes.

"Mrs. Ellis . . . I'm sorry to have to do this now, but if we want to catch this perpetrator, time is of the essence." She didn't answer, so he continued. "I'm going to have to ask you a few questions. Is that going to be okay?"

She nodded her head but still couldn't speak.

"Could you tell me why your husband went to the drugstore so late at night?"

"Pills for my back," she finally managed to say. "He was picking up a prescription for me."

"You've been here the whole time? You didn't leave the house?" he asked.

She nodded.

"Can anybody confirm that?" She shook her head. Then he leaned back and studied her carefully. He seemed to make a decision, then continued on. "What I want you to know, Mrs. Ellis, is I'm not going to let this hit-and-run go unsolved." He waited, then added, "That's a promise. Me to you."

Somebody hit Chandler and drove away, leaving him to die alone? The idea was preposterous. Chandler was . . . He always seemed so . . . Charmed.

"My own wife was the victim of a hit-and-run, three years ago," Robert Butler was saying. "So while most people won't understand what you're going through right now, I want you t'know I understand exactly how you feel."

She looked at him, not really processing much of this. They were just words that buzzed in her anguish. The detective was looking at her with sad understanding, as if they shared a secret.

Then this soft-spoken, plain man picked up his Bible, opened it to a dog-eared page, and began to read, first from Philippians 4: "Rejoice in the Lord always, again I say, rejoice." His voice was soft, soothing. "And the peace of God which passeth all understanding shall keep your hearts and minds through Jesus Christ. I can do all things through Christ who strengthens me."

He continued reading the Bible to her, how long, she didn't know. At first it just annoyed her, but then she began to listen to his carefully selected passages.

"Hebrews 9:27: 'And as it is appointed unto men once to die, but after this the judgment: so Christ was once offered to bear the sins of many.'" Then: "Acts 9:41: 'And he gave her his hand, and lifted her up; and when he had called the saints and widows, he presented her alive. And it was known throughout all Joppa; and many believed in the Lord.'"

His words began to finally soothe her. They cut into her grief with gentle wisdom. She listened, locking onto each sentence, holding tight to the ideas he was reading to her, as if they were slender ropes spun by God that somehow led to Chandler.

Afterward, when she thought back on it, it seemed odd that a police detective working a violent crime detail would sit in her living room and read from the Bible after destroying her life with a few declarative sentences.

Only later did she find out that after Bob Butler's wife was run down and killed, he became a born-again Christian. He carried his Bible with him everywhere, right along with the North Carolina state penal code. Later still, she found out that his fellow detectives at the Charlotte P.D. called him "Bible Bob" behind his back. He had become something of a department joke, reading scripture to grieving relatives as well as unrepentant criminals.

But during those first minutes after the horrible realization of Chandler's death fell on her, crushing her, he tried to shield her from the pain by reading to her from the Bible in his soft, comforting drawl.

And finally, "Revelations 14:13: 'Blessed are the dead which die in the Lord from henceforth. Yea, saith the Spirit, that they may rest from their labors; and their works do follow them.'"

CHAPTER

12

I MAY HAVE HAD TOO MUCH TO DRINK ON THE plane. At least my flight attendant, a smartly turned-out fruit cup named Denny with minty breath and plucked eyebrows, thought so. He cut me off somewhere over Denver. Back in the pre-9/11, dot-com wizard days, I would have given this prissy asshole some primo grief, but since the World Trade Center went down, flying has become a contact sport with bomb-sniffing dogs and cavity searches. These days, if you even get out of your seat too fast, your fellow passengers will knock you into a bulkhead, and the crew will take you off the plane in handcuffs.

So I cut Denny some slack and sat there nursing the last one, trying hard not to think about Chandler and the rented Taurus and what a gross, horrible thing I'd done.

Of course, it was a little like being in the desert and saying you weren't going to think about water. Once you say it, that's all you *can* think about. So I played tag with my thoughts, a terrible game of mental "gotcha," where my conscience, or memory, or whatever it was, kept catching up to me, and each time it did, I had to readdress a new menu of negative terms that described me. *Check, please.*

But of course I couldn't leave . . . couldn't get off the plane until it landed. Worse still, I couldn't bear my own company. I wanted to get away from myself. If it could have helped, I would have asked Denny to move me to a new seat.

L.A. was hot, smoggy, and ugly. I say this as one who loves this fast, transient, slightly glitzy city. Normally L.A. is my kind of place. An hour from skiing or the beach, enough fun and glitter to keep you endlessly diverted. Booty, in short-shorts, whizzing by on Rollerblades almost everywhere you looked. A town designed for insincerity and bullshit. My town. But today it all looked different. As I deplaned, everything felt different, darker and less interesting.

Then I did something I swear you wouldn't believe. I stopped at an airport book stand and bought a copy of *Hustler*, a skin magazine with pictures of naked hookers in high heels doing squats and editorials so simplistic it's like they were written in crayon. I took it to my car, which was parked in the big lot across from American Airlines, and drove until I found a liquor store on Century Boulevard. There are plenty on that boulevard of broken windows. I stopped at the first one I saw and bought a bottle of blended scotch, took it to the car, and had a few stiff ones right out of the bottle. Then I opened my April edition of *Hustler* and had a handkerchief date with myself right there in the front seat.

Why I did this is anybody's guess ... some three-hundred-dollar-an-hour Beverly Hills shrink would probably say I was trying to confirm my sense of self, or that sex, even self-administered, is a subconcious confirmation of life ... a validation of my existence. Or maybe I just needed to get my mind off of what I'd done for a few minutes. At any rate, there I was, parked behind the liquor store, looking at shaved pussies, working on a dishonorable discharge.

The problem here is, I couldn't really get hard, which is generally not a problem for me at all. I'm a charter member of the diamond-cutters club. But all I had going here was a modified flounder. I finally did a soft ejaculation and closed the magazine, zipped up, and began looking around to see if I'd been spotted. Then lethargy and despair descended. Somewhere in the back of my mind, the old Chick started heckling me. *What's the problem, CB? Can't get a good chubby anymore?* The question began to haunt me. Doubts about my own sexuality hovered and I began to wonder if killing Chandler had somehow altered me, taken the pump out of my python.

A friend of mine once boiled man's existence down to one short sentence. "You know what life is all about, Chick?" he asked. "The cars, the houses, the great clothes, the rings and watches ... Know why guys need all that stuff?"

"Status?" I answered. We'd been drinking in the men's bar at the Jonathan Club, where he was a member.

"No, not status."

"What, then? What's it all about?" I grinned drunkenly, thinking he was about to give me some funny punch line.

"It's about getting laid." He saluted me with his drink and continued. "Boil it all down and that's all it is. You go out and buy a sexy car or a big pinky diamond. Why? So your brother-in-law will think you're hot shit? No way. All that stuff, everything we do, everything we buy—it's all just about getting laid. Take that outta the equation and life becomes a zero-sum experience."

It's strange that such monumental truth, such soul-defining wisdom, would be learned in a bar. But I swear, I've held everything I've ever experienced up to that simple equation, and it's bulletproof. No exceptions.

Follow the bouncing ball.

Why did I buy the house in the six hundred block of Elm? Answer: So people would know I had money.

Yeah, but what people, Chick? Ugly people? Old people? Male-type people?

Well, no, not exactly.

So why would I spend three million I don't have, on a house I can't afford . . . put myself into a hole, and cause myself endless sleepless nights? Why do that if I'm not trying to impress the guys I play golf with? Who *was* I trying to impress?

Yeah, Chick, who?

Well, the house was a great investment. Property values in that neighborhood are . . .

You're lying. Who did you buy it for? Not for Evelyn. She was already married to you. So who? Let's hear it Chick. Stop hedging.

Well . . . I guess I wanted other girls to know I had it.

Yeah, but what girls, Chick? We talkin' porkers here?

No, not porkers. Pretty girls. California beauties. Great-looking west side squid. I bought it so pretty girls would look at me and smile and wish I wasn't married so they could sleep with me. They'd covet what I had and find me desirable, because if you want the absolute truth, I don't find myself all that desirable. I think I'm a loser with nothing I really care about, so I need those things to help prop up my self-esteem—my self-image. My unspoken message is, Take a ride on the Chick Best Express. Maybe once you see everything I have, you'll spread 'em and let me deliver a load.

So that was the whole enchilada. Boil it down and, just like my friend said, everything we do or buy is just about getting laid. So it followed then that I'd killed Chandler Ellis because I wanted to sleep with Paige. Because of that fantasy, I'd committed a murder.

But what if God gets so angry he takes the starch outta my monkey?

What if, from now on, because of psychological stress or guilt, or some other Freudian malady, I'm cursed to limp-dick my way through the rest of my life?

WHAT IF I CAN'T GET IT UP ANYMORE?

I took another deep swig of scotch.

"You've gotta stop drinking so much," some ghost from my past whispered in my subconscious. Grandma, my father . . . the long gone dot-com wizard . . . somebody.

I pulled out of the liquor-store parking lot into a brown smoggy day.

You see what I was doing here, don't you?

I was determined to punish myself. Determined to make myself pay a price for what I had done. Losing my hard-on was just about the worst thing that could happen—the worst thing that I could imagine. But back then, twelve hours after I killed Chandler, I thought it was just temporary, a stress-related anomaly. Back then, I still thought I had something to live for. Back then, I was just getting started. It was only the first day of my slow drive through hell.

CHAPTER

13

PAIGE WOKE UP EACH MORNING AND FOR A SECOND would think everything was fine, but then her memory would return, crashing into her like a rogue wave, knocking her spirit flat, leaving her unable to rise. It left her dead inside, consumed by a feeling of complete loss. She felt used up and hollow. She would often lie in bed for an hour, unable to get up and face the day, looking at the black horizon that was now her future. How could she get up and slog through that darkness day after day?

The intense anger came later.

She would finally make it out of bed and wander into the bathroom, look at her tangled, sleep-tousled hair and tearstained, bloated face. For a moment, she would contemplate what to do with the mess. She generally just ignored it, grabbed for a scrunchie, and pulled her hair back and knotted it. No lipstick, no eye shadow, no powder. She would then wander downstairs, pale and wan, clutching the banister with a vacant expression, looking like the tragic ghost in a black-and-white movie. Her heart was sinking. She was totally unable to cope.

Each morning her friends showed up to console her—mostly people from the school where she and Chandler taught. Teachers and administrators filled her house wearing anxious expressions. Nobody knew what to say to her, so they mumbled nonsense clichés: "Only the good die young . . . God only takes those who have finished their work." She would nod and whisper her thanks.

They would hold both her hands in theirs and look deeply into her eyes, searching for some spark of life, some evidence that their well-meaning sentiments had raised her spirits. But Paige's eyes remained vacant, her whispered responses hollow.

These interactions were predictable and ultimately useless to her. But she felt an obligation to be there for her friends, to help them with their mission of mercy on her behalf. Without her pretending to be encouraged by their efforts, the whole scene would have been even more hopeless. So Paige made the best of it. As she struggled to entertain them, at least they forced her to point her thoughts outward, away from the suicidal depression that burned inside.

And there were things that needed to be done.

There was a funeral to plan, people to call, out-of-state friends to contact who might not have heard, although everyone *must* know by now. The network news shows had been running clips for days.

The first forty-eight hours passed in a blur of faces and decisions.

They picked a cemetery and then a gravesite. She bought two—one for herself right next to his. She couldn't wait to fill it.

They picked the clothes that Chandler would wear. Someone stupidly suggested his quarterback jersey. But she would never do that. He had moved way beyond football. She spent an hour in his closet before she finally selected the suit he'd been married in. It hadn't necessarily been his favorite outfit, but it was hers. She loved the way he looked in that suit.

By Wednesday, she had taken care of most of the essentials. She booked a minister, the pastor at their Episcopal church. She picked the pallbearers, mostly people from the school, along with two cousins Chandler had been close to. His best friend in college, a wide receiver named Clarence Rutledge, helped her organize it. She picked the time—2 P.M. Saturday. She made hotel reservations for Chandler's mother and father.

She had been reading the Bible, looking for a verse that Chandler liked so she could put it on the cover of the memorial program. She had narrowed it down to a few but hadn't decided on which one yet.

On Wednesday afternoon she went down to the Charlotte Police Department for a meeting with Detective Butler. He was waiting in the lobby with a tight smile. He didn't smile so much with his mouth as he did with his eyes. She liked that. He understood the weight of her grief because he carried it himself.

He didn't hold her hands in both of his and mutter platitudes like her nervous friends at home. He told her she looked very tired. Honesty. He took her upstairs to a noisy detective squad room and they sat in his cluttered cubicle. There were pictures of a woman with a plain but friendly face displayed in ornately engraved silver frames. In several of the snapshots, older children in their twenties stood next to her. Bob Butler was pawing through a box at his feet, searching for something. He looked up and caught her staring at the photos.

"Is that your late wife?" she asked.

"Yep," he said, and the tight smile returned. "I'm sure you want to get through this as quickly as possible. You told me that Chandler went to the drugstore to get medicine for your back. We found the bottle." He continued searching the box and finally held up an evidence bag. "This the stuff?" He showed her the plastic bottle full of pills sealed in the baggie.

"Yes, that's it—Darvocet. I have a back problem from running. Normally I get Percocet when it flares up, but Dr. Baker couldn't prescribe it without seeing me again so he prescribed this to hold me over." She thought she'd already told him that, but repeated it anyway to fill the silence.

"Okay." He put it back in the box. "Just give it to me quick—by the numbers. He left your house driving the Suburban. Go from there."

"Yes, it was twenty minutes after eleven . . ."

"That doesn't track. The woman who found him in the parking lot called the paramedics. The call was logged in at exactly eleven-twenty. It takes fifteen minutes to get to Walgreens from your house. I know 'cause I drove it. Another five to pick up the meds . . . "

"Right. Then working back, it must have been around eleven when he left."

"Then, what? No calls from him or anything? Like maybe from the car on the way, asking if you needed anything else?"

"No sir."

"Call me Bob."

"Okay."

"Did he ever mention having any enemies?"

"You think somebody did this on purpose?" she asked. The idea had never occurred to her.

"Well, it's never a good idea to take anything at face value. Coulda just been an accident where the driver panicked and took off. Coulda been something more complicated. I like to look at everything."

"Well, no . . . Everybody loved . . . They loved . . . Everybody . . . " She couldn't finish. She felt herself sliding over the edge. Bob saved her.

"You know what I think you need?"

"What?"

"Coffee. Lemme get you a cup." He got up and left her alone to pull herself together. She fought the tears down, battling them like a warrior, finally managing to slam the door hard on her emotions. She wasn't going to come unglued. Not in the office of the man who would try and catch Chandler's killer. That wouldn't help. She wanted this murderer brought to justice. She needed to stay calm and precise because suddenly she had stopped feeling empty. Suddenly, she was filled with a need for vengeance.

And then, the first flash of white-hot anger. Her face burned with rage, and it startled her. For the first time in her life she was angry enough to kill the one who had done this to Chan. The feeling passed, but in its wake Paige was left shaken by the memory of its fury.

Detective Butler was back a few minutes later with two Styrofoam cups full of coffee, packets of sweetener, and nondairy creamer. He lay everything, along with a plastic spoon, down in front of her.

"Is that good?" he asked.

"Yes sir."

"Bob."

"Bob."

He smiled at her, with his eyes this time as well as his mouth. "Okay. No enemies?"

"No."

"He taught at North High. Any problems there?"

"No."

"L.D. kids. That's like troubled children, right?"

"They're kids with learning problems; they're not troubled. You can talk to them. They loved him, at least most of them did. He . . . he . . . " She started to tear up again. First tears, then rage, now tears again. *Get ahold of yourself,* she thought angrily.

"Okay. Not troubled kids—learning disabled. Got it," Butler said, writing in his notebook. Then he looked up.

"And nothing noteworthy or out of the ordinary happened in the day or two leading up to the event?"

She shook her head and he made more notes.

"Okay, that's it for now. Good job."

"Have you got anything?" she asked. "Are there any, you know, clues or anything?"

"Yes, we have a few leads."

"Would it be . . . Is it possible for me to know what they are?"

"Sure." He leaned back and looked at her. A sleepy look crossed his face. "You weren't planning on getting a divorce or anything, were you?" he drawled, unexpectedly.

"Huh?"

"Everything okay in the marriage? No girlfriends in Chandler's life, no fights where stuff got thrown?"

"Fuck you." The rage suddenly returned. Who did this skinny jerk think he was?

"Perfect answer," Butler said, made a note, then looked up and smiled apologetically. "Gotta ask. Wouldn't be doing the job 'less we looked at everything. Even though I believe you, I'm still gonna check around. Just to make sure. Everybody's a suspect 'til I get my focus. All of this is for Chandler, just remember that. In a wrongful death, my job is to speak for the dead. I'm Chandler's last advocate. He's my guy now . . . my client. I gotta look at everything. If you'd killed him and I didn't check on your relationship, then I would've let my guy down."

"Give me a lie detector test." She was still smoking mad. *Did he really think she was a suspect?*

"Don't need to. At least not yet. For right now, 'less your friends tell me different, your anger was all I needed to see."

She sat across from this man with his rumpled suit and cracker smile and felt her anger recede. In retrospect, she knew he was right. He had to look at her. It was possible that she could have done it, or hired someone to kill Chandler. She took a deep breath to calm herself and nodded.

"So, we friends again?" he asked.

"Yes."

"Okay. Here's what we got. CSI's found some paint fragments on his body. We're analyzing it now. We've got one good tire impression. A Firestone with what looks like a factory flaw across the midline tread on the right side. The preliminary paint analysis should be able to give us the make and color of the car. Looks like it was blue."

"That sounds like you have a lot."

"Better than nothing. We're looking for a blue car, probably with some right front fender damage and a cut center tread on one of the right-side tires. So that's something."

"That's wonderful," she said again, then asked, "How long will they let you work on this? I know that once an investigation is a few weeks old, the police will make it a cold case and stop working it. You have to stay on this until it's solved, Detective Butler. Don't let them take you off."

"Where'd you get that?"

"I read a lot of crime novels."

"Okay, here's the headline. You wanta know how long I'll work the case? I will work it until thorns start popping up on orchids and butterflies grow fangs. I will work it until my brain turns to applesauce. In short, Mrs. Ellis, this guy who hit your husband has got a bulldog on his ass—excuse the language. I won't quit. This folder will never be off my desk. I ain't necessarily the smartest cop on the force, but I'm sure the most stubborn. If I don't solve this case and you come up here unannounced two years from now, Chandler's folder is gonna be sitting right here—right in front of me. We square on that?"

She nodded, clutching her purse in both hands. For the first time, Paige felt a glimmer of hope. "But why? You didn't know him."

"Because we didn't catch the one who ran over Althea, didn't get whoever did that. Course, I couldn't work that case. Out of policy for me to work my own wife's death. These guys around here gave it both knees, but we never cleared it. Chandler is gonna get better service. Got my promise."

She left by the side door and drove back to the house, feeling somehow better. But the memory of the white-hot anger lingered. She'd heard that anger often followed the death of a loved one, but she certainly hadn't been prepared for it to be such murderous rage.

There were ten cars parked out front when she arrived. A flower delivery van was wedged in the driveway. More flowers . . . just what she needed. She walked up the stairs to the front door and confronted the crowd of anxious friends. They hovered and fretted. Lots to do. Plans to make. "Do you want to rent the extra room at the mortuary for the reception after the funeral or use the rectory at the church?"

"Who's going to call all these people from out of state and tell them when the funeral is?"

"I will," she said, suddenly needing something to do. She took the stack of file cards. One of her friends had gone through her Rolodex and separated out business and personal contacts, then written a name and number on each card and alphabetized the stack. She went into Chandler's office and sat by the phone. The top card read:

BEAU AND SUE AVERY, MIAMI, FL

She started dialing, telling friends when the funeral was. Ten cards down she finally hit Chick and Evelyn Best.

CHAPTER

14

ONCE I GOT HOME FROM CHARLOTTE, I FOUND out that our Talmudic attorney, Jube Shiver, had managed to get Melissa's bail set at twenty thousand. We had to put down 20 percent, so in my absence, Evelyn charged it on her trusty card for all occasions, the good old black Amex. Once Evelyn bailed Melissa out of Juvie, our grateful daughter immediately skipped her bond, or, to put a better face on it, she disappeared, and nobody quite knew where she was. According to my wife, it was my job to try and find her. That meant I had to call Big Mac. I got him on the phone after trying at least six times. I shouldn't have wasted the effort.

"Look, man, I ain't the bitch's babysitter," was the way he addressed my question as to her current whereabouts.

"Mr. McKenna, I am not suggesting that you are. It's just that if Melissa has some crazy idea about running and not facing these charges, then things will only get worse. She needs to put herself in the hands of our attorney and fight this in court."

Before you say, "Duh, Chick"—or more to the point, "Why don't you take your own fucking advice?"—let's remember that Melissa was only facing a possession with intent to sell charge, and I was facing second-degree murder. In life, the way you choose to deal with any given problem is usually in direct relationship to its degree of jeopardy.

"If I see your bang-tail daughter, I'll tell her, but I'm fuckin' tired a gaffling with that bitch. What a dumb-ass move leaving her meth in my crib. Now I got major heat coming down on me. Fucking pisses me off."

"Yes," I said softly. "I can certainly see how it might."

Okay, okay. I know. Don't even go there. But the guy scares me. So, I couldn't find Melissa. God only knows where she was.

Evelyn and I got into a huge fight a day later. It was about Mickey D and the American Express account, which was a collective topic as well as a selective one. My no-limit Black Card had just been canceled because of the Hawaii trip. I'd failed to stay current. The less valuable Optima Card was only good for up to ten grand. Four had gone for Melissa's bail, but Evelyn spent another six—and wait till you hear what it went for. She maxed it out by prepaying a two-room, high-roller suite for her and Micky D at the Bellagio Hotel in Vegas. It was for the coming weekend, and cost twenty-five hundred a night. Apparently, Mickey D was going to compete in the Mr. USA bodybuilding show there. She spent another thousand on new clothes for the occasion. She wanted to be there to root Mickey on. Rooting, in case you forgot, is something hogs do.

Why was this happening?

Did Evelyn really think I was going to finance a trip to Vegas for her and this walking woodpile, who I'm now absolutely certain is wet-decking her?

You're probably saying to yourself: "Why all this anger, Chick? You don't even like her. Since you're working up to a divorce and you don't want to make love to her yourself, what's the problem if her trainer fulfills your sexual obligation? Once you hire the private detective, Mickey D is gonna get a starring role in your divorce anyway. It's win-win." I'm sure that's what you're thinking. Am I right?

So here's the deal on that. It's about respect, okay? The fact that I'm thinking about divorcing this angry woman, and would probably be thinking about it even if Mickey D wasn't in the picture, just isn't what it's about. If you think it is, then you're missing the point completely.

Not to be overly simplistic, but let's say I've got a car that I don't drive any longer because there are things about it I don't like. Let's further say that I have a newer, better car that I enjoy driving much more and I'm even thinking of getting rid of the first one. Does that mean I'd let some asshole I hate drive the old car around when I'm not using it? See the problem?

So I said no to the Vegas trip. Mickey D could get somebody else to oil him up before his big pose-down.

Of course, Evelyn went completely off the tracks over this.

"Nothing is going to happen, Chick. It's just a sporting event."

Right. It's a sporting event like eating shit is a dining event. Standing around in a bikini brief, glistening like an oil wrestler in a strip joint, does not, in my opinion, qualify as a sport.

But Evelyn was in full rant; her pinched features turned blood red with anger. "You know, Chick, you sit around all day bitching about everything. The business sucks, the gardeners suck, the way I want to train sucks, Melissa sucks. But what do you do? What interests you besides complaining?"

"Lotsa stuff!" I shouted.

"Not a fucking thing. Nothing! You got no hopes or dreams, no hobbies or interests. You're as boring as a boiled chicken dinner. Why don't you go do something? Anything. Why don't you try, just for once in your goddam life, to work up some enthusiasm for something?"

This from a woman who finds emotional fulfillment in measuring her own biceps. I'm telling you, it's over. I'm absolutely done with this marriage.

The argument raged, but I didn't back down. I didn't relent. In fact, I was sort of beginning to enjoy it, because it took my mind off everything else. But the thing about fighting with Evelyn is you have to be ready for it to turn dangerous. She's tough, and on a whim will attack you physically. So when I argue with her, I always keep some furniture between us.

The next morning I was still pissed. I left before she got up. I climbed into my new Porsche Targa, backed out of my driveway, and just drove around. I was dreading going into the office. Everything down there was a shambles. I was also dreading ever having to go back home and face Evelyn and my problems with Melissa. I was dreading turning on the news and hearing about Chandler, dreading running into Mickey D or Big Mac, dreading not being able to get it up next time I tried. I had nothing at all to look forward to.

I was about as low as a guy can get, down at the bottom, French-kissing the drain. Evelyn said that I had nothing in my life—nothing worthwhile that I cared about. While these words were shouted in anger without much thought, from a woman with the emotional complexity of a truckstop waitress, there was a modicum of truth in what she'd said.

Amongst all my possessions and accomplishments, I *didn't* really have anything I cared about. Nothing *did* interest me. I had only one ambition. I wanted to be admired by others. When you stop to think about it, that's a pretty worthless goal.

Okay, here's another embarrassing admission, which I'm sure you've already figured out anyway. Under all my strutting and boasting, I had been depending on other people to grade my paper—to validate me. And with bestmarket.com falling on its head, that wasn't happening much lately. Since I wasn't proud of my accomplishments, I was left trying to be proud of a bunch of possessions, which, once purchased, had instantly begun to depreciate at about 20 percent a year.

So despite all of Evelyn's bullshit, there was some truth in her accusations. I let a bunch of hucksters on Madison Avenue define me. I wore Armani because David Beckham did, or the Breitling Navitimer because Travolta wore one and "It's the instrument of professionals." See the problem? Even my status-heavy black Porsche Targa, which I bought because it was a car "with no substitutes," now just seemed like an overpriced Hamburg penis symbol. Despite all those flashy possessions, I was pretty much lost. I wanted other people to want what I had, and nobody seemed to care. Pathetic.

I drove around the UCLA campus with the top down, hating myself in my hundred-thousand-dollar sports car. I was a psychiatric joke—a middle-aged Balsa Boy who couldn't get it up, hoping college girls would think my car was cool and smile at me. Of course, they didn't think I was cool. They looked at me like I was a guy delivering a pizza. I couldn't take a full day of that, so finally I headed home, arriving around noon. When I got there, thankfully, Evelyn was gone and the phone was ringing. Maybe it was Melissa.

I had to run for it and caught it just before the answering machine picked up.

"Hello?" I said, out of breath.

"Chick?" a woman replied.

"Who is this?" I didn't recognize the voice.

"It's Paige Ellis." And right then, my heart leapt. I'm not sure whether it was from fear or joy. Fear, because what if she knew I'd done the hit-and-run on Chandler? What if she was about to accuse me of it? Joy, because the sound of her voice sent a pure streak of ecstasy through me. You can see how tangled up I was inside.

"Paige?" I swallowed. "Hey, how you been?" I was trying to sound lighthearted. But immediately, I knew that was a mistake. Chandler's death had been a national news story. I should have been sad—should have told her how sorry I was.

"You haven't heard?" Her voice seemed small. "It's been all over the TV."

"Heard what?" I had no choice now except to play dumb, but I gotta tell you, this was really sounding lame.

"Chandler was killed," she whispered. "A hit-and-run two days ago. Somebody just . . . just drove over him and then ran away."

"Oh, my God!" I was trying not to deliver the line badly. "My God, Paige. How awful."

"Chick, I'm so, I'm just . . . " Close to tears now.

"Oh . . . I know, I know," I said, cooing these words. But to be honest I was really angry with myself for the bungling way I was handling this.

"I just called to tell you that his funeral is on Saturday at two. I know you probably can't come, but I just wanted you and Evie to know about it."

"Saturday," I said numbly. "No kidding . . . " I was still at a loss. I'd killed her husband and now Paige was inviting me to his funeral. The insanity of it was mind-boggling.

"Gee, Paige, I'm so . . . I'm so sorry . . . so terribly, terribly sorry." You can see how weak all this was. I was floundering, but in the back of my mind, I wanted to make my opening mistake sound better, to clean up my mess, so I took a shot.

"The reason I probably hadn't heard about it is I'm smack in the middle of a big financial thing at the company," I ad-libbed. "We've been kinda locked behind closed doors working on a big deal for the past week and I haven't seen much, if any, TV."

As soon as this was out of my mouth I cringed. Another mistake. Obviously there were dozens of people who knew that I'd flown to New York to meet with the gnome in the shiny pants and hadn't been locked behind closed doors for a week like I'd just said. See how tough it is to get this shit right?

"Paige? When's the funeral again?" I needed to change the subject and get off this.

"Oh, that's so sweet, Chick. But you don't need to come. It's so far for you. I just . . . wanted you and Evelyn to know that it's Saturday afternoon at All Saints Episcopal Church here in Charlotte. If you send something, don't send flowers. I've got enough flowers to open a shop. But we'd love a donation to Chandler's learning foundation."

"Right. Right . . . I'll do that. I know this is a horrible time for you, but I'll pray for you, Paige. I'll pray for Chandler."

I'm sure God was up there waiting for *that* fucking prayer. But there you have it. That's what I said. She was on the verge of tears again. I could hear it in her voice and her breathing as she thanked me.

I had an overwhelming desire to ease her suffering. So, unexpectedly, without even planning it, I heard myself say, "Don't worry, Paige. I'll be there. I'm never too busy for a friend. I'll help you get through this. I'll see you Saturday. You have my promise."

After we rang off, I stood there, realizing I had just agreed to go to the funeral of a man I'd killed.

Sometimes, I swear, I amaze myself.

Of course, that phone call changed everything.

An hour earlier I'd been fuming over the fact that Evelyn wanted to go to Vegas with Mickey D. Now I couldn't get her off on that trip quick enough.

The funeral was Saturday at two. I checked and there were no red-eye flights from L.A. to Charlotte, but I could fly into Atlanta if I got out of here right after Evelyn left for Vegas on Friday night. Evelyn said that the Mr. USA Oildown was a two-day thing, which meant she and Mickey D wouldn't be back in L.A. until late Sunday. With the time change from the East Coast, I could easily beat her home Sunday night.

My mind started racing while I paced, making plans. I even thought about what I would wear to the service. No kidding. Two days ago, I'd killed this guy, and now I was worrying about a sexy look for his funeral. None of the shallowness of these thoughts was lost on me, either. Even though I was appalled at myself for this line of thought, I decided to wear my new black Armani with the three-quarter-length European cut. It's a long line and takes some pounds off. Not that it matters, but I look damn good in it.

I picked up the phone and booked the Friday night red-eye flight on Delta, then reserved a room at the Atlanta airport Hilton. I could get a few hours' sleep, rent a car, and easily make the drive to Charlotte in the morning.

Evelyn arrived back home at five. I knew she'd been at Gold's Gym helping Mickey with his pre-contest routine because she was in her spandex gear, her eraser-sized nipples clearly visible, protruding through the thin sports bra. When she saw me she threw her purse down angrily on the side table in the entry.

"Y'know what, Chick?" she fumed. "I've been thinking about it and this is total bullshit. The money in our charge account is half mine. This is a fucking community property state. If I wanna spend our money, I can spend it any way I want. I don't have to get your permission first."

"You're absolutely right," I said, taking her starch out faster than a Tijuana laundry.

"I am?" She seemed stunned. Over the past year, about the only thing we'd agreed on was not to exchange birthday presents.

"Yes, you are," I said softly. "I acted badly. You're interested in bodybuilding. Your trainer is about to enter a very important national contest. Of course you'd want to be there to see him compete. It was wrong of me to say what I did. I apologize. I think you should go."

"Really?" She was standing in front of me now, her long, tapered legs slightly spread, her expression puzzled. Evelyn wasn't used to this kind of stuff from me and was immediately suspicious. I had to rein in my Mr. Reasonable act, or run the risk that she'd totally reject it.

"I'm going to trust you and Mickey to be adults," I said, trying to get back on the right side of the line.

"I'm not fucking him, Chick."

She was such a delightfully subtle creature.

"I know you're not. I know that. I'm sorry I made a big deal out of the trip to Vegas."

She was still distrustful, studying me suspiciously, the way you'd study a large, black spider in the back of your cupboard, not quite sure if it was dangerous or how to handle it.

"This is for real?"

"Yeah, yeah . . . I want you to do the things that interest you and I'll try and find things to do that interest me."

"I'm not sleeping with him. I don't even find Mickey D the least bit attractive."

Boy, how dumb did she think I was? But I let her have that round. I just nodded and smiled and tried to look supportive.

Anyway, without giving you the whole play-by-play, it went down pretty much the way I wanted. She and Mickey were on the phone immediately, making plans. The conversation lasted for an hour. I found out later that some of his weightlifter friends and some girls who were competing in Miss Fitness USA were all going to follow each other to Vegas. A rolling steroid party.

Evelyn sat at her desk and was bright and animated as she talked to Mickey, waving her lacquered nails over the phone like a voodoo priestess blessing goat entrails. All thoughts of our bail-jumping daughter were left in the dust as we both planned for the weekend.

It occurred to me that Evelyn had not mentioned Chandler's death. It had been on the news for two days, and yet, not a word about it from her. I wondered how she had missed it. On the other hand, if she knew, why hadn't she said anything? I chewed on that for a long time. After careful deliberation, my guess was she hadn't heard. I could think of no reason why she would fail to mention it if she had. So, how the hell *had* she missed it?

I had my suspicions there as well. They went like this: I knew that Mickey D didn't have a TV, because Evelyn had wanted to loan him one of ours, a while back. My guess? Evelyn and the man she didn't find the least bit attractive had been over at his place while I'd been in New York trying to save our business. Since there was no Melissa to worry about, she'd probably just moved in with Mickey for a few days so she could set his hand brake for him.

Well, okay, that's fine. I'm through worrying about it because once this all settles down, I'm gonna give Evelyn a standard California drive-by divorce. She can have half the community property, which right now, with all my liabilities, comes to minus eight million. If there was ever a cheap time to shed this marriage, now was that time. In case you're bad with math, her half of minus eight million is zip.

She left for Mickey's apartment Friday, with a big smile, carrying her luggage, which was just one gym bag. My nudist wife probably wouldn't be wearing much in Vegas, despite the fact that she'd just hit the charge account for a thousand dollars in new clothes—probably bought herself some snappy new nipple jewelry.

After she was gone, I turned on the answering machine, packed my overnight bag, and left. I had plenty of time to catch my flight.

With all of this going on, I still never once thought about Melissa. I know, I know. I should have been out on the streets driving around, trying to find her before she ruined her life, but I was so fucked up at this point, I had lost sight of my priorities. So I was off to LAX, my mind reeling with the possibilities that lay ahead.

A funeral probably isn't the best place to strike up a new relationship with the widow, but I wanted Paige Ellis more than I'd ever wanted anything else in my life.

I wasn't thinking straight. On that Friday night in April, I didn't have a clue what I was doing.

CHAPTER

IT WAS HARD FOR PAIGE TO CONCENTRATE AT THE funeral. Her mind was filled with gruesome images of Chandler's dead body, produced by the open casket viewing that she'd had the previous day. Her friends told her that she should look at Chandler in death—that it would help her say goodbye and accept the fact that he was gone. She had long ago learned that most sentences containing the word "should" were downers, but she'd ignored her own counsel. Now her last memory of him was the ghastly, chalky-looking face that rested on a silk pillow in the coffin. That memory of him, for the moment, had replaced all others.

It didn't look like Chandler, either. The embalmers, working from photos, had made him too thin and stern. Chandler had always been lit from the inside. A kinetic spirit who seemed to glow. Sometimes, when she'd had an open period at school, she would sneak by his classroom and peek through his door. He was so focused when he taught that he often didn't even see her. Watching him work with his L.D. students was like watching a magician perform.

When he first took over the class, he'd been told by the principal that 90 percent of the kids were already lost causes—delinquents who never came to class, or anger-management cases that he was supposed to just sit on and keep out of trouble. But Chandler beat those odds by turning their anger into excitement. He found ways to inspire them, and most became interested students. The ones who played hooky would find him on their front porches with a deal. Come to school for a week; if you don't like it, I'll pay you fifty dollars. He held contests to challenge the kids who refused to read. The prizes were field trips to baseball games. Unorthodox, but he almost never had to pay up. He challenged these kids, but more importantly, he gave them his respect.

The lump of clay lying in the casket in the mortuary's slumber room just wasn't Chan. Paige had to concentrate hard to erase that waxy memory from her mind. She wanted to remember Chandler alive, holding her hand and looking into her eyes. She wanted to remember their lovemaking, their laughter.

She liked to remember the times they ran together on the river path. Chandler was quick, but she was the distance runner and usually left him around mile six. "Where you been, buddy?" she'd grin when he finally chugged in.

"You cheated," he would joke as he bent over, gasping for breath. "You stayed in shape."

She remembered the sand squeaking between their toes as they walked the beach at sunset. They talked about everything: current affairs, art, religion, sex. They argued with each other—mostly politics. He was the Democrat, the limousine liberal, a dove: "We shouldn't try and solve the world's problems with force!" he would say. She was the army brat—a fiscal conservative, the hawk: "We should stay the course and kick some Al Qaeda ass!" They argued, they challenged each other, they laughed, they made love, they discussed thoughts so personal that both of them knew they could never be shared with anyone else.

The day after he died, she began an oil portrait of him, but had stopped, because even with all her talent and all her focused love, she couldn't capture him. He was so much more than the sum of his parts.

The funeral was mercifully over in an hour. The people who spoke seemed loving and sad, but to be perfectly honest, she'd only heard parts of what they'd said. Chandler's parents, Peter and Sophia Ellis, had flown in from Los Angeles immediately after they heard. Chandler's father was a tall, handsome man with wavy hair and a strong jaw. Physically, he always reminded her a little of Billy Graham. At the gravesite, he talked about Chandler as a boy, playing in the backyard of their house. He told of a time when his son had found a bird with a broken wing and how he'd nursed it back to health. It never flew again, but he'd kept it as a pet and even taught it to eat from his hand. Chan's first disabled student.

Peter Ellis broke down at the end of his remarks. His wife, Sophia, had taken so many sedatives that she seemed disconnected and far away.

Clarence Rutledge spoke last. Paige could have kissed him, because not once did he mention football. Instead, he talked about Chandler's devotion to L.D. children—how, at Georgetown, he donated hours, working in a clinic in Washington, D.C., after classes.

Ashes to ashes, dust to dust.

Dirt was laid on the casket by the minister and it was finally over.

She remembered walking with Chandler's parents to the limo and the ride from the gravesite back to the church where the reception was being held. Even though she was always surrounded by lots of people, she had never felt so alone. Paige's father had been an army colonel, and after he retired, her parents began a life of travel and recreation. But they died in a boating accident in Florida when she was nineteen. She was their only child. Except for an aunt who was now very ill in a convalescent hospital, and one cousin, in the army, she had no family.

As they exited the limo and started inside the rectory for the reception, she felt a hand on her arm.

"Paige?"

She turned around and was surprised to see it was Chick Best.

She reached out to take his hand, but he grabbed her and hugged her instead. He seemed almost desperate. He was holding her tightly, squeezing her until she had to finally struggle to pull away. "You came. You came all the way from California," she said, finally disengaging.

"I told you I'd be here."

She started looking around. "Where's Evie?"

"Couldn't make it. Just me."

"Thank you so much for coming," she murmured.

Then other people were pulling at her, offering condolences. Chick stood there awkwardly, as if he had something more he wanted to say, but then she was swept away by the crowd heading into the reception.

They were served sparkling wine and hors d'oeuvres. People stood in little groups, talking about Chandler and Paige in low voices. She overheard snatches of their conversations: "He was so young . . . They were so right for each other . . . So much in love . . . "

Sometime toward the end, she felt a hand on her arm and turned again, to find Chick Best standing there. He was now holding a glass of wine, looking slightly out of place in a long, three-quarter-length black coat, which she knew was the rage in Europe, but—in her opinion—looked ridiculous on him. He was too short for the style; it made him look like a Quaker.

"I'm . . . Is there anything I can do to help you?" he asked softly.

"No, no . . . I'm fine. Well, not fine, exactly. Pretty shitty, actually. But there's really nothing, Chick. I think this is something I have to get through alone."

"Look, this may not be the best time. I know how stressful everything is, but I assume you're inundated with financial issues right now and I can . . . "

"Paige . . . " a soft male voice said, interrupting Chick in mid-sentence.

When she heard that deep, soft voice, she knew it was Clarence Rutledge. She turned away from Chick and faced him. Clarence had tears in his eyes.

"I loved him so much," Chandler's old wide receiver said. He was tall and handsome, and had just graduated from Georgetown Law School.

She reached out and hugged him. The two of them stood wrapped in each other's arms for almost a minute. She could feel Clarence sobbing through the embrace. Then he pulled back.

"My parents came," he said. "Chan used to stay with us in D.C. in the summer before football and during our two-a-days in July. My folks were very fond of him. They want to meet you." Then he led her toward an aging African-American couple.

She forgot, until she was being introduced, that she had just walked off and left Chick standing there.

Later, after the reception, Paige was with several of the other teachers from the school walking out to the church parking lot. She just wanted to go home and lie down. The whole thing was too much for her. Just then, she noticed Chick Best again, hovering near her limo in his three-quarter-length coat.

"Uh, Paige . . . If I could have just a moment, there was something I wanted to discuss with you."

"Oh, Chick, can't it wait?" She knew he meant well, but she needed some space.

"Well, I guess it could," he said, hesitantly. "But I have to leave first thing in the morning. Maybe I could take you out to dinner tonight."

"I'm really bushed, Chick. It's been a frightful day."

"Right," he said. Her teacher friends, three middle-aged women, were standing there listening to all this.

Paige saw a frustrated look pass across Chick's face. "Would you mind terribly if we had a moment alone?" he said, rather sharply, to them. She thought the remark out of place, but before she could object, her friends turned quickly away, heading toward their cars. Now Paige was forced to stand in the parking lot while Chick tried to tell her what he wanted.

"You know how sorry Evelyn and I are," he began.

"Thank you, Chick."

"And I wanted you to know that nothing, nothing is too much for you to ask."

"That's very sweet of you, but I'm fine, really. I'll get through this." She wished she could get away from him. Since Chandler died, she had invested all her energy in making other people feel better. She was finally out of emotional currency. She needed to go home. She needed to be alone.

"I'm very good with business," he was saying. "Figures, accounts, all that."

"Oh, I know you are, Chick. You're wonderful with that." *What on earth was he getting at?*

"I just wanted you to know if you need help on the probate for the estate or any financial stuff that you might not understand, I can stay and we can work on it or I could fly back here on a moment's notice, to help you."

And now he grabbed both her hands in his and held them insistently.

"Really. It's what I do. I want you not to worry about any of it. Just turn everything over to me," he said.

"That's so sweet of you, Chick. But . . . "

"No, really. I'm serious."

"Yes, of course . . . "

"Anything at all. I just want to help. It's all I want."

"Of course. If I need anything, I have your number." Now she was getting frustrated with him. He was gripping both her hands tightly. She tried to back away.

"I could stay an extra day, if that would help," he continued.

Why wouldn't he leave her alone? She just wanted to get away from these hovering, clutching people. "I'm *fine*, Chick," she snapped at him. Didn't he know the probate would be handled by the Chandler and Ellis family estate lawyers? She certainly didn't need any of his help on that. "I think Chandler's father's lawyers are taking care of all that," she said.

"Oh, I . . . It's just . . . "

"Please, I need to go. I need to lie down. It's very nice you came." Then she tried to give him a quick hug, but he grabbed her again, squeezing her to him. She finally had to put her hands on his chest and push him away. "Give my love to Evie," she said.

It seemed an odd encounter, but almost immediately she forgot about it as more friends stepped forward to claim her attention. People embraced her. People asked her if there was anything they could do . . . if they could run her errands or help her with thank-you notes for all the flowers, until she wanted to scream. But she didn't. She smiled politely and plodded on.

"I think I need to get some rest," she repeated over and over, but these friends wouldn't let go of her either. They meant well, but they were smothering her.

"I'm fine," she kept saying. "I'll get through this. I know I will."

But it was pure bullshit. She knew she wouldn't get through it, and she certainly wasn't fine.

She was devastated.

Her life, like Chandler's, was over.

CHAPTER 16

SO GOING TO THAT DUMB FUNERAL WAS ONE OF my all-time biggest boner moves. I admit it. From the very start, I was off balance, off my game. But in her grief, Paige was more beautiful, more endearing to me, than she had ever been, and I remind you that I was already so smitten that I had murdered her husband to make her more available. Now my lust, love, or passion, whatever it was, overwhelmed me.

Going back over it, I got to the funeral with an hour to spare. I ended up standing in back of a crowd of Paige and Chandler's family and friends, surrounded by Chandler's high-school students, listening to one drippy story after another. The hands-down prizewinner was the one his father told about Chandler fixing a bird's wing. As this saccharine tale unfolded, a bunch of tenth-grade dropouts and high-school teachers cried. I was going to need an insulin shot when this was over.

The memorial program had a verse from Proverbs inscribed on the front. The minister said Paige had picked it because it had been one of Chandler's favorites, something about it being better to be poor than rich. So even in death this guy was pissing me off.

I won't bore you with my feeble attempts at communicating with Paige at the funeral. What the fuck was I thinking? Here I was, standing with a bunch of people I didn't even know, trying to explain to her how I could help her with her financial affairs, when she had the best legal assassins in the world at her disposal. I felt as out of place as a Buddhist monk in a strip club. I was standing there trying to blend in with a bunch of schoolteachers who thought it was appropriate to wear brown tweed to a funeral.

In between bouts of social awkwardness, I stupidly kept hitting on Paige. Eventually, I got pushed into a corner with another man who looked as out of place as I did. But we were hardly a matched set. I was stylin' in my Armani long line; he was dressed like a tractor salesman, in tan pants and a fifty-dollar blazer. He had the worst salt-and-pepper, out-of-style flattop I've ever seen. It looked like his barber had used a lawn mower on him.

"Beautiful service," he said, not really looking at me, but keeping his gray eyes on the people milling around in the rectory.

"Yeah, great," I replied.

"What'cher name?" he asked. So I told him.

"Not from around here, are you, Chick?" he asked.

"Flew in for the funeral. Got here like an hour ago."

"L.A., right?"

Now I sort of turned to look at him, because how the hell could he have known that? I'd never met this guy.

"It's the accent," he smiled. "Flat vowels—that's always West Coast. I'm guessing L.A. 'cause a the tan and the little Valley thing you got going there, putting the word 'like' in a sentence where it don't belong."

"*Doesn't* belong," I corrected coldly. If he was going to fuck with my grammar, I'd fuck with his.

"But I'm right, no? It's a hobby a mine tryin' ta guess where people are from by their accents."

"Yeah, you're right. I'm from L.A., the carjack capital of the world."

"Yeah, I read about that. I also read you people kill each other over bad lane changes." He smiled benignly. "What's the deal with all that?"

"Footballus-interruptus," I smiled. "We're all still pissed the Rams moved to St. Louis."

"Right. Good one. That explains it."

He smiled back at me—bad teeth, heavy tobacco stains. A real hode. I was just about to leave when he stopped me with his next question.

"What's your connection to the deceased?"

It seemed to me like a funny way to put it, calling Chandler "the deceased." It was almost as if he hadn't known him at all.

"Friend," I said. "What's yours?"

"I'm protecting his rights. Making sure he gets the best that the city of Charlotte can provide."

"I'm sorry, what? You're with the city?"

"Yes, sir, work for the city." Then he went on. "So you knew Chandler in L.A. before he moved here?"

"Hawaii. We met a few months ago, became friends."

"Musta been some quick friendship. Only known him for a few months. Flew all the way in from L.A. for his funeral."

"Yeah . . . yeah, we . . . I'm doing some Internet advertising for Paige, so naturally . . . "

I stopped. Something was wrong about this guy. He looked at me as if he could see beneath my skin, his eyes suddenly like lasers, peeling off surface paint.

". . . So, naturally, you came." He finished my sentence for me.

"Yeah," I said. "What exactly is it you do for the city?" I asked.

"I investigate homicides."

"Oh . . . " How could I have missed it? The bad haircut, the cheap clothes, the bowling-alley personality. Cop. I was standing here like a moron, shooting the shit with the very guy who was employed to catch me.

I'm not one to spend a lot of time worrying about bad karma, metaphysics, or spiritual payback, but even for me this was a little spooky. For a second, I stood looking away from him, trying to figure out how to take it from here. I'd already sorta stepped in it by telling this guy I'd only known Chandler for a few months—telling him I came all the way from L.A. If I'm such a recent acquaintance, why would I be at the funeral? Of course, you can see the problem—there was only one easy answer to that question. The old Mickey Spillane favorite: "The killer always returns to the scene of the crime." Of course, I was just at the funeral, but it's really the same thing, isn't it?

I glanced at my underdressed companion and found him still staring at me with those sharp gray lasers. Except for the eyes, he didn't look all that smart. Maybe the steel glint I was seeing was just mean, North Carolina stubbornness. After all, the brothers in this state had been marrying their first cousins since the Civil War. Inbred people are supposed to be stupid, stubborn, and mean. At least that's what I was hoping.

I kept trying to ease my way out of this, but for the moment I was stuck in the conversation, so I plunged on. "So you're investigating Chandler's death?" I said, trying to make it conversational.

"Not his death. Coroner investigates the death. I'm investigating his murder."

"Murder? I thought it was just a hit-and-run."

"Second-degree homicide."

"Oh."

Silence descended while I tried to decide what to say next.

"Why are you at the funeral?" I finally asked.

"Always go to the funeral."

"Really?"

"Yep . . . yep, ever time."

He actually said "ever" instead of "every." I was starting to feel slightly better. He obviously had never gone to college.

If you're gonna commit a second-degree homicide, I guess it's better to be investigated by an undereducated, inbred, southern cop than some knuckle-cracking Harvard criminologist.

"You're here because you think the killer might show up?" I asked. I don't know what I was doing. Why was I leading him on like this? It was almost as if I was intentionally trying to get myself caught. Of course, acting dumb but interested could also serve to throw him off. After all, like I said, . . . Make that *as* I said, . . . he didn't look too bright.

"Yep . . . more times than I can tell you, the killer shows up. These perps think they gotta put flowers on the coffin. Sometimes, it's a complete stranger. Sometimes it's a good friend, sometimes just a recent acquaintance." He paused, smiled, then added sleepily, "Like you."

I smiled back, but my heart, I swear, was pounding on the walls of my chest like a deranged mental patient trying to get out. Then he went on, still smiling, "There's something, some inner force that seems to make these people want to come to the funeral."

"Really?" I was scrambling for a casual attitude.

"Yep."

"What do you suppose it is?"

"Well, I'm not a psychiatrist. I'm just an underpaid flatfoot, but I expect it's two things, maybe three."

"This is fascinating."

"Ya think?"

"Like, yes . . . " I said and then smiled at him. "So come on, what are they?"

"Like, okay," he smiled back. "One is hubris. Some killers just want to put it all out there. They're sayin' 'I'm smarter than all a you blue flannel assholes. I can watch the coffin go into the ground, stand right here out in the open and you'll never get me.' So, hubris is the first one."

"And the next?"

"Stupidity comes next. Some killers are just plain box-a-rocks stupid. They want to experience the funeral because they hated the victim, or they had some fiscal or personal reason to commit the murder, and they don't think any cops are gonna be here looking at who shows up. So stupid is the next, pure and simple."

I nodded. Of course, this was the category I so neatly fit into. But I was committed to this line of questioning, so I asked him what the third was.

"The third is 'cause it would be inappropriate not to come. Cause suspicion. Brother, husband, wife . . . that kinda thing. Course everybody in that category is gonna get a hard look from me anyway."

"Paige obviously didn't do it," I said, rushing to her defense.

"Pretty sure a that, are ya?"

"You kidding? She loved him. She worshipped him."

He took out a notepad and started writing.

"What are you doing?" I asked.

"I'm writing that down. Don't want to forget it," he said, and right then I had a shiver of fear. It went down my spine and chilled my balls.

Why did this smartass remark frighten me? I'll tell you why. It frightened me because this cop had obviously decided to start fucking with me. He was being sarcastic and offhand. Two things about that: One, it told me he had already formed a healthy dislike for me, and of course this is the last thing I needed. The second thing was even more distressing than the first. That little piece of sarcasm gave me a glimpse of the man looking out at me from behind those gray eyes. He was not some stupid, inbred country bluecoat. He was a shrewd, smart, cold-blooded son-of-a-bitch.

In that brief second, I saw this ending badly. In that moment, I suspected that this narrow-shouldered man in the fifty-dollar sport coat might one day actually arrest me for Chandler's murder.

CHAPTER

17

BY THE END OF MAY, THE ANGER THAT HAD SPORAD- ically been hitting Paige settled on her like a vengeful cloak. She needed to get it out, so despite her painful back, she enrolled in a full-contact martial arts class. Her instructor was a half-Asian, half-German roughneck named Hans Mochadome— Moch. She was athletic, and the four hours a week she spent in the dojo helped to take the rage away as she methodically tried to beat the shit out of her quick, agile classmates.

Paige also decided to take the next school year off. She was in no frame of mind to teach kindergarten. Whether she even wanted to stay in Charlotte was still up for grabs. It had been her hometown after her parents died, and when she and Chandler decided to get married, he had agreed to relocate there for her.

But now she felt maybe she needed a change. The lone-liness since Chandler's death was overpowering and the anger debilitating. She knew she was terrible company and in a bad place emotionally.

Six weeks had passed since the funeral and she was still clobbered anew every morning by the stark realization that he was gone, that she was all alone.

Her religious beliefs precluded suicide, but her memories made going on seem pointless. She had two general conditions—sad and angry. When sadness hit, she more or less just sat. Sat in her house with all of Chandler's things. Sat in the park watching other people's children play. When she was angry, she went to the dojo and tried to kill anybody stupid enough to stand in front of her.

She slept on Chandler's side of the bed, not changing the sheets for the first two weeks because his smell was still there. She sat in the back of his closet with his clothes hanging over her, crying until she had no more tears.

Bob Butler made weekly visits and brought her up to date on the investigation. At first these visits seemed to calm her, to take her out of these two polarized moods. With Bob Butler, she was seeking retribution. With him, she could look toward the future. Admittedly, that future only encompassed catching the asshole who ran down Chandler. But it was still a step out of lethargy and anger.

"The paint is from a blue Taurus," he told her a week or so after the funeral. They were sitting in a little cafe across from the dojo where they often met. She was in her sweats; he was wearing the same outfit he always wore, the frayed blue blazer and tan pants.

They stirred their mochas as he continued. "The good thing about it being a Taurus is, Hertz, Budget, and Avis all rent 'em. Buy 'em in bulk. If our killer rented the car, that could be a break 'cause they keep records of every rental. I'm working that angle."

"That's great, Bob," she said, trying to find some enthusiasm. There had to be thousands of blue Tauruses.

"Well, it's a lotta damn cars, but I'm gonna take that time period around the killing—the tenth through the fifteenth of April—and send an e-mail to the district headquarters of all a them companies, and ask 'em if any cars came back smashed up around those dates. Then we sort through those and check the names back."

"Do you think that will tell us who did it?" A useless, dumb question, but she asked it anyway.

"Well . . . might . . . can't never tell. They're pretty careful checking cars back in, lookin' for damage, so if it was some rental and it was dented, there'd be a record. Course maybe it ain't a rental. It could just be some civilian car, but hey, it's a place to start."

She smiled and took his hand. "Thanks," she told him.

He embarrassed easily and now he looked away. His ears, which stuck out badly, turned bright red. "It's no trouble. Least I can do, Mrs. Ellis."

"Paige," she instructed softly.

He always wanted her to call him Bob, but insisted on calling her Mrs. Ellis, almost as if he needed the formality to define the relationship. He was humble and sweet and his motives were pure. He wanted only to catch her husband's killer. She knew he was doing it for his dead wife, Althea, as much as for her. There was something very Old World and sentimental about Bible Bob Butler.

Next, he went over a list of names he had collected at the funeral. There were half a dozen people he was curious about—most of them out-of-town friends of hers and Chandler's. Somewhere toward the end he looked up and said, "What about this guy, Charles Best?"

"Chick?" she said. "What about him?"

"He said he met you guys in Hawaii less than a year ago, then he comes all the way from L.A. for the funeral."

"Yeah?"

"Recent acquaintance seems kinda funny, is all."

"He's just a very caring person. Actually, it was sweet of him to come."

"So there was nothing strange going on there?"

For the first time since the funeral, she thought about the way Chick had wanted to help her with the probate of the estate—how he seemed almost desperate about it, and how he had pleaded with her in the parking lot of the church. It definitely seemed unusual then, but now she decided it was nothing. Everybody had been acting strangely. "He's just a good friend," she said.

Bob Butler put the list away. "Okay, then. Guess far as I can see, the killer didn't show at the funeral. Don't tell Angela Lansbury."

They sat quietly for several minutes and sipped their coffees.

"Are we really going to find out who did it?" she asked, hopefully. "'Cause with all this karate I'm taking, if you catch him, I want the first two out of three falls."

Bible Bob smiled at her as he absently stirred his mocha. The spoon clicked dully in the thick pottery mug. "Then stay in shape, Mrs. Ellis," he said softly. "'Cause I'm gonna set that meeting up for you."

CHAPTER

18

I DON'T MEAN TO SOUND LIKE A WHINER, BUT THE months following Chandler's funeral were more painful for me than you can imagine. We finally found Melissa. In typical Melissa "go fuck yourself" fashion, she was sleeping under a bridge off the 134 freeway. The way we found her was, one of her whacked-out, homeless girlfriends overdosed on a spoonful of Mexican Brown, curled up in a ball, and caught the big bus. Melissa was asleep near her when the cops and the paramedics arrived to bag and tag the body, then started pulling that sad bunch of runaways out of their cardboard boxes and rolled-up blankets. There was enough space paste hidden under that off-ramp to lift the whole bridge ten feet off the ground and set it down sideways.

So we got Melissa back. Blessing, or curse? You decide. Since her court date hadn't come up yet, she technically hadn't skipped bail, but her bondsman, a tattooed, gap-toothed, ex-prizefighter named Easy Money Mahoney, told me he knew that Melissa planned to split, and that in his opinion, she had no intention of meeting her court date. If he was going to continue to hold her paper, his insurance company wanted the whole twenty grand in escrow—a no-fault bond, he called it. See how this is going? Everything was hitting me at once. So now I had to convert the last of my company IRA account to keep her out of jail. And what did I get back from Melissa in return? A lotta fucking attitude, that's what.

"They're just my friends," she snarled when I asked why she was hanging with a bunch of addicts under the bridge.

"Your 'friends' have more tracks than the Southern Pacific," I said accusingly.

"My dad, the great seventies drug guru. You got all the fucking answers, don't you?"

It went on like that. It was endless.

Melissa was just being Melissa—pissed off, making us bleed. It seemed to amuse her that I'd had to cash in our last worthwhile asset to keep her from being put back in jail. Amused Melissa—pissed-off Evelyn. There was no way to win with those two.

Speaking of Evelyn, I was seeing less and less of my scowling wife.

Here's the story on the Mr. USA Contest. Mickey D had come in fourth, and for Evelyn, that was a big deal. She got to wear his cheesy runner-up medal around the house occasionally.

"Mickey shoulda won," she'd grumbled. "It was supposed to be an all-natural show, but they only did random drug tests, so this other guy—who anybody with eyes could see was on steroids—didn't have to take a piss test, and he stole it."

Like Mickey doesn't shoot enough gym-juice to bench-press a school bus. Our daily conversations had started to become short and angry.

"Where you going?" Me.

"Out." Her.

"When you coming back?"

"None of your damn business."

"Could you please go to the market? There's no food."

"What's wrong, Chick? Your fuckin' legs broken?"

It was cold enough in our house to go ice-skating. Occasionally, the girls from *Hustler* and I would sneak into the bathroom, lock the door, and check on the Bishop.

Nothing. Limp as a spruce willow.

I borrowed some Viagra from a friend of mine. He gave me two 50-mg little blue pills. He said to cut 'em in half. Of course, I ignored this advice. In my world, more is invariably better, but 50 mgs proved to be too much. In fifteen minutes, my heart was racing—fluttering like a hummingbird. It scared the shit out of me, but I sorta came up to half-mast. I sat there on the toilet looking at the sorriest erection since Michael Jackson's wedding night. But at least I wasn't hanging limp at six-thirty. Progress . . . kinda.

Oh yeah, and I had begun drinking much more than before. It started almost from the first day I got back to L.A. after Chandler's funeral. I'd pound down a few shots before noon, to get the knots out of my stomach, toss back a couple more at lunch, and then engage in some serious elbow-bending in the evening. By six, I was usually giving my tonsils a good shellacking. I don't think I started drinking like that just because I killed Chandler. I think it was also because I longed to get in touch with Paige and now I couldn't. After the funeral and my run-in with that rumpled cop, I was afraid. Half a dozen times I almost called, but froze, my hand shaking as I gripped the receiver, trapped between longing and fear. So I got drunk instead.

Evelyn started calling me an alcoholic. I wasn't quite up to taking social criticism from a woman who spent her afternoons between the legs of a semi-literate steroid monkey. And she wasn't even trying to hide it anymore. So, when she called me a drunk, gentleman that I was, I called her a cocksucking, wall-dancing whore.

We were really having a ball, Evelyn and me. I swear, if I coulda gotten away with it I would have strangled her. I was starting to fantasize about murder. But before you make a big deal out of that, let me say I believed I was way too smart to fall into that kind of trap. So in the beginning, every time I thought about killing her, I just pushed the idea aside.

Anyway, the four months after I ran over Chandler were a living hell.

Only one bright spot. Remember Marvin Worth, the CFO at bestmarket.com? Well, he'd managed to convince one of our large account receivables, a movie-production company, that it would be better to take over our dot-com than to let it slide into Chapter 11, where they'd only get ten cents on the dollar for what we owed them.

Gladstone Pictures was the name of the outfit. It was a Canadian conglomerate and a producer of action movies. We'd sold hundreds of thousands of their DVDs and were into them for four mil, plus a mil in interest, before they cut off our credit and started screaming at us.

Somehow, Marvin Worth had managed to talk these Canucks into taking over my company for the five million dollars we owed them. Hardly a thrilling prospect, because as you may remember, a few years ago my dot-com was valued at six hundred million, but I'd also been down as low as two with that ridiculous offer from Walter Lily. So the five mil sounded okay under the circumstances. Trouble was, the deal stipulated that we had to assume all the current liabilities and indemnify Gladstone against past debts stemming from old disputes and future lawsuits. As I told you, we owed over eight million, so the bottom line was after the sale, I'd be left with an unrecoupable deficit of around three mil.

Then good fortune struck. The leaseholder on the buildings and warehouses we rented went broke. A complete bankruptcy. Since they were no longer a corporate entity, Marvin found a way to break our lease, which was on our books as a four-million-dollar liability.

Putting it all in context for you and leaving out the legal subsets—because, while fascinating, they're probably way over your head unless you have a high degree of business sophistication—I could now sell the company and stand a good chance of coming out of it almost two million dollars to the good.

Two million dollars. Not exactly a fortune, but at least enough to get me started again—enough to set up some new offices and get a new game going.

Maybe you can see where this is heading. My problem now was going to be Evelyn. If I didn't divorce her, I was pretty sure that as soon as she saw the two mil in the bank, she would divorce me. California is a community property state, so she would get half. Once I paid the freight on both our lawyers and their expenses, my two mil was going to be cut down to almost nothing.

That was the box I was in. "Barkeep, 'nother round, please."

Anyway, despite all this, I was determined not to do anything stupid. I mean, the easiest, cheapest way out of this would be if Evelyn just sort of left the picture—if she married Mickey D. But even I couldn't hope for that kind of luck. Evelyn was way too smart to marry a poverty-stricken weightlifter, no matter how impressive his cuts. She would wait until she had her half of whatever I managed to salvage, then she'd move in with him. See the problem?

So that left murder.

But, as I've already discussed, that just wasn't a viable option. The husband is always the prime suspect, and I'm not anxious to end my life fighting off a squad of tail-gunners at Soledad State Prison. Chandler aside, I'm not a killer. So I knew I had to stop thinking about killing Evelyn. It wasn't an option, because I knew I'd get caught. I knew that. So let's move on. We're moving on. Okay?

The day we were going to sign the deal with Gladstone Pictures, I had to drive Evelyn's car because she had stolen mine. Why did she take my car? Because Mickey D liked the Porsche Targa, that's why. He thought he looked sexy in it with the top down; he and Evelyn cruising around in muscle tees and wraparound shades. Whenever they went to the beach, he'd always talk her into stealing my car. I'd go out to the garage and the fucking Porsche would be gone. No note from her, no "May I borrow your car, dear?" It was community property, and as she'd already so plainly told me, she could do what she wanted with it.

So with the Porsche gone, I had no choice but to take Evelyn's Mercedes SL600. But she never washes it, and the thing was filthy. I knew I might have to take one of the Gladstone executives to lunch after the signing, so I stopped at a car wash on the way to the office. I went to the drive-through on Adams.

To begin with, this place is an ethnic war zone—a sink-hole. It's staffed mostly with pissed-off African-American parolees—black teenagers in blue jumpsuits who glower as you pull in. You're white meat. They're the meat-eaters. Let the games begin.

They don't want to work there, and they squeegee your windshield like they're swinging a razor at you, but they have to hold down a job or their P.O.s will throw their criminal asses back in the pecker palace.

I ordered the wash and hot wax, and was standing by the manager's office, watching Evelyn's gold Mercedes convertible go through the whirling brushes. Behind me, through an open door, I could hear the manager, a Hispanic man called Juan, in a discussion with two other men. I glanced around and saw them. Juan was a fat, short Mexican with bad skin. He was sitting behind the desk. Across from him was a middle-aged, overweight white guy, who, it turned out, was a county parole agent. He stood next to a sullen black teenager—ripped and muscled. This kid was projecting enough silent anger to start a riot.

Here's the story I overheard while waiting for Evelyn's car: The black banger was ready to get out of jail on state paper and needed a job to make his parole requirement. His P.O., the white guy with the big gut, was saying, "Delroy has good recs from his CUS," which he explained was his custody unit supervisor.

I heard some papers rustle and then the manager said, "Says here you got a history of violent crimes, Delroy. Carjacking, pulling guns and shit, threatening people's lives . . . I run a car wash. I can't have you standing around here scoping other people's rides."

"My homies put me up on that, man. But once I got popped and did my nickel, I know dat ain't for me. I ain't gonna fall behind dat kinda shit no mo', know what I be sayin'? I ain't about ta be go an get myself rolled up on no major felony, dat's for damn sure."

Or something like that, 'cause to be honest, he spoke so low and with such a ghetto accent, it was very hard to understand him. It sounded like pure jailhouse bullshit to me.

"Says here, you shot a guy once when you were jackin' his ride," Juan said.

"Mr. Hernandez, that be a real sad story. Know what I'm sayin'? That guy was frontin' me off, y'know? I had no choice. Hadda cold deck d'nigger, but, I'm through wid'dat, now," the ex-con said. "Ain't gonna be no more crime in my time. Gonna get me a piece a'da rock."

Juan was waffling, so finally the parole officer made a deal to close it. "Just give Delroy a try. He'll work for the first two weeks at half pay, till you're sure. You'll like Delroy. He wants to turn his life around. Ain't that right, son?"

"Yessir, not be doin' no dumbass kamikaze shit no more. Here on, I'm down for what da white-shirts say."

There was some more paper shuffling and talking that I couldn't make out, then I heard a chair scrape, and they exited the office behind me. I got a closer look at Delroy as he went past. He was a hard-looking, ebony-skinned, teenaged asshole with boxed-out gold front teeth, who looked like he'd kill you for your pocket change. He had a tattoo on the back of his neck that I already recognized, because Big Mac had the same one on his bicep.

B2K: Born to Kill.

This town is a jungle. Sometimes people die just because they said the wrong thing in a bar or at the water ride at Magic Mountain.

"Hey man, you're cuttin' in. Go to the back of the line."

"Eat shit, asshole." BLAM-BLAM-BLAM.

It's all about survival.

Cut off some guy like Delroy on the freeway and you've cashed your last supermarket coupon. That's what life in L.A. had become—kill or be killed.

As I left the car wash in Evelyn's Mercedes, I pledged to myself that I was through being a target. From now on, I was taking control of my life. From now on, these assholes had better get out of my way or take what's coming.

I had already killed one guy. Fuck with me and you could be next.

CHAPTER  19

IN EARLY OCTOBER, PAIGE GOT BACK TO THE POR-trait of Chandler. She was working with more emotional distance now. She found solace in trying to capture the strong, flat planes of his face. She finally liked the way it was turning out.

Given the circumstances, she was surviving pretty well. She had lost five pounds, along with her appetite, and was beginning to look gaunt, so she had been working half-heartedly at putting the weight back on.

In the afternoons, when it was cooler, she ran down by the river. She found herself stretching the distances out, keeping her pace brisk and taking pleasure in the fact that as her endurance grew, she didn't tire. The daily run and the dojo workouts exhausted her and she slept soundly, descending into a muscle-tired REM, where the painful dreams of Chandler didn't follow.

But the rage always lay just below the surface. She had a stress fracture in her left wrist from blocking her karate instructor's side kick, known as a *yoko-geri*. She also had one on her right forearm from a missed *tettsui-uke,* a bottom fist-block. Her sensei had wanted her to take a month off and let them heal, but she'd ignored the advice and stayed in class; both injuries got worse until finally an orthopedist ordered her to give it up for six months. So she concentrated on her running and pushed her distance up to ten miles a day.

Bob Butler still phoned her each Wednesday to set a visit. He would bring her up to date over coffee or Cokes, but his attitude was starting to suggest failure.

"I'm beginning to think maybe I ain't gonna get this guy after all," Bob sadly admitted one afternoon. "Just finished goin' back again, recheckin' everything, recontacting rental car companies, asking them to check fender damage again.

"Same answer: no blue Tauruses with busted fenders at none a them big car agencies, so that means most likely, it ain't a rental. Now I'm checkin' paint stores and tire stores in the Tri-State Area."

They were sitting on a wrought-iron bench near the aqueduct, watching two tugs work a huge oil tanker as it slid up the river. One was in front, the other trailing, each nosing the tanker occasionally, then running along beside it bumping and herding the mammoth ship like busy sheepdogs.

"Tire stores?" She was puzzled.

"Well, it's a long shot, but if he's smart, this perp could know we can do a pretty good job at matching treads we recover off a bodies, or from tracks on the pavement. If our driver knew that, maybe the perp coulda went and changed tires."

"Isn't that going to make him harder to catch?" she asked.

"Maybe could be yes, maybe could be no." He then turned and looked directly at her, finding her gaze with friendly gray eyes. "Here's what I'm hopin'. If this doer changed the tires, that means he talked to somebody, and maybe that somebody will remember. Since the perp just ran Chandler down, could be that he or she was real stressed, acting strange. The tire store might help me get a sketch. I'll show it to you and we'll see if you can make the identification. If you can't and it turns out to be a stranger, at least we got something to show around."

She nodded and swung her eyes back to the huge ship that was now sliding by directly in front of them, its massive hull taking away the view. "How many hundreds of tire stores are there?" she asked, not really expecting an exact answer.

He pulled out several computer sheets. "Here's all the names off the Corporation Commission's computer. That's just the ones that contain the words "tire" or "tread" in the corporate filing." He handed it to her. She was surprised by the number of listings.

"Counting the chains and the independents, there's five hundred in the state of North Carolina alone," he said. "'Bout the same in South Carolina and Virginia. After I run through all'a them, I'll punch out the auto parts stores that sell tires, and last, the gas stations. But that's gonna be a pile a places, so I'm hopin' I score with the list you're holding first."

"Lotta tire centers," she said bleakly.

"Yep," he nodded. "Gonna take a heap a doin', but since the rental car thing was a bust, I have to go after this angle. Gonna check paint and body shops, too. Got a similar list a'them. Figure the front end a'that car musta got pretty damaged. Since the TV people put it on the news that Chandler was run down by a blue Taurus, the perp hadda know we made the car. So he puts the car in his garage for a month or two, doesn't drive it, then when the heat has died down, he takes it out, gets the front end fixed, probably sells it after that."

"It's a lot of work, Bob."

"Nah," he grinned. "I live for this stuff." But he was blushing again, his ears turning pink.

She reached out and took his hand. "Bob, you can't possibly know how grateful I . . . "

But he cut her off. "Don't say nothin', Mrs. Ellis. It's just my job."

Of course, she knew Bob had been ordered to put the case aside. He had a folder full of fresh crimes that his homicide supervisor had directed him to focus on. Nobody on the Charlotte PD thought there was much chance of ever solving Chandler's hit-and-run. While it stayed active, Bob could only put a minimal amount of time in on it each week. But that didn't stop him. He had given her his promise, so he was working it on his off-hours, on weekends and holidays. Working it for her and for his dead wife, Althea.

"You need to take some time off. Take a vacation," she told him. "Now you're the one looking tired."

"What'm I gonna do, Mrs. Ellis?" he said, sadly. "Where you think I should go? Maybe to some Caribbean hotel all by myself, sit in a room and just look at the TV?"

"Don't you ever think about getting married again?" she asked him.

"No, ma'am," he replied. He reached for his Bible and started thumbing through it. "Bible says I gotta play it this way. Lotta people think I'm nuts, but that don't matter t'me 'tall." He found the verse he wanted. "Mark 11 says, 'Whosoever shall put away his wife and marry another, committeth adultery.'" He closed the Bible and looked up at her. "Can't go against the scriptures."

"I think that means while she's still alive, Bob," Paige smiled.

"Yep. Ya might be right, but y'see, in my mind Althea *is* alive. She'll never die. Think about Althea ever day . . . think about her, talk to her . . . So it's not like I'm alone. But I can't take her on a vacation either. Can't walk on the beach with her, hold her hand, or go swimmin'. So I figure I just might as well stick around here and catch this guy who hit Chandler."

She watched him as he stood and picked up his Bible.

"Best be gettin' started. Workin' only weekends is gonna take me a mess a'time t'get through all these."

"Thank you, Bob," she said. "I can't tell you how much it means . . ."

"You're welcome, Mrs. Ellis," he said, blushing again. Then he turned and walked back to his car—a rumpled man clutching a Bible who had the softest gray eyes she had ever seen.

CHAPTER  20

I SOLD BESTMARKET.COM IN LATE SEPTEMBER AND managed to get out of that burning building with just a little under two million dollars. But as I sailed out the door, I had mixed feelings. It was like bailing out of your corporate jet at twenty thousand feet. It felt good when the chute opened, but it hurt like hell to watch something you once loved fly on without you.

However, I had bigger problems—much bigger.

Just before the company sale became final, I learned that Evelyn had hired a forensic accountant. What, you might ask, is a forensic accountant? It's a guy who specializes in hunting down hidden assets.

Here's how I stumbled onto this despicable fact. I'd started to record Evelyn's phone calls, so when she and Mickey talked, I would have an incriminating tape of them planning one of their Vaseline parties. I'd removed the speaker element from the garage telephone so Evelyn couldn't hear the background change when I picked up the receiver and started recording. You see, back then I was still counting on getting a divorce. But all I'd managed to record were conversations where Mickey D and Evelyn discussed his body. Believe me, it was a gagger listening to hours of that drivel.

"Mickey, I really don't think you need to work on rear delts anymore. Your shoulders are simply gorgeous. I'd stick with lats and traps, and keep pounding out crunches, keep the ab work up."

They went on endlessly with that shit. As far as I was concerned, the tapes absolutely proved they were doing the sheet dance. But I also knew that since they hadn't actually discussed screwing, the recordings would prove very little in a court of law. You had to know Evelyn to get the drift, to understand the subtext.

During one of these phone tapings, when she thought I was out of the house, she called some guy named Paul Delmonte. When I heard his name I thought, who the fuck is *this* asshole? But it quickly came out that he was a forensic accountant she'd hired to dig through my bank records. Apparently he was checking for wire transfers to hidden off-shore accounts. He told Evelyn he suspected me of hiding funds someplace like the Cayman Islands, which in fact I was. He said, if he could prove I did it in anticipation of a divorce, then it would constitute criminal fraud.

After listening to this, I came to the hard-fought realization that it was time to step up and deal with this bloodless marriage once and for all.

You're probably asking yourself, what the hell does that mean? Good question. But before I explain, just hear me out, okay, because my chain of logic is important.

Since my recorded phone conversations with Mickey D hadn't done the job, I'd been flirting with the idea of hiring a P.I. to follow them around and gather evidence for the divorce, get some long lens shots of Evelyn over at Mickey D's place, going at it. But the more I pondered this, the more I realized that hiring a private detective was potentially a big mistake.

While naming Mickey D as a correspondent would be helpful in a divorce action, it wouldn't solve the problem of dividing up my estate. As I already mentioned, California is a community property state and the courts take a very hard line when it comes to dividing up assets. I had been carefully siphoning off some of the two million from the sale of the company, working up phony expenses, which I could deduct as costs from the total, wiring the proceeds to the Caymans. That's the criminal fraud her accountant was talking about. I doubted the D.A. would file on it, but it would definitely weigh against me in a divorce action.

As soon as her accountant found the money, it would eventually get returned. Then Evelyn would destroy me— use the fact that I'd tried to embezzle from her to gain sympathy with the judge. Once that happened, the odds were good she'd get even more than her half. Plus, I'd be stuck paying for her divorce lawyers and accountants, as well as a lotta other stuff. Bottom line: After federal and state taxes, I'd be lucky to net a few hundred grand. You can see how grossly unfair all this is.

But wait—it gets even worse.

I have a friend who does divorce law. I got him drunk one night, and without letting him suspect I was thinking of dumping Evelyn, I lured him into a discussion on California divorce. I couldn't believe what this guy said. He told me about something called "goodwill." Wait till you hear about this piece of bullshit. Goodwill is not something one person has for another. In a California divorce, a dollar amount can be attached to my reputation as a businessman—my "goodwill" in the marketplace. The way this goes, since Evelyn was my wife while my reputation was being built, she potentially shares in any money it might eventually produce. That means even my future earnings are at risk. Can you believe this?

Then my lawyer friend tells me the bad news on personal property. All of *my* personal stuff—my car, my golf clubs, everything goes on the pile—gets sold and divided up. But everything *she* owns—all her stuff—is *not* personal property. It's all "gifts." That's right, you heard me. The jewelry that we couldn't afford that she bought for herself without telling me is not community property. It's a fucking gift!

I can feel my blood pressure going up again just thinking about it. But I wasn't going to let her get away with it. I wasn't going to let her stand there with one hand on my wallet, the other on Mickey D's schlong, and just pick me clean. I'd worked too damned hard. So what's the answer?

Okay, let's revisit the idea of maybe getting somebody to take Evelyn off the count.

Now you're probably saying, *"You can't be serious, Chick. You mean you're actually going to kill her?"*

Just stick with me for a minute, okay? When you boil it all down, the criminal fraud, the goodwill, the fact that she ends up with everything I sweated and sacrificed to earn, what other choice do I have? It's either that or walk out of this thing with nothing but the lint in my pocket and the potential that whatever I earn in the future is partially hers.

So yes. The answer is you're damn right. I was definitely thinking about it. However, the more I examined the idea, the more I realized this was the most complicated logistics problem I'd ever faced. Obviously, I didn't want to do it myself, but the more I thought about it, the more I realized that hiring a hit man was not an acceptable option either. If I tried that, several things could conceivably happen, all of them bad.

One: The guy I tried to hire could turn me down. Then if I got somebody else to do it, the first guy would know I was behind the killing, and he would own me for the rest of my life. He could blackmail me or, worse still, if in the future he were to get in trouble for some criminal action himself, he could sell me out to the D.A. to get his sentence lessened.

Two: My hired hit man could say yes to me, do the job, and then come back on me demanding more money later. If he's a professional killer, what am I gonna do? Say no? I couldn't go to the cops. I'd be fucked.

Three: In order to find a killer, I'd have to put the word out on the street that I was looking for somebody. More and more, I read that the cops often find out about these things, street rumor being the profitable growth industry that it is. If the police got wind that I was looking for a hitter, they could send in some undercover cop with a shaved head and an eye patch to meet me in a bar. Once I try and hire him, I'm toast. Intent to commit.

I'm sure there are more problems, but these were enough to scare me off the idea of trying to hire professional help. I also realized that I had no friends or family who had the credentials or inclination to go that far out on a limb for me. That meant if I wanted her dead, I had no other choice but to do it myself. I had to kill Evelyn with my own hands.

Over the next week or two I tried to think of the best way to do it. I tried to plot it out, using cold, hard logic, making myself go over it time and again.

I finally came up with the following plan:

I decided I would do a carjacking, and during the crime, I would shoot Evelyn through the driver's side window of the car.

Why did I decide to do it that way? Because carjacking is the new crime du jour in L.A., and during many, the dumb-ass vehicle owner dies fighting for the keys to his Suburban. Also, most if not all carjacks are stranger crimes, not committed by family or friends.

So here's how I did it.

On Friday morning, the second week of November, I went out to the garage and discovered that the Porsche was gone. Evelyn and Mickey D were off buzzing Malibu with the top down, looking hot and sexy, cruising the strand in matching Lycra. I had been waiting for the right day, a day when they borrowed my car, but a lot of other variables had to also be in place.

I hurried back inside and looked at Evelyn's calendar. Luck was with me, because she had a hair appointment scheduled for four-thirty that afternoon. So far so good. Evelyn can't drive a stick shift, so that meant Mickey would drive her home and switch back to his car. He parks down the street. After he left, she'd drive her Mercedes to her hair appointment.

I went down the hall and checked on Melissa, who kept Bride-of-Dracula hours staying out all night and sleeping all day. My angry daughter was cutting Zs in her room, dreaming of biker rallies or crystal meth orgies—whatever. She needed to be here for my plan to work.

Then I put on a pair of driving gloves I had bought for this occasion, went back out to the garage, and wiped down the inside of Evelyn's car.

I had an old army .45 hidden in my closet that I'd found in the weeds of a vacant lot behind our house a few years before. For some reason, when I found it, I didn't turn it in to the police. Why had I kept it? Well, I'm not exactly sure. Maybe I thought there would come a time when I would need an untraceable firearm. Maybe I just liked the way it felt in my hand. Maybe it was something as simple as finder's keepers. Or, here's a big one. Maybe all of this was written down in the big book for me. Maybe my killing Evelyn was part of our preordained personal destinies.

I figured this gun had been ditched by somebody who had a criminal record. It had probably been stolen or used in a crime. At any rate, the important thing was, it couldn't be traced back to me.

Shortly after I found it, I bought a box of .45 ammo, went out to a shooting range and test-fired the thing. It worked fine. I didn't hit much, but in the army I'd learned that .45s were designed for use up close and not as target pistols.

I loaded it, making sure to wear gloves when I put the .45 shells into the clip. I've read my share of Michael Connelly and T. Jefferson Parker crime novels. I'm no dummy, and I understood it's possible for the cops to get a print hit off an ejected cartridge.

Once I had the car prepped, I put the gun, sans the loaded clip, under the seat, wrapped in a bunch of old newspapers. Then I put on jeans, a T-shirt, dark sunglasses, and a ball cap. With this disguise in place, I drove her car back to the car wash on Adams.

Delroy, the eighteen-year-old carjack-felon I'd overheard in the manager's office a month ago, was still working here. He was a finisher, which was perfect. Delroy was standing with another sullen youth, holding a chamois and a bottle of Windex, scowling at the line of cars like they were constipated turds.

I counted cars and timed it so when Evelyn's Mercedes came off the line at the end of the wash, Delroy would be next up and get the car. He opened the door, flopped in behind the wheel, and drove it to a place where he could wipe down the water spots and do the tires and windows.

I walked over and watched him work. Delroy wasn't a happy guy. He was careless and left water spots everywhere. As I neared him, his animal magnetism hit me—his vibe. He was a menacing kid with impressive arms, which he displayed, having ripped the sleeves off of his blue car-wash jumpsuit. He exuded a murderous aura, if there is such a thing.

"Can y'get the dash?" I asked him.

He glared at me. "Say what?"

"There's still a lotta dust on the dash," I said.

He shot me his murder-one stare. "Ain't no fuckin' dust on your dash, Jim."

"Do I need to get the manager?" I said, hoping this wasn't going to turn into some kind of altercation. He held my gaze for a few seconds, but finally turned with insolent grace, yanked the door open, got in again, and ran the rag carelessly over Evelyn's gold leather dash.

"You didn't clean the rearview mirror," I complained.

"Shee-it," Delroy muttered as he hit it with some Windex, then wiped it dry.

"You moved it," I persisted.

"The fuck?"

"You moved the mirror. I just saw you. Straighten it back. You should leave it like you found it."

"Hey, Mayonnaise, do I look like yo' fuckin' nigger?" he muttered, but he straightened the mirror.

When he finally climbed out of the car, I pointed under the seat. "What about all that?" I said, indicating the edge of the wad of newspapers poking out from under the seat. "Could you get that trash out from under there? I paid to get this car cleaned."

By then, Delroy'd had enough of me. He was sparking anger, wondering how he could take my head off and not go back to prison for it.

"I guess I'll just have to get Juan," I sniveled, starting toward the manager's office.

Delroy growled something at me that I didn't hear, but as I turned back, he had already begun to fish for the trash under the seat. With elaborate fuck-you slowness, he started to remove the rumpled-up newspapers. As I mentioned, I had hidden the .45 in the middle of the wad, and Delroy quickly found it. He pulled the gun out, held it pointed carelessly in my direction, and grinned as if I'd just signed up to get my asshole stretched.

"Got yourself a strap under here, m'man. You licensed to pack this chunck a chrome? Still wanna talk to Fat Juan?" He kept smiling, the gold-boxed front teeth glinting in bright California sunlight.

"Just put it back," I ordered.

He held it for a long time, trying to make me think he was about to shoot me right there on the car-wash finishing line. Of course, the clip wasn't in, so nobody was going to get shot. At least not yet.

"Put it back," I said firmly.

Slowly, Delroy replaced the gun under the seat, smiling at me the entire time, like finding the gun had somehow made me his personal property—his yard bitch.

I pushed past him, got in the car, and drove home.

Once I arrived, I grabbed a pre-packed backpack that contained a plastic raincoat, a change of clothes, shoes, hat, and socks. Then I checked on Melissa again. My angry daughter was still zonked. So far, so good.

I went into the den and poured myself a stiff scotch on the rocks for courage. Then I sat in my upholstered club chair and waited for my adulterous wife to come home.

CHAPTER

21

A LOT OF THE GREAT FEMALE MARATHONERS today, like Ethiopia's Getenesh Wami and Kenya's Helena Kirop, are from high altitudes and hot climates. The heat and thin air helps them with their training. Paige, on the other hand, trained in Charlotte, North Carolina, which was at sea level and freezing cold in winter. Wami and Kirop are light and almost seem to be built out of titanium, with no upper body—all legs and narrow shoulders. They carry what weight they have in their thighs and butts. Paige, on the other hand, had broad shoulders and carried her weight high. She'd started out in college as a middle-distance runner, so her strides tended to be less fluid and more choppy, but since Chandler had died, she'd been training more diligently, and her split times on 10Ks had come down to just under seven-minute miles—6:49 to be exact.

Since that terrible night when she learned of Chandler's death, her runs had been an oasis of sorts, where she could focus on the effort, and everything else faded away. As she ran, her mind miraculously cleared, and the Mean Reds were blown out of her like noxious exhaust. She began to contemplate her future. But the lingering anger—the Mean Reds—were always right behind her, chasing her like a swarm of gnats, waiting for her to slow down so they could engulf her again.

Paige ran in the evening along the well-lit clay path down by the river, smelling the damp, mist-wet ground, pushing herself harder and faster, trying to develop enough clarity to begin to chart the next act of her life. She was trying to view herself not as a victim, but as a work in progress.

One thing was damned sure. Chandler wasn't coming back. He was part of her past. If Paige intended to go on, she needed to establish some goals and pick up a more positive attitude.

It was November, on a Friday, almost seven months to the day since Chandler had died, and Paige was about four miles into her run, when she finally decided that she had to get out of Charlotte. Everywhere she looked there were painful memories. The restaurant where she and Chandler had gone to celebrate after they'd bought the house; the movie theater where they'd held hands and talked afterward about having a baby; the parks where they'd walked and shared their feelings. Even the dry cleaner that kept losing his favorite shirt. There were also her friends who still treated her like a broken thing. The constant reminders of what she'd lost were everywhere, and when she saw them, they would drive her to the ground, where she would curl around her grief like a wounded animal.

She knew she had to leave. But where should she go? Where could she start her new life? Paige hadn't gotten to that part yet.

But her runs allowed her to stop marinating in Chandler's death, and if only for an hour, she was finally focusing on the future. She knew she would never find anybody to replace Chan, but she had to get on with life, had to reclaim what was left of Paige Ellis.

So, on that Friday, she finally made the decision to leave. It was an important first step.

When Paige returned from her run, she saw Bob Butler's car parked under a streetlight in front of her house. She slowed her pace as soon as she saw the gray Crown Victoria with her sad detective slumped in the front seat, waiting.

Right after Chandler died, she had looked forward to Bob's visits. They had pushed her out of the early stages of grief and forced her to contemplate the future, even though that future only encompassed the gristly act of vengeance.

Bob and Paige had pledged to catch the bastard. But lately, as her mind steadied and her emotions stabilized, she was beginning to have second thoughts.

Bob Butler had shown her how lack of closure could poison you. Bob was living proof of what could happen if you let yourself wallow in grief. She could still see the remnants of who he had once been, but his emotions had calcified. He was lost inside his Bible. There were fewer and fewer things that entertained or interested him. Where once there had been a lively enthusiast, she now only saw the skeletal fragments of what she thought was his former self. Paige was determined not to let that happen to her.

Worse still, despite his monumental, even heroic effort to find Chandler's killer, it was clear that Robert Butler was getting nowhere. This quest was all tied up in his emotions about his dead wife. This manhunt was something they were doing more for him now than for her. She could almost chart his failure in the stoop of his shoulders and the lower angle of his chin.

With no new breaks in the case to report, they often ended up giving their weekly meetings more weight by lapsing into long psychological discussions about loss and death. It was a subject where Paige still had no sense of proportion. They were both just venting.

She slowed and stopped a few hundred yards behind the gray sedan, and for an instant, had an urge to take off and ditch him. Catching Chandler's killer was no longer the sole answer for her. Vengeance had become a destructive emotion that kept her wallowing in despair.

But for the moment, they were still mired in it, so she jogged up to his car, stuck her head in the open passenger window.

"What's up, stranger?" she said, through a smile she didn't feel.

"I think I'm finally getting somewhere," he said. "Get in and listen to what I just found out."

CHAPTER

 22

I'D BEEN SITTING IN THAT DAMN CLUB CHAIR FOR almost an hour when I finally heard Mickey D pull my Porsche into the garage. I heard them talking and laughing, then heard Mickey walking down the drive. He's short and wears Cuban heels, so when he walks his shoes clack; it's easy to hear him coming and going. His car is a piece-of-shit Camry, and to keep up appearances, Evelyn makes him park it just around the corner. Subtle as the Gay Pride Parade, these two.

Then Evelyn entered the house. I saw her walk down the hall to get her car keys out of the dish in the kitchen. She looked in the den and saw me pounding down scotch shooters, slumped in my chair, but she didn't bother to acknowledge my presence. She walked right past. But that's okay, Evelyn, 'cause you're about to get your wheels cleaned.

Evelyn passed the doorway again, heading out. This time she didn't bother to look in at all. I heard her unlatch the back door and walk into the garage. She started the gold Mercedes and pulled out.

I rocketed up out of my chair, and still clutching the bottle of scotch, I grabbed my gloves, my pre-packed backpack of fresh clothes, and a box containing the now-loaded .45. Then I followed her into the garage. I waited until she'd cleared the drive, then climbed into the Porsche and checked to make sure the lovers hadn't left the gas tank on E. Then I followed her.

My hands were shaking as I drove. I don't know if it was from anticipation, excitement, or fear. It took us about forty minutes, with the traffic, to get to her hair salon in the Valley.

I knew once I stepped out of the Porsche and started to do this, there would be no turning back. I couldn't approach her wearing a ball cap, dark glasses, and a plastic raincoat, aim a .45 at her through the window of the Mercedes, then get cold feet and say, "Sorry, just kidding." This would have to be, as they say in show biz, a one-take master.

It was about four-fifteen when she pulled in and parked behind Salono Bello. The hair salon is located in a strip mall on the north end of Van Nuys Boulevard. The guy who does her hair is a narrow-hipped sword dancer with a hair transplant. His name is Mr. Eddy—not Eddie, not Ed—Mr. Eddy. I love this shit.

I parked a block away in an alley and walked up the street to a spot where I could see her getting out of her car. I couldn't do the deed right then because, at that exact moment, some Mexican delivery guy was all involved in unloading boxes from his rusting van.

I found a spot up the street where I was out of sight but could see the parking lot and Evelyn's car. I opened the backpack and put on my leather gloves, then pulled the baseball cap low. I opened the bag and took out the plastic raincoat. The clothes I was wearing were old, and even though I had the raincoat, I was planning on dumping everything after the shooting to defeat paraffin tests and blood splatter evidence.

Then I settled down out of sight in some heavy bushes and watched the back of the hair salon. Salono Bello was a little too far out on Van Nuys Boulevard for its upscale clientele. Liquor stores and rundown apartment complexes were closing in on the strip mall, surrounding it like graffiti-painted savages.

Mr. Eddy had told Evelyn he was giving up his lease and moving to a shop on Lankershim. I was glad he hadn't gotten around to it yet. This area was a perfect setting for a carjack murder. The politically correct way to describe the block would be to say it was "mixed." A better description would be to say it was being totally overrun by ethnic assholes.

I continued to watch the parking lot behind the hair salon. It was late in the afternoon and there were only three or four cars there. The sun sets early in November. My guess was around five o'clock. I figured that since Evelyn was getting her two-month dye-job, she wouldn't be out until after dark—around six. The parking lot should be empty by then. I kept telling myself, *Relax, Chick, this will work out fine.*

Only trouble was, my hands wouldn't stop shaking. My palms were sweating in the leather gloves. My heart was beating too fast, and I kept pulling on the bottle of scotch I'd brought, looking for relaxation and courage. Time oozed.

Finally, at five-fifty-five, Evelyn came out with Mr. Eddy and stood at the back door of the salon. They paused to talk.

After they finished their chat, she gave him a peck on the cheek. He tittered, cooed, and waggled his fingers at her as he made a graceful pirouette and went back inside to close up. Evelyn hurried to her Mercedes.

From here on, my recollection of the event gets kind of hazy. I mean, I remember what happened, but it's sort of surrealistic. Time became abstract. I was more than a little hammered on scotch, and remember thinking it's probably not such a good idea to try and commit a first-degree murder while half in the bag. But I was already too far into this to abort. I waited until Evelyn was inside her Mercedes with the motor running, then I walked up to the car.

She was starting to pull out of her parking space when she saw me. She stopped the car and frowned, her expression pinched and mean. I walked toward her, holding the gun low and out of sight behind my leg. I swear I still didn't know if I could do it. My mouth was suddenly bone dry. But to gain resolve as I closed the distance, I was concentrating on all the things I hated about her. Standing naked on the hotel balcony, screwing Mickey D, wasting more money than a Hollywood charity, taking all my dot-com profits and blowing them on jewelry she never even wore, hiring a forensic accountant to get me arrested for fraud—the whole depressing array of complaints I had built up over the past two years.

As I got closer, she started rolling down the window. "What the fuck are you doing here?" she growled. "You look ridiculous in that getup."

"I came to give you this," I said theatrically as I pulled the gun out from behind my leg and pointed it at her.

You won't believe this, but she actually started laughing at me. No kidding . . . she sat there and just laughed.

"Who do you think you're kidding with that?" she said, glancing at the automatic. "What a fucking moron you are, Chick."

That did it. I'm pointing a gun at her about to take her shitty life and she laughs and calls *me* a moron?

I pulled the trigger.

I wasn't at all prepared for what happened. To begin with, the .45 roared, reverberating with deafening impact in the enclosed concrete strip mall. Blood spewed, blowing back all over me as Evelyn flew sideways, all the way across the seat of the car toward the passenger door, taking the unrolling seat belt with her. It finally snapped to the end of its length. She hung there in the belt. With half of her head gone, she was undoubtedly dead, but then the seat belt slowly retracted, pulling her toward me. She came relentlessly back across the seat, like the murderous corpse in a mummy movie. As she neared, I could see the hole I'd put in her forehead, which was about the size of a nickel, but the bullet had exited, taking the back of her head with it and breaking the far window. She finally settled back into the driver's seat, where she sat dripping blood and cerebral fluid. It was gruesome and horrible.

"Holy shit," is what I think I said. But I couldn't stop now. I couldn't freeze up. The gunshot would bring people. They would see me. I opened the door, reached in, unhooked the seat belt, and dragged her out of the car. I threw her onto the pavement. Then I jumped into the idling Mercedes and roared away.

I couldn't believe how much blood and brain tissue was in there. I didn't count on there being such a terrible mess in the front seat. When I had imagined it, there wasn't any blood or cerebral tissue at all, but now, the whole dash and seat were oozing with gore.

I drove up into the hills and parked in a deserted spot I'd picked out earlier. I had chained my BMX Black Mountain trail bike to a tree well off the road almost a week ago.

Here's the story on the BMX bike: It had been Evelyn's gift to me two Christmases ago. She wanted me to ride it, get back into shape—more grief about my body. That was back when we were still occasionally bumping boots together. She once told me after sex that she was repulsed by my flab. As I remembered this, I had a moment of pure joy that she was out of my life forever. Now, all I had to do was finish the job.

I didn't have to wipe down the car, because I'd been wearing gloves, and even if a print of mine miraculously survived, so what? After all, it was our Mercedes.

I went to work stripping the car using the small Mercedes toolkit in the trunk. I pulled out the radio and the CD player. I took the airbags and the phone. I'm not much with tools, as I'm sure you've already guessed, but most of this stuff was easy to remove, except for the radio, which I accidentally broke when I pulled it out of the dash.

I stripped off the bloody raincoat and all my clothes and changed into the fresh duds I'd brought. Then I rolled everything up and put it in the backpack. I put on the pack, dropped the .45 near the car, climbed on my bike, and rode down out of the mountains.

I peddled for at least fifteen minutes. I was peddling like mad and I thought my lungs would explode. Finally I made it to a gas station that I'd picked earlier because it seemed like nobody in the place spoke much English. Using my fractured Spanish, I asked one of the Mexicans who worked there to watch my bike.

"*Mira esta bicicleta,*" or something. He nodded and I called a cab. I went to an address in the Valley about a quarter mile from the murder scene, paid the cabbie, and walked the rest of the way to the hair salon.

When I got to Salono Bello, it was six forty-five. There was a coroner's van there, and cops all over the place. Looky-loos were ringing the crime scene. I had parked my Porsche a block away, in an alley. The cops were still working by Evelyn's body and hadn't gotten around to canvasing the neighborhood yet. I got into my car and drove back to where I'd hidden the radio and the airbags. I threw them into the trunk and drove to the gas station, then threw my trail bike in the back of the Porsche along with everything else. Then I drove up to the Hollywood Reservoir, and after I made sure nobody was around, slung the radio, phone, and airbags out into the water and watched them sink. I grabbed the backpack full of clothes, walked up into the woods above Lake Hollywood, and set fire to everything using a can of lighter fluid I'd brought with me. Then I buried the ashes. I got back into the car and was home well before eight.

For my alibi to hold up I had to be able to prove I was at home from around five-forty-five until now, give or take half an hour. That's where my angry daughter came in. Melissa was still asleep, so I sneaked into her room and reset her clock to six-oh-five. Then I woke her up.

"What the fuck do you want?" she said, typically pissed, as she rolled over and glared at me out of one bloodshot eye.

"You know where your mother went?" I asked.

"Fuck, no." She looked at the darkened window. "What time is it? I'm meeting Big Mac later."

"I don't know. Is that clock right?" I asked, pointing at it. She turned a bleary eye toward the dial.

"Yeah . . . five past six?" she said.

I looked at my watch. "Six-oh-five exactly," I confirmed. "Go back to sleep. I'm just getting worried about your mother. When do you want me to wake you up?"

"Eight . . . nine . . . I don't know."

I turned off the light and sat on the floor outside her room until I could hear her steady breathing again, then I sneaked back inside and reset her clock to the right time.

I wasn't sure how long it would be until the cops arrived. I knew I would be their prime suspect until they located and dusted the car and gun and came up with Delroy's prints.

Then I jumped in the shower and lathered up.

While I was washing, a strange thought hit me. I had been completely destroyed when I killed Chandler. It had tortured me for weeks. After I'd run him down, I'd had to pull over and vomit. I couldn't even get an erection. But with Evelyn, I didn't feel a shred of anything—no nausea or guilt. No remorse or sadness. I simply felt free.

Was that a gain or a loss? It felt like a gain, but I was smart enough to realize it was probably a loss.

As I stood under the spray, washing myself clean, I was so happy I couldn't keep from smiling.

You see, I was already looking forward to calling Paige and telling her about my horrible, unexpected tragedy.

PAIGE & CHICK

I THOUGHT BOB BUTLER HAD AGED TERRIBLY IN the months since Chandler died. He looked tired and drawn sitting in his car in front of my house. He had lost weight, and I could see new lines framing his mouth, cutting the skin around his eyes. As I looked at him sitting there, smiling, ready to tell me his good news, I wondered if I could go through another meeting where some promising clue he found turned into a disappointing dead end.

"Come inside, I've got some coffee on," I told him.

"No, no . . . I wanta get going. Got me two hundred miles t'go, and I want t'get there 'fore it gets too late."

He leaned over and opened the passenger door, so I slid in. The car smelled like fried grease and old socks. Since Althea died, Bob had fewer and fewer nights when he went home. He had turned his car into temporary living quarters.

I suspected he was either sleeping in the backseat or on a couch at the precinct house.

"Let's hear the news," I said, trying to keep it upbeat, while not expecting much.

"Remember the sheet I sent to all them tire stores?" he asked. "Well, I got a hit." He pulled out a fax and handed it to me. On the top of the page, in letters that were designed to look like tire treads, it read:

DALE'S TIRE TOWN
NEWPORT NEWS, VIRGINIA
WHERE THE RUBBER MEETS THE ROAD

I scanned the fax and saw that it was from somebody named Dale Winthrop. He wrote that on April 13th of this year, he had sold four new Firestones to a guy in a blue Taurus with a busted-up right front fender. The fax said that the tires he took off the car still had more than an inch of good rubber left.

"That's wonderful," I said, curbing my emotions as I handed it back.

"This guy sells four tires to a Taurus driver in April," Bob continued. "The thirteenth is the day after Chandler was hit. Takes about four hours to get to Newport News, so let's say our killer does the hit-and-run here between eleven and eleven-thirty that night, drives up there, arrives around four in the morning, waits until eight when the guy opens up, and switches all his rubber. It fits the timetable. Why would this guy with the busted-up blue Taurus change four perfectly good tires? That's my question."

"It's a wonderful break, Bob," I said. But inside, I was conflicted. This was going to lead where it would lead, but at the end of the day, it wouldn't bring Chandler back. I still wanted the killer caught. I just didn't want to lose myself in the process.

"I'll call you if I get anywhere with this guy Dale," Bob said. "I've already got an artist with the Newport News PD on standby. Gonna try and get Dale to describe this guy in the Taurus so we can get a sketch. I'll call if it jells."

I gave him a hug and held his hand. It felt thin.

"You're not eating. I want you to come in and let me make you a sandwich. You can't drive all the way to Virginia with no food or sleep."

"I'm fine, Mrs. Ellis," he said, smiling at me. Bright light danced for a moment in his soft gray eyes. "I'm gonna get this bird for ya, just like I promised."

I patted his hand and got out of the car.

"I'll call you tomorrow morning," he said, then started the Crown Vic and pulled away. I watched him leave until his taillights disappeared in the dark mist.

Despite Bob's news, as I walked into the house the Mean Reds were buzzing over me, trying to find a way back in.

I opened the refrigerator and pulled out an ice-cold bottled water, then went out to sit on the back porch. My legs were still quivering from the run. Rubbery, fan-sized leaves on the huge magnolia trees behind my house rattled loudly in a gusting breeze. It was a familiar sound and setting. I was desperately trying to pick a new path, but once I'd stopped running, the same tiresome questions caught up to me. How could I leave Charlotte? This was our house. How could there be life without Chandler? No matter how badly I wanted to move on, the emotions over my husband's death were still raw, and they haunted me.

Snap out of it, girl, I lectured myself. *You gotta get on with this.*

But, as always, every time I stopped moving or sat and contemplated, I was trapped by memories of our past and the enormous realization of what I'd lost. Once that happened, I always started to sink.

Self-pity . . . Longing . . . Despair.

Then came the anger. Just like always.

CHAPTER

HOW LONG WOULD IT TAKE THE FUCKING COPS
to show up? Chick wondered. He had been sitting in his living room waiting for over two anxiety-building hours, cursing LAPD incompetence.

Then, at 10:15 P.M., finally a knock at the front door. He got up and walked past Melissa's room, where she was still on her bed sawing lumber. She'd said she wanted to be awakened at nine, but he hadn't done it because she was part of his timeline and alibi. He knew once she got up, she would fly out of the house without so much as a "See ya later." He took two deep breaths before he opened the front door.

Standing on the porch was one of the most implausibly handsome men Chick had ever seen. He was olive-skinned, dark-haired, with a sculpted jaw, complete with a cleft chin. He had seawater blue eyes and was dressed in a charcoal-gray suit, cinnamon shirt, and maroon tie. He looked like he just stepped out of a fucking Calvin Klein ad. Chick hated him on sight.

"Charles Best?" the man said solemnly.

"I go by Chick and I don't take meetings on my front porch. Call my office." He'd planned that opening line, thinking it showed the right degree of indifference. The man on the porch ignored this and waved toward a car parked out by the curb. The passenger door opened and a second man, who'd been waiting inside the vehicle talking on a cell phone, got out and joined them. This one had narrow shoulders, dandruff, and male pattern baldness.

"I'm Detective Sergeant Apollo Demetrius," the handsome cop said, pulling out a badge and showing it to Chick. He motioned toward the second man. "This is my partner, Detective Charles Watts."

"Police?" Chick asked, trying to look and sound confused, like, "What on earth would the police want with us?"

"May we come in please, sir?" Apollo Demetrius asked.

Chick nodded and stood aside. The two policemen entered his antique and crystal plush-pile foyer and stood in the entry for a minute, looking at the expensive layout. Chick could almost read their thoughts: *This guy has money. He's got lawyers on speed dial so be careful.*

"What's this all about?" Chick asked, arranging what he hoped was a look of mild consternation on his face.

"Is your wife Evelyn Best?" Demetrius asked.

"Yes, she is. Why? What's wrong?" Chick had cautioned himself not to go for the Academy Award here and overact, but he needed to show some concern and perhaps just a dash of impending fear. It's not every day two cops show up at your front door asking about your wife. He thought he'd hit just the right note—confused, startled, but not yet overly alarmed.

"I'm afraid I have some bad news," Demetrius continued. "You might want to sit down." Chick waved this off, so Demetrius went on. "Your wife was killed in what appears to be a carjacking around six-fifteen this evening. She was shot in the head behind a hair salon in Van Nuys." These words passed over the detective's sensuous lips like velvet bricks. Brutal information delivered as smoothly as a pickup line in a singles bar.

"She was . . . she was . . . what?" Chick looked at them, his mouth agape. He put his hands to his face, then dropped his head into them. *How little is too little? How much is too much? Don't overdo it . . . Don't underdo it.* It was a hard balance to strike. Since he felt absolutely nothing, it all had to be performance. Instead of concentrating on real feelings, he was focused on behavior, which he knew might cause him to come off as emotionless and mechanical.

He moved away from the matinee-idol detective, trying to get some distance from the man's probing stare. He knew he was being carefully evaluated by both cops, and it made him tense. His body language seemed stiff and jerky, even to him. Then he had a sudden wave of flop-sweat. *Was he already fucking this up?*

"Are you okay? Can we get you anything? Some water?" Demetrius asked.

Chick sort of shook his head, breathing through his mouth, trying to look like he was in some kind of emotional free fall.

"Why would anybody . . . ? It can't be . . . Are you sure it was her?"

"Yes. Her stylist, Edward Paul, heard the shots, identified the body, and pinned the time of death for us. He saw your wife's murderer driving off in her car, but didn't get a good look at the shooter. The car was just turning the corner. She was already dead in the parking lot behind his salon when he found her."

A strange incongruous thought flickered. *Mr. Eddy's last name was Paul . . .* He'd never known that. *So why not Mr. Paul?* That was what went through his head, but he sobbed and said, "Oh . . . oh . . . my God . . . Oh . . . no, not Evelyn . . . " *Too much? Too little?* He was flying blind. He was hyperaware of his every movement, like a bad actor in a high school play.

"We have some questions," Demetrius said. "I hope you won't take this the wrong way, but we need to establish where everyone was. Could you tell us where you were about six o'clock?"

"Right here. I was right here in the house." Trying for shock and dismay. Maybe pulling it off, maybe bungling it badly.

"Can anybody confirm that? Was anybody here with you?"

"Uh . . . no . . . Well, my daughter was . . . " Chick paused. "I mean, she's here."

"Can you get her, please?"

So Chick got up, and with what he hoped was an anguished expression on his face, walked down the hall to his daughter's room. The plain-looking detective followed so he could monitor what was being said. Chick found Melissa sprawled on her bed, still zonked. That girl had honed the art of sleeping to a razor's edge. She could sleep through a cat fight, or more to the point, through a crystal meth raid.

"Melissa, wake up," he said, shaking her by the shoulder.

"Lemme alone," she growled, and rolled over, facing the other way. "Can't I get a moment's peace in this fucking house?"

Great, Chick thought, *let's show this eavesdropping detective what a tight, happy little family we are.*

"Your mother has been murdered," he said bluntly, going for maximum effect, trying to shock her into some sort of grieving response. He saw her breathing stop, saw her back freeze, then after ten seconds or so, she rolled over and looked at him.

"Huh?" Her eyes were slits of unpleasantness, her hair a two-day nest of bad grooming. Her face glittered with metal as she studied him with sleepy, suspicious eyes.

"Somebody carjacked her at Salono Bello. Shot her dead . . . took the Mercedes. The police are here." He said it softly, sounding sad while at the same time trying to get the gravity of the situation across to her.

"No shit?" she said, struggling to sit up.

No shit was hardly the appropriate response. "Oh, my God," or "Oh no, not Mom, please." But Melissa's first words were "No shit?" She was hopeless. But at least she was sitting up now, looking at Chick. "How the fuck?" was her next stab at communication.

"I just told you. She was carjacked. Shot." He plowed on. "The cops want to talk to us. Get out of bed."

She scowled at him. "The police? I didn't do anything." Then she got up, put on her robe, and stood in the darkened bedroom. "Did they also shoot that shithead, Mickey D, I hope?"

Chick didn't answer, but thought, *Good going, Meliss. Exactly what we needed.*

The plain-looking cop retreated from his listening post in the hall as Chick led his scowling child back into the living room and made the introductions. "This is Melissa . . . Detective Demetrius, and Detective . . . what was it again . . . ?"

"Watts," said the ordinary-looking cop.

"I already told her what happened," Chick said, then realized that this was all becoming very matter-of-fact, so he added, "My God . . . my God . . . I still can't believe . . . " just to let them know he was in major heartbreak here, in deep shock at hearing the horrible news.

"We're trying to establish where your father was at the time of the incident," Demetrius said. "Can you attest to his whereabouts this evening, say, starting any time after 4 P.M.?"

"How the fuck would I know?" Melissa said. She was scowling while looking at them, but Chick could read her like the morning paper. She was already trying to figure out what this murder would do to her life. Would it change anything? Would her credit card get frozen?

"Your father said he was here," Demetrius added. "Can you confirm that?"

"I was asleep," she scowled. "How the hell would I know?"

It wasn't going at all the way he'd planned. Chick thought her attitude was atrocious, and he could read shock at her behavior on both cops' faces. But they had a job where they witnessed the worst of mankind, so they waited patiently without comment. Chick didn't want to prod her, but Watts was writing everything down in a spiral crime book, and Chick desperately needed Melissa for his alibi, so he tried to jog her memory.

"Wait a minute. Didn't I come in earlier to wake you up for your date? What time was that? Do you remember?"

"Huh?"

At this rate, they wouldn't even need a trial. They might as well just drag the electric chair over here and plug it in.

Chick tried again. "Remember, I woke you up? I think it was about . . . "

"Let her tell it, please," Demetrius interrupted.

"Okay, yeah . . . I guess I remember." Melissa was snapping out of it. A look of feral shrewdness came into her eyes. "Six o'clock or six-oh-five . . . something like that. He came in and woke me up for my date."

"You're certain?" Demetrius asked, a little disappointment creeping into those two words.

"I said it, didn't I? You think I'd lie?"

Shit, Chick thought.

"I don't know, Miss Best, I just met you. Your mother was murdered. You don't seem very upset."

"I just woke up!"

Chick thought it couldn't possibly be going much worse, but that was Melissa. She hated both of them. Forgetting for the moment that he had pulled the trigger, Chick was irritated that Melissa wasn't at all bothered that the woman who had given birth to her and raised her had just been brutally murdered. Out of the corner of his eye, he saw Demetrius and Watts exchange a private look.

"Look, give me a lie detector test if you don't believe me," she suddenly blurted. "The cops never believe anything I say, anyway. They always think I'm lying."

Of course they absolutely believed her confession about the crystal meth when she *was* lying, but that's another story. The idea of a polygraph test was the last thing Chick wanted to introduce into this conversation. Next thing, the cops would want him to take one too. He was hoping they'd find the Mercedes, find the gun, get Delroy's prints off both, and solve this thing quickly, put it behind him before anybody started asking for a polygraph.

"A lie detector test might be a very good idea," Demetrius said. "Would you also agree to take one, Chick?" Now using his first name like they already owned him. "Just to get this part of the investigation behind us?"

"I guess," Chick said, thinking he'd like to strangle his daughter. But killing both members of his immediate family on the same night was probably a bit much, even for him.

Demetrius's cell phone rang and he answered it.

"Yeah. Yeah. Okay, good. Have them call a unit from Valley impound, but don't hook it up. Notify CSI, and get a forensics team to the site. I'll be there in twenty." He hung up. "We just found your wife's car," he said, watching Chick closely. "It was ditched up in the mountains above Glendale."

"Is that good?" Chick asked, trying to sound like a confused citizen who had just lost his wife and didn't know his ass from a pound of Philadelphia cream cheese. *Too much?* He didn't know—couldn't read anything in their blank expressions.

"The car is the crime scene," Demetrius finally said. "It could be very important. I'll set it up for you both to take those polygraph tests. How's tomorrow sound?"

"Uh . . . well, Thursday would be better . . . "

"Why?" Demetrius asked, looking at him coldly.

"I'm very upset right now, that's why."

"We both want to catch this guy, don't we, Chick?" Demetrius was smiling slightly, as if he'd just caught Chick in a criminal inconsistency. After a moment's hesitation, Chick nodded.

"Good. How 'bout we just set it up for the first available time tomorrow, then," the handsome detective said. Watts closed his spiral pad and both of them stood. As they walked toward the door, Demetrius spun around unexpectedly and faced Chick. "Everything between you and your wife okay, Mr. Best? No fights? No problems?"

"No. Everything was fine."

"Who's this Mickey D person your daughter just mentioned?" Watts asked.

"That's Mickey DePolina. He's a family friend. Our personal trainer."

"Nothing going on between your wife and her trainer?" Watts persisted.

"Of course not. Evelyn and I were very much in love."

Behind him, Melissa groaned theatrically. Maybe he'd throw caution to the wind and just go for the double H with these two cops as eyewitnesses.

"I've already asked for a technician to come out here and give you a GSR test," Demetrius said. "He should be along any time."

"A what?" Chick was confused.

"It's a Gunshot Residue Test. We use paraffin to check your hands for barium and antimony to establish if you've fired a gun recently. Don't take it the wrong way. It's standard procedure. We always start by eliminating family members first. We'll hang around till he gets here."

"You gonna test me?" Melissa said, her eyebrow studs climbing her forehead like fishhooks in two furry caterpillars.

Then Chick heard a car pull up out front.

"That won't be necessary," Demetrius said coldly. "We'll get back to you tomorrow." When they opened the door, Chick saw a plain sedan parked at the curb. A lab tech got out and unloaded two boxes from his trunk.

"We're very sorry for your loss," Demetrius said without much sorrow.

"Thank you for your sympathy," Chick said stiffly, and watched as they walked down the steps to their car, pausing to talk to the technician on the way. Chick turned and saw Melissa smiling at him.

"Caught a real break with this carjack, didn't ya?" his angry daughter said. "Looks like somebody went ahead and did it for you."

CHAPTER 25

"PAIGE, I DESPERATELY NEED TO TALK TO YOU," A man's voice said, without an opening hello or even identifying himself.

I was standing in my living room. "Who is this?" I asked, trying to pick the voice out of my memory bank of old friends.

"It's Chick," he said, his voice so small, so sad, I could barely hear him.

"Chick?" Why on earth would he be calling me at nine in the morning—six A.M. L.A. time?

"You're the only one I could think of to call," he whispered. He seemed to be sobbing. Then he said, "Evelyn was murdered . . . carjacked. Friday night, somebody put a gun . . . they put a gun in her car window and then . . . and then they just shot her." Another sob followed this horrible news.

"Oh, my God, Chick . . . I'm so sorry." My heart went out to him. I remembered the desolation of waking up the morning after Chandler died, knowing something was wrong. Then, as the memories returned, having to come to grips with his death all over again.

"These first days are the toughest, the absolute worst," I said. "Waking up to the loss each morning, it's impossible. I know exactly what you're going through, Chick."

"Nobody else understands. Nobody I know has been through this, except you."

He sounded devastated. Lost and broken. I took a breath and tried to come up with the best way to handle this.

"Do you want to talk? Would it help if we spent some time right now and talked about your feelings?" I didn't quite know what the best form of therapy might be. We shared an almost identical tragedy, but I didn't know Chick and Evelyn that well so I wasn't sure I should be spewing out a bunch of helpful hints with no intellectual perspective.

"Evelyn really loved you, Paige," he suddenly said unexpectedly.

"That's so sweet," I answered. But what I was thinking was, how could that be? We barely knew one another. I'd always felt there was something strange and sort of self-absorbed about Evelyn Best.

"We had so much together," Chick was saying. "Evelyn and I always knew what the other was feeling. She knew what I was thinking even before I would say it. I can't believe she's not here, not with me anymore." A sob followed this, then he went on, "And the way she was with Melissa . . . such a wonderful mother."

"I don't mean to start giving a lot of unsolicited advice, Chick, but if I were you, I'd make sure that Melissa talks to someone. Children deal with these things in different ways from adults. You don't want her to bury it. Her emotions over this need to come out."

"You mean, like a psychiatrist?"

"A psychiatrist or even a good friend who she trusts and will open up to. Somebody to help her get in touch with her feelings."

"I just . . . I just . . . " and he stopped.

"You just what?"

"I just . . . I wanted . . . "

"Whatever you want, I'm there, Chick."

"It's not fair," he said, his voice almost a whisper. "It's too much to ask."

"If you don't tell me, we'll never know. What is it, Chick?"

"I want . . . what I want is to talk to you."

"You can call me anytime. We could even have a set time, a phone schedule, and talk every day."

"I was hoping . . . What I wanted is . . . I wanted to see you."

"You mean you want me to come out there?" Thinking, *My God, is he serious? Fly out to L.A.?*

"I shouldn't ask you to do that, should I?" His voice seemed to recoil, as if I had just physically hurt him. Suddenly my response seemed horribly selfish. And then a strange thing happened. I got angry at myself. I had just spent seven months trying to muddle through Chandler's death. I had relied heavily on my friends to get me through. Chick had even flown back here for Chan's funeral. Why was I looking for a way to duck this?

"If you want me there, I'll come," I finally offered.

"That's stupid, isn't it?" he said. "It's too much to ask."

"Nonsense." This time I put a little more *oomph* into it.

"I . . . the police are still investigating," he said. "They found her car up in the mountains last night. They say the killer stripped it, took the radio—the air bags—stuff like that. I think they found the gun, too. At least, that's what they said on the news. It's strange . . . The police lab people did some tests here Friday night, but they haven't talked to me since."

"Tests?"

"They said it was a formality. A Gunshot Residue Test to see if I'd fired a gun recently."

"Oh my God, Chick, that's horrible. You mean they're treating you like a suspect?"

"They told me it's routine—that they always try and eliminate the immediate family first. But I passed and Melissa was with me during the time of the killing so I don't think they really suspect me. It's just hard to go through it, is all. I was hardly in a mood for any of that last night . . . Last night I just wanted to curl up and die."

"That's absolutely unbelievable that they would treat you that way on the night she was killed," I said. But then I remembered the meeting at the station the day after Chandler died, when Bob Butler had asked me about any possible trouble in our marriage—if Chandler had any girlfriends or affairs. I remembered how furious I'd become, asking him for a lie detector test after telling him to go fuck himself. So the fact is, Bob Butler had checked me out just like the L.A. cops were checking out Chick. Bob had said he owed it to Chandler. *Speaking for the dead,* he'd called it.

"Anyway, I don't know when the funeral is going to be," Chick continued. "The police haven't released her body. I'll call you and let you know," he said softly. "Maybe, if it's not too much trouble, you could come for a day or so. It would really help to have somebody here who understands."

"I'll come," I said firmly. "I'll be there, Chick."

Then we lapsed into a prolonged silence. I wondered what on earth I could tell him beyond what I'd already said. Maybe just having someone who had gone through it and was still standing would give him a reason to hang on.

"Want to hear something really silly?" he finally asked.

"If you want to tell me, yes, of course."

"Sometimes, when we were dressing to go out, we'd be getting ready in separate dressing rooms and we'd meet in the hallway and when we came out we'd be wearing the exact same colors. I'd have on a black suit and a purple tie—she'd come out of her bathroom in a purple dress with a black belt and scarf. Happened all the time. We used to laugh about it."

"You guys were on each other's wavelength. Sharing moods. It's the sign of a good marriage," I said. But it was obviously the wrong thing to say because I heard him start to sob.

"Oh Chick," I said, "I'm so sorry."

"I've got to go," he said, "I'm coming apart here."

"You'll get through it, Chick. I'll come out there and help you!"

"Okay, bye." And he was gone.

I decided right then, if I was going to help him, I should go out to Los Angeles now. Now was when he needed me, not later. I decided to try and do for him what my friends had done for me.

Then a very strange thing happened. I heard a voice in my subconscious.

"Don't go," the voice said. It sounded like Chandler, and it startled me. *"Don't go to Los Angeles,"* the voice repeated.

But how could I not go? I'd just given Chick my word.

CHAPTER

26

SERGEANT APOLLO DEMETRIUS SHOWED UP AT
Chick's house again on the Monday following Evelyn's murder. It was a day after the glorious phone call with Paige
where she promised to come to L.A.

"Do you know anybody named Delroy Washington?"
Demetrius asked. He was sitting in Chick's beautifully fur-
nished living room, leaking his Aqua Velva scent and mascu-
line vibe all over the place. The cold-eyed, ordinary-looking
Charlie Watts wasn't there.

"Delroy Washington . . . ? No, I don't think so," Chick
said, going for puzzled confusion.

Then Sergeant Ain't-I-Hot-Looking Demetrius took
some photographs out of his briefcase and laid them out
on the coffee table. Six mug shots of glowering, black
teenage assholes. They all had Afro-hip haircuts—fades
with Zs cut into the sides. One or two had cornrows or
dreads. Ghetto styles that screamed "Fuck you, Whitey."
They all wore sullen expressions with angry eyes. Of course,

Delroy Washington was right there in the mix, top row, far right side.

"This is what we call a six-pack," Demetrius said. "Not abs—pictures. We use them for eyewitness identifications. All these guys have been chosen because they are about the same age and build. One of them is a possible perp. Take your time and look them over, sir. See if one looks familiar."

Chick noted that he'd gone from "Chick" to "Sir"—a definite step in the right direction. He was no longer at the top of Demetrius's suspect list.

"He could be a guy who came to the door, selling something, or maybe he worked at some garage where you or your wife park your cars, a valet service. You might not know his name. Could be a vendor you use. Guy at the corner market. Anyone there look familiar?"

Of course, Chick wasn't about to claim Delroy Washington. The last thing he needed was for that angry asshole to say, "Yeah, I know this guy, too. He had a .45 stashed under the seat of a gold Mercedes I detailed at the wash."

Chick needed to keep his distance from Delroy until the angry gangster lawyered up. With all the physical evidence Chick had planted, he was pretty sure the lawyer would go for a plea bargain and agree to a nice second-degree murder, rather than take a chance on murder one with special circumstance. A plea bargain would be neat and quick. It would clear the case without ever involving Chick.

"Should I know him?" Chick said after pretending to study each picture carefully.

"If it was a random jacking, then no, but sometimes these gangsters steal on demand. Somebody orders a gold Mercedes like your wife's, and they target the vehicle in advance. That might have produced a contact."

"None of these guys look familiar," Chick said, straightening back up.

Apollo Demetrius gathered up the pictures and returned them to his worn leather briefcase. "Okay, good enough." He got to his feet.

"Do you think one of those guys did it?" Chick asked. "They look very young."

"In the ghetto, youth is not necessarily a condition of innocence," Demetrius said, sounding for a minute more like a criminology professor than a cop. "I've got Pee-Wee G's in my gang book who are barely out of puberty and they've already skagged two or three rival homeboys . . . We got adolescent killers standing ten deep at Juvenile Hall. The juvie-rancho up in Saugus is a cesspool of homicidal, preteen violence. You wouldn't believe what's being raised in the inner city and getting passed off as human."

The detective started toward the door and Chick hurried to follow.

"So one of these guys did it?" he persisted, hoping to hear more.

"Yep. Think so . . . got the murder weapon. It's an old forty-five. It's what we call a street gun. Serial number was filed. A cold piece. I can't get an ownership trail. One thing it does have is Delroy Washington's prints all over it. We also found his prints inside your wife's car, on the back of the rearview mirror. Got a ten-point match—Delroy left more ridges and swirls on that crime scene than they got on the jewelry counter at Macy's."

"Prints on the back of the mirror?" Chick asked, trying for naive confusion.

"Asshole steals a vehicle, first thing he does is readjust the mirror so he can use it. On nine out of ten of these jacks we get a clean set of prints off the back of the rearview." Apollo paused, then added, "I think this is pretty much a slam dunk. Washington has a yellow sheet full of violent crimes. He has two prior carjackings. Shot one of the drivers. A nonfatal wound, but he went down on an attempt to commit. He's also been down on two previous felony assault car thefts, both class-A beefs because he likes using a gun."

"He shot somebody before Evelyn?" Chick asked, sounding appalled.

Demetrius nodded, "I think we gotta great chance of setting him up for the needle. This is a lying-in-wait, special-circumstances murder. If the D.A. will file it that way, this kid could hit death row. If he won't, we're gonna lock Del up permanently on a third strike. But to do that, we've gotta take him all the way to trial, because his P.D.'s not going to plead him on a third strike. That means you're gonna have to be ready to testify. You up for that, sir?"

"Oh," Chick said. "Well, of course . . . " But he hadn't counted on a trial. Even though he'd been wearing the baseball cap and glasses, there was a chance Delroy would remember the Mercedes, or worse still, recognize him in court. Of course, if that happened, it would be Chick's word against the word of a three-time loser. *Sure I went to the car wash on Adams. That's undoubtedly where he must have seen Evelyn's car . . . Gun under the seat? Is he kidding? I don't even own a gun. I'm an Internet executive.*

Still, Chick wished it could just be bargained off like he'd planned. That way they'd all be done with it. Nothing, when it came to Evelyn, was ever easy. In death, she was still causing him problems.

"The D.A. is ready to charge Delroy. We'll know how he's gonna file it in a couple a days. I guess we can forget all the other stuff, the lie detector test, the backup interview. We got our guy."

"Thanks," Chick said, looking sad, despite the fact this was the best fucking news since *People* magazine called in '98 to say they were doing a story on bestmarket.com.

"When will you release my wife's body? I'm trying to plan her funeral." He hoped he'd packed enough grief into that sentence to get it past Demetrius's smell detector. Of course, who could smell anything but Aqua Velva anyway?

"I think the coroner's done. We'll let go of her remains today or tomorrow. You can go ahead and make your arrangements," Demetrius said.

"Thanks," Chick said again, looking sadly down at the carpet, thinking murder wasn't all that tough if you thought things out. Planned without emotion and followed through methodically, murder could actually be a viable option. You just had to do it carefully and make sure all the facts were served.

And look at the high level of karmic improvement here. Delroy Washington, a mean, angry asshole who had achieved nothing in his short antisocial existence, other than fouling the L.A. Basin with violent crimes, was off to end his life behind bars. Evelyn, who had achieved no worthwhile skills beyond her bone-jarring dead lifts and rock-hard biceps, was also gone, removing a shitload of negative energy. Delroy was going to serve Chick's murder sentence, so that Chick could go on and make further, worthwhile contributions to the gross revenue product of L.A.'s business and tax environment, completing a perfect circle of positive fiscal and psychic energy. How can you beat that?

Chick walked Demetrius out of the house. They stood on the front porch and the detective shook Chick's hand.

"Must be hard," the handsome cop commiserated, turning from a suspicious asshole to a sympathetic friend in less than two days.

"I loved her very much," Chick drooped sadly.

"I hope it helps, knowing we got the doer."

"It helps, more than I can tell you," Chick said.

"Be sure your daughter doesn't skip her court date on the twenty-eighth for her meth possession bust. She's a first-time offender and if she plays it smart, she should come out of that with a suspended sentence. She's a minor, so after she turns eighteen, her record will be sealed. That bust won't even show up. But if she gets cute, she'll get hammered."

"Thank you," Chick said, surprised he knew about Melissa's pending legal problems.

Demetrius turned and walked down to his car, taking the dimpled chin and Aqua Velva reek with him. Detective Watts wasn't sitting out there in the front seat, making cell calls. Demetrius had come alone. The visit had been a wrap-up interview.

Chick watched as the detective drove off, then turned and walked into his overpriced split-level house and shut the massive oak door.

Case closed, he thought. Then a huge smile spread across his face. Evelyn was finally out of his life and Paige Ellis was coming all the way from North Carolina for the funeral.

He poured himself a tumbler of scotch and sighed. *Could it possibly get any better than this?*

CHAPTER

27

IT WAS TWO IN THE AFTERNOON WHEN MY DELTA
flight from North Carolina landed at LAX. My overnight case
had been a few millimeters too large to pass through the
post-9/ll airport screening apparatus in Charlotte. I could
have probably blasted it through with a well-aimed *hiji-ushi-
rate*, but the woman on the screening machine snatched the
bag off the conveyor and had it checked before I could perform my bad-ass elbow strike.

According to the e-mail I'd received from Chick, Evelyn's funeral was on Saturday at 10 A.M. at Forest Lawn in
the Hollywood Hills. I e-mailed him back before leaving for
the airport informing him that I would be staying at the
Langham Huntington Hotel in Pasadena. I'd chosen
Pasadena because Chandler's parents lived there. I didn't
want to impose on my in-laws and just show up, bags in
hand, but I certainly wanted to pay them a visit.

I was at baggage claim waiting for my luggage, admiring
a beautiful, ninety-degree, smog-free L.A. day, when I heard
my name being called.

"Paige! Paige Ellis. Over here."

I turned, and over by the door behind the ropes, saw Chick Best. He was dressed in a charcoal suit with a cinnamon-colored shirt and maroon tie. His sunglasses were pushed up on his head movie-star style. I certainly hadn't expected him to come to the airport to meet me. In fact, I didn't quite know what to make of it. I hadn't even given him my travel arrangements, so how had he known what flight I'd be on? Spooky. But there he was, just the same, so I smiled and waved.

I retrieved my bag, pulled out the handle, and wheeled it past the bored luggage-checker and out to the curb.

Chick hugged me. I could feel his breath on my neck.

"This is so sweet of you," he said.

I had a vivid memory flash of the uncomfortable encounter after Chandler's funeral, when Chick had wrapped his arms around me and wouldn't let go. But this time, he quickly turned me loose and held me at arm's length. I was looking into sad brown eyes. He smiled weakly.

"These past few days have been an absolute horror," he said. He had what looked like a fresh haircut. I could see white around the ears where he'd just gotten it trimmed. He reeked of aftershave—Aqua Velva, I think.

"Are you holding up okay?" I asked, feeling awkward in his presence. In Hawaii, I was pretty much only focused on Chandler. Other than two dinners on Maui and a few moments at my husband's funeral, I hardly knew this man.

"Come on, we'll talk once we get out of here," he said and led me across the crowded terminal and into the parking structure. A black Porsche Targa was parked with its top down near the exit turnstile. He popped the trunk, took my bag, and dropped it inside.

"I made reservations for you at the Beverly Wilshire. It's close to Rodeo Drive, good stores. Evelyn shopped there all the time, and you won't have far to go by cab to get to my place, or you can rent a car if you'd rather not mess with taxies."

"I'm not much of a shopper, Chick. Didn't you get my e-mail? I'm already booked at the Langham Huntington in Pasadena."

He smiled as he opened the passenger door and let me in. "That's the old Ritz-Carlton, right?" I nodded. "Great hotel, but a helluva long ways away," he said, pulling down his wrap-around sunglasses and sliding them onto his nose. "It's all the way out at the end of the 110. Even if you use the 210 or try to go over Coldwater, you're gonna hit killer traffic most times of the day."

"I want to see Chandler's family and they live out there. Since Evelyn's funeral is at Forest Lawn in Hollywood, I figured I could just shoot right out the 210 to the 134 and hang a left on Forest Lawn Drive by the river and I'd be there."

I could see I'd surprised him with my encyclopedic knowledge of the L.A. freeway system. I got to know my way around out here pretty well right after Chandler and I were married. We'd spent a lot of time in L.A. while Chan was working with his family's attorneys, setting up the learning foundation.

"Okay," Chick smiled, "the Langham it is, then." He pulled out of the parking structure and drove onto the freeway heading east, toward Pasadena.

It was one of those L.A. days that made you want to move here. The Santa Ana winds were blowing and had swept the basin clear of air pollution. The few flags I saw stood at right angles, rippling and snapping in the stiff breeze. In honor of the day, convertible tops were down, sunglasses flashing, blonde hair flying. A regular Pepsi commercial. It was November, but it felt like springtime. The grass at home was already beginning to freeze at night, turning brown with the first chill of winter, so despite the circumstances, it felt liberating to be here.

"They caught the guy," Chick said, not taking his eyes off the road. "Black kid named Delroy Washington with a long record of carjacking and gang violence. Cops think it was random. He saw her car, went over and shot her so she wouldn't be able to identify him later. Took the Mercedes and ran."

"That's awful," I said.

"Y'know, sometimes I just sit and think what if she hadn't gone to the Valley to get her hair done? What if she'd canceled her appointment, which she often did? Or what if her hairdresser had moved the time, told her to come a half-hour earlier or later? What if she hadn't been in Van Nuys at that exact moment, and had never run into this angry, screwed-up kid? I keep trying to make sense of it, but what it comes down to is Evelyn was just at the wrong place at the wrong time and hit the double zero. Even so, I still can't keep from thinking, what if?"

He looked over. I couldn't see his eyes behind his wraparound sunglasses, but I could imagine what was reflected there. I had asked all the same unanswerable, self-torturing questions. What if I hadn't gone running that evening? What if my back hadn't flared up? What if I'd decided to just tough it out with no Percocet, instead of calling Dr. Baker and getting him to prescribe Darvocet? Then Chandler wouldn't have gone out to pick up my medicine. He wouldn't have been in that drugstore parking lot, wouldn't have been crushed by the hit-and-run driver.

"There's no answer to the what ifs, or the whys," I finally told him, "any more than there's an answer for why some people get cancer and others don't. It is what it is. It's just life."

That sounded like a lame platitude even as I said it, and if he was like me, he was probably still too close to Evelyn's death to deal with it philosophically.

He nodded slowly but seemed unconvinced. "It's just . . . being at home without her . . . it's like punishment. Did you feel that way?"

"Exactly that way," I said. "But where else can you go? How do you hide from your feelings?"

"Exactly," he said. "And then, there are all the funeral arrangements. I've been trying to handle that. It's so hard to even know what to bury her in. I keep thinking, does it really matter? She's dead. Does it make a difference if she's in her pink summer dress, or the green A-line she liked so much? What about jewelry? I know it's silly, but some part of me wants it to be exactly right. It's sort of like the final communal gesture I'll ever make for us."

I was surprised at that one. Chick had never seemed very metaphysical to me. More of a business accounting type. But he was absolutely right. I'd felt all the same things he was feeling.

"Somebody actually suggested that we bury Chandler in his football jersey," I said.

"Ridiculous," Chick said. "Evelyn liked to work out. Maybe I should bury her in a sport bra."

We were both suddenly smiling—laughing at the idea of what other people thought was the essence of a person's life.

"Part of me just keeps looking for answers," he went on. "Part of me is looking for a place to stash all this anger I have for Delroy Washington. Sometimes I pray he'll get the needle and I'll be standing behind the glass watching. But I also know that's not going to help me get past this. I can't bring Evelyn back by punishing some angry kid who's just a violent product of our own societal mistakes. Suffice it to say, I'm confused. Sometimes I sit in my backyard and look at the trees, see the wind blow the leaves away, and wish I could just sail away with them, get out of here on a gust of air. Does any of that make sense?"

"Perfect sense." I reached out and squeezed his hand in a gesture of support as we were swept along in the flow of sixty-mile-an-hour L.A. traffic.

Chick pulled his hand away so he could shift into a lower gear. The Porsche growled and buzzed around a Vons produce truck.

"Is there anything I can do to help you with the funeral arrangements?" I asked.

"Just being here is help enough. Having somebody who's been through this to talk to . . . it's all I need."

I looked over at Chick's profile. His eyes were still hidden behind those trendy glasses. I wondered who was really inside there. I decided one way or another, I would do everything in my power to help him get through this.

Big mistake.

CHAPTER 28

JORDAN WEISMAN WAS ONE OF THE ACE COM-
puter programmers at bestmarket.com before the company
sold. Chick pulled a guilt trip on Jordy and he had finally
agreed to hack into all the major airlines' computers to find
out what flight Paige Ellis would be on from Charlotte. Jordan didn't like pulling hacks, but Chick b.s.'d him saying he
was doing a new start-up and there might be a job in it for
him. Jordan came through in less than thirty minutes.

After that, Chick spent the next six hours going for the
perfect ensemble. Nothing seemed exactly right, so he ended
up driving to Bloomingdale's and buying a cinnamon shirt
and maroon tie. He already had a charcoal suit, so what it
came down to was he had pretty much ended up stealing
Apollo Demetrius's entire look, right down to the Aqua
Velva.

Chick then spent almost forty minutes trying to select
the right watch. He was a watch collector, an aficionado of
world-class timepieces. Over the years, he'd bought every

expensive or trendsetting chronometer available. He had Breitlings and Piagets, Rolexes and Cartiers. Over fifty watches were displayed in velvet-lined cases with glass tops in his walk-in closet. Each polished mahogany box contained six timepieces. He remembered reading somewhere once that sociopaths often had a fascination with clocks . . .

He wondered, *Are my fifty watches trying to tell me something?*

Finally, he selected the Breitling Navitimer, the same model John Travolta wore in their ads. Sporty, expensive, but not ostentatious. He snapped it on and set it.

His mind was swirling with anticipation and resolve. Only one lingering fear . . . if he got lucky . . . if he pulled this off . . . if he could talk Paige into it . . .

COULD HE GET IT UP?

He washed down a Viagra, waited twenty minutes for it to hit the old bloodstream, and then with his heart racing picked up the girls from *Hustler* and headed to the bathroom.

Nothing.

Not a quiver.

He was deader than an opening act at the Laugh Factory. Then, just as he decided to stop, he got a slight tingle down there. Not one of his old Chick Best blue-vein specials—but he was at least getting some blood flow. Flop-sweat gathered on his brow as he coaxed this poor wobbler up. It rose weakly, like a patient at a rest home. Finally, he was at half-mast, hanging out over the toilet seat, barely erect.

He couldn't believe this was happening. Paige Ellis was actually on an airplane, heading to Los Angeles to see him, and he couldn't get a decent hard-on. He was in the middle of a heavy dose of self-administered performance anxiety when he finally decided to give it up and stop. He zipped up, rushed out of the bathroom, and entered his den to fire down two scotch shooters. As they hit bottom, the knot in his stomach lessened.

Okay, jerking off was one thing. Making love was another. The old Love Master would grow some wood when the time came, but, to be perfectly honest, Chick was becoming sexually panicked. At the same time he was committed to this course of action, determined to push on.

So he went to the airport and stood at the Delta baggage claim, waiting, and then finally saw her walking with self-confidence up to the carousel. She was so beautiful, so slender and fine, that his heart actually clutched when he saw her. He waited while the bags began coming off, watching the way she stood as a few people talked to her, asking dumb questions like, "Is this the luggage from flight 216?"

She was the most amazing person he'd ever encountered . . . a fantasy and a reality. An object of lust and at the same time the gold standard for feminine perfection . . . well rounded, talented, incredible. His descriptive words for her were endless.

Chick felt diminished by her presence, unworthy and outclassed. He had spent his entire adult life trying to be worthy of other people's admiration. He had acquired the symbols of success, while always looking right and left, jealous of all the things other people had. Now, as he watched Paige Ellis, he finally realized that she was what he had been after all along. He'd been put on earth to be completed by her. She was the yin to his yang . . . no sexual pun intended.

When he could bear the ecstasy of watching her no longer, he called her name. She saw him, waved, and dragged her little bag over. They'd hugged and he'd led her to the car—and then the first minor setback . . . The fucking Langham Hotel in Pasadena.

She wanted to stay way the hell out on the east side of town. How could he just drop in on her out there unannounced? What could he say? "Oh, hi. I was just walking in the Rose Bowl parking lot, which is only twenty fucking miles from my house, and I thought I'd swing by and see what you were doing." Impossible.

He'd tried to confuse her with his line of freeway bullshit. Most out-of-towners panicked when you slung L.A.'s confusing array of freeway numbers at them, but she'd come right back with, "I'll just take the 210 to the 134, hang a left on Forest Lawn Drive by the river."

That was another thing: Evelyn was shit on directions and it had always pissed him off. Even though she was born here, Evelyn could never remember a freeway number. Whenever they were trying to meet at a restaurant, she'd say stuff like, "It's easy to find, Chick . . . can't miss it. Take the freeway—you know the one I mean—it's right by where I get my nails done—and then get off near the shoe store where I buy my Prada sandals. Go past that cute antique shop where they give you coffee mocha, turn left, and you're there . . . " Ridiculous. Paige didn't even live here and she was right on the old button. Everything about her impressed him.

And then she had reached out and held his hand, squeezing it while he drove. It shot a volt of electricity up his arm, straight into his heart.

Chick also felt that after a shaky start with Demetrius, he'd finally hit a pretty good post-death performance stride. Just the right amount of heartsick grief and moronic psychobabble over Evelyn's brutal murder.

All that stuff about, "What if she'd changed her appointment?" "What if she'd decided not to go?" That stuff was really on target. Paige was eating it up.

Of course there were a few other, more accurate what ifs. What if his angry wife hadn't been spending money they didn't have, on clothes she wouldn't even wear? What if she hadn't been screwing her trainer and turning his marriage into a sexless sham?

Mickey D, by the way, hadn't even called to find out about the burial—a testament to the depth of that Vaseline-lubricated, penile-inserted relationship. If there was a bookmaker's line on shallow behavior, Chick would have given the points and bet the house that Mickey D wouldn't even bother to come to the funeral. The side bet was that he would probably also call sometime next week and offer to buy the gym equipment for ten cents on the dollar. What an asshole.

They had finally pulled up at the Langham Hotel in Pasadena, and Chick waved off the doorman so he could get her luggage out of the trunk. He had his droopy, sad-eyed victim thing down pretty good now.

"Well, you've had a long flight and I've got a million things to do," Chick said. "By the way, I thought the scripture you put on Chandler's Memorial Program was perfect. It seemed to capture the essence of him. I've been reading the Bible, looking for something for Evelyn." This was such bullshit he couldn't believe he was saying it. He was thankful he hadn't removed the cool Silhouette darks. If there was anything in print that captured Evelyn, it wouldn't have been in the Bible, but in the Book of Human Conceit, somewhere between Larcenous Debt and Lustful Behavior. But, in preparation for this moment, he had found one Bible passage that he thought seemed deep and sensitive, so he reeled it off from memory.

"Last night, I found something in Proverbs that sort of got me. 'For her proceeds are better than profits of silver. She is more precious than rubies, and all the things you may desire cannot compare with her.'" He looked down at his shoes as he finished.

"That's very beautiful, Chick," Paige said.

"Yeah. Well, maybe it's the right one." He turned sadly and moved away from her, stopping beside his car door before finally looking back.

"Well, see ya." He started to get into the car, wondering if she was just going to let him drive away. She couldn't be that hard-hearted. Even pound puppies didn't look as sad and lost as this.

"Chick, I came out here to help. Are you sure there isn't anything I could do for you?"

"*Finally,*" he thought. He was behind the wheel of the sleek black roadster, and looked up, giving her his best angle. "I don't want to impose on you, Paige. It's so sweet you even came at all."

"I want to help. That's the main reason I'm here."

"Well, I'm going to pick out the coffin now, but I could sure use some help on the flowers and stuff . . . "

"I can do that."

"They have a shop right there, at Forest Lawn. They told me they can do wreaths or sprays, anything I want. Evie loved spring flowers—purple jasmine, especially." He looked down sadly. "Purple was her favorite color."

"Why don't I come and help you?"

"Are you sure? It's been a long day for you. You just got here."

"Chick, of course I'll help. What time do you want me to be there? I'm renting a car from the hotel agency."

"Is five-thirty too early?"

"Five-thirty is perfect."

Chick couldn't believe how well this was going. By the time they'd finished picking out flowers, it would be six or six-thirty. After a stressful time selecting wreaths and bouquets for his poor dead wife, what could be more natural than two friends going out to dinner to try and get past the horrible specter of Evelyn's passing?

He had just the place. The Bistro Garden on Ventura Boulevard. A little wine, a little pasta, the special fish dish they did only for him. He felt his package twitch. Nothing overt, just a little throb and some subtle stiffening. His

johnson was telling him, "Hang in there, pal, all is not lost."
He was beginning to pitch a nice little tent in his boxers.

He put the car in gear, waved, and roared out, giving the
Porsche a little extra pop of the clutch for effect, laying a
chirp of rubber just like the sexy hero in one of Jerry Bruckheimer's blockbusters.

CHAPTER

 29

CHICK WAS DRINKING WAY TOO MUCH. WE HADN'T even ordered dinner and he was already on his fourth scotch. I looked across a white tablecloth littered with unused bone china and crystal goblets. Chick was beginning to slur his words, but showed no sign of backing off on the liquor.

"Damn people. Vultures. Who do they think they're kidding? Like it makes any damn difference what kind of box she's buried in." We had already been through this once. He was talking about the account supervisor at Forest Lawn, who Chick was convinced had tried to embarrass him into upgrading Evelyn's coffin, from a medium-priced box, known as a Heaven Rider, to a top-of-the-line, mahogany monster with silver handles called the Eternal Rest.

"They prey on your grief," he slurred, "saying it will be her accommodation for eternity. Like I'm gonna fall for that bullshit guilt trip."

"They were just showing you what was available, Chick. The choice was always yours." He grunted and downed his scotch, the ice clicking against his teeth. Then he held up his glass for a refill.

"I think we should order," I said. We'd been at the Bistro Garden for almost an hour and he'd shooed the waiter away twice. Emotionally, he was all over the place. At times, it was like this next part of life without Evelyn was going to be unbearable, and then he would suddenly change. He'd start talking about a new business venture and his eyes would sparkle, as if he were about to begin a wonderful new journey. It was very strange.

He nodded for the waiter and then insisted on ordering my meal for me.

"They do a special whitefish for me in a Mexican red sauce. It's not on the menu but you'll love it."

I nodded okay, because the truth was, I was very tired and it sounded quick. It was three hours later in Charlotte and I was still on Eastern Time. The more Chick drank, the bigger the bore he became. I just wanted to eat and go back to Pasadena, fall in bed, and pull the world up over my head.

"*Pescado blanco de mejor para dos,*" Chick said. The waiter nodded and wrote it down, then turned and left.

Chick smiled at me. "Named the dish after me ... *Pescado blanco de mejor.*" Then he translated, "White fish à la Best. Their idea, not mine."

"Very flattering," I said, feeling, with this admission, we had definitely run out of things to discuss.

While we waited for our meals, and after Chick's fifth scotch arrived, he began talking about all his private club memberships, finally working his way around to a very exclusive bird-hunting club he belonged to in Mexico, called *La Guerra*.

"Only very important corporate executives and famous actors belong," he boasted. "Very hard to get into this place. It's beautiful, but remote. They fly you down in chartered planes. It's got its own private airstrip. Cabins are rustic, but it's top-drawer all the way. The five-star chef is from Paris—the works."

"It sounds fascinating," I said, trying to stifle a yawn.

The fish arrived and it was excellent. After that came dessert, which Chick also ordered for me. Peach cobbler. Also great. Mercifully, the check finally arrived and we were out of there.

"Chick, are you sure you're all right to drive?" I asked.

He furrowed his brow, as if the fact that he'd had five drinks and was about to get behind the wheel hadn't even occurred to him. But now that realization dawned. "You think I overdid the scotch a little?"

"You've had quite a few."

"Since Evelyn died, I've been leaning on the booze a little too much." Then his eyes turned pensive. "I'm sorry if I got a little loaded here. It's just . . . sometimes I feel . . . "

"It's okay. You don't have to apologize. I understand. But, Chick, drinking too much isn't the answer."

"You're so right. I'll stop."

"I don't mean to be preaching at you," I said. "It's just . . . you'll never come to grips with Evelyn's death by anesthetizing yourself."

"You're right, of course. Thank God you're here to help me. What a wonderful friend you are, Paige. You know exactly the right things to do and say. You're a saint."

Pointing out the obvious to him should hardly qualify me for sainthood. Then he reached for my hand and held it. A troubled look passed across his face, a dark cloud of sudden anguish.

"Do you ever feel as if Chandler was put on earth just for you? That, without him, you would have been only half of something, only part of what you were meant to be?" He was looking right into my eyes as he said that. "Because that's the way I feel," he continued. "I feel like Evelyn was put here to complete me. Put here to address my shortcomings, my lack of focus, my bouts with shallow behavior."

"You're not shallow, Chick," I said, wishing the valet would hurry getting my damn car up to me.

"Are you kidding?" he said. "Not shallow? Have you been listening to me tonight? Country clubs and hunting lodges, cheesy T.V. actors I sometimes play golf with. Like who cares, right?"

I just smiled. I wasn't going near that one.

"But I've always been a sucker for stuff like that. I always wanted to belong, so I can get tricked by nonsense. My father died when I was young so I had no role models. I went through a midlife phase where I tried to buy acceptance. But self-worth can't be bought. It has to come from inside. Evelyn's death has finally taught me that."

I nodded because I felt that was absolutely true. When Chandler had donated his inheritance and formed the learning foundation, I'd asked him why he was giving away his fortune so freely. He said L.D. kids were what he wanted his life to be about. He told me that it seemed to him that over the past decade people in this country had been striving for all the wrong things. "American society is shallowing out," he'd told me. "More and more it seems to be about nothing." Chan was right. Nobody knew who won the Nobel Prize for Medicine; instead we choose to be entertained for a month by the whole Anna Nicole circus or the shallow antics of Paris Hilton or Britney Spears. What the hell happened to cause such a shift in our society's values?

Chan said, "If I'm really going to be happy, I have to invest and devote my life to something important that I truly believe in."

That was why he gave his fortune away. Yet by Chick's own admission, only now, after his wife's death, was he learning that true happiness can't be bought, that it has to come from inside you.

The cars arrived, and Chick told the attendant to repark the Porsche, that he'd call a cab. I offered to drive him home but he said it was exactly in the wrong direction, which it was.

"You're bound to be exhausted," he said. "I can pick up the Porsche in the morning."

I got into the Mustang and drove off.

On the way to Pasadena I fished my cell out of my purse to check messages. The battery was fried and I had stupidly not packed my charger, so I was officially incommunicado.

When I returned to the hotel, there was an envelope under my door. I ripped it open and found a fax from Bob Butler.

Dear Mrs. Ellis:

I tried to reach you, but your cell phone isn't picking up. I'm sending this fax instead. Good news. I found the tire store where the hit-and-run driver switched his Firestones. I had a sketch artist work with Dale Winthrop, the owner, but she said that since it was seven months ago, his memory of the man is not very good. The enclosed sketch may not be too close.

As I was leaving, I checked my office and we got lucky again. I just got a response from an auto body repair shop in New Jersey, Top Hat Auto. An estimator there, named Lou LaFanta, remembers a redo for a right front fender on a blue Taurus about the same time of Chandler's death. I'm on my way up there to talk to him now. Hopefully he can improve on my sketch and tell me something new.

Yours truly,
Detective Robert Butler

P.S. The Lord with his great and strong sword shall slay the dragon that is in the sea. Isaiah 27:1.

I held up the faxed sketch. It was of a middle-aged white male. It looked like nobody I had ever seen before.

CHAPTER  30

CHICK COULDN'T BELIEVE WHAT A RAGING ASS-
hole he'd been at dinner. It wasn't until he was standing outside the restaurant and the cold night air sobered him
slightly that he was able to accurately review the mindless
stream of bullshit he'd been spewing at Paige all evening. He
vaguely remembered seeing flashes of disinterest and disappointment passing across her face, along with a few stifled
yawns. His drunken response had been to amp it up, drop a
few more actors' names, and tell her about some other
worthless club, or Rotary award he'd won.

He'd planned to talk only about Evelyn at dinner, to
discuss his innermost fears about being left alone without
her. He had cautioned himself—don't come on to her this
time. He'd seen the disastrous results that had produced at
Chandler's funeral. And then, like a complete dick, he'd just
ignored his own counsel, forgotten everything that had

been working so beautifully, and reverted to his old "Don't-you-love-what-I've-got-and-don't-you-wish-you-had-it" bullshit.

Thank God his mind had finally cleared and he was able to come up with his prepackaged closer about Evelyn completing him. But he knew he'd lost ground and now needed to go proactive.

He had seen a paperback book in her purse when she'd opened it to get her lipstick . . . *Death of a Loved One* by Dr. Emily Eaton. It occurred to Chick that since he had absolutely no emotions on the loss of Evelyn, that book might be very useful in telling him how he should pretend to feel. He stopped at Book Star on Ventura on the way home and picked up a copy just as they were closing.

Once he got to his house on Elm, he found Melissa in the front room slumped in front of the television. She was watching some horrible MTV rerun of a Spring Break special, starring Jerry Springer, who was on a stage in Cancun convincing teenage girls to take off their tops and wrestle each other in a vat of Jell-O, while a bunch of drunk college guys were yelling, "Jer-ree, Jer-ree, Jer-ree . . . "

What passed as entertainment these days baffled him.

"Melissa, could you turn that down for a minute? I need to discuss the funeral tomorrow," he said.

She didn't turn it down. Didn't even look up from the program.

"Melissa, we need to arrive together," he continued. "The service starts at two. A limo will pick us up at one-thirty sharp. We need to be on time."

Nothing. She was smiling as one of the topless girls on the TV slipped in some Jell-O on the stage and almost fell off the riser.

"Melissa, are you listening to me?"

"Of course not," she said. "I'm tuning you out completely. It's how I survive your pathetic bullshit."

He crossed the room and turned off the TV. She snapped her head around and glared at him. "I was watching that."

"I'm talking to you. We've got to leave at one-thirty tomorrow. The limo driver from Forest Lawn is going to be here and I would really appreciate it if you'd dress respectfully for the event and leave all the face metal at home. It's your mother's funeral. Try not to show up looking like an ad for fishhooks."

She scowled angrily. "Maybe this hasn't occurred to you Pops 'cause you're so busy trying to bang that Ellis bitch, but I don't give a shit what you want."

That one really rocked him because Chick had no idea his intentions were so transparent that even his stoner daughter was able to spot them.

"I'm gonna wear what I want and I'm bringing Big Mac," she continued.

"He's not invited. This is your mother's funeral for God's sake." But Chick didn't have to think for long to know what was on her mind. She planned to roll up to the gravesite on the back of that tattooed asshole's Harley, both of them wearing biker leather. Anything to humiliate and embarrass him.

"If you're planning on showing up and making a scene, then don't come at all," Chick finally said.

"Not come to *Mommy's funeral*?" Sarcastic and deliberately over the top. She followed this with a sly smile. "Gee, Daddy, what a strange thing for you to say."

"Melissa, I'm not kidding."

"Neither am I."

Chick stood there wondering what the hell he was supposed to do. There was certainly no controlling her. If she was willing to claim that meth bust and risk playing pet the kitty with a bunch of weight-lifting prison lesbians, then taking Big Mac to Evelyn's funeral was obviously nothing to her. He thought, maybe if he offered money . . .

"You've been pestering me for months about new winter clothes," he said. "What if I clear your credit card. You can go up to five hundred dollars."

"Hey, my cooperation is gonna cost a helluva lot more than that."

A fucking protocol negotiation over her own mother's funeral. He couldn't believe it! But he was trapped, so he went on. "How much then?"

"It's going to be awkward," she said, chewing a cuticle. "Big Mac really wants to go. He was hoping to sit next to Mickey D, who, by the way, called today to say he's coming— no pun intended. Instead of worrying about Big Mac, maybe you ought to call the Mick and make sure that asshole doesn't show up oiled like a pole dancer in one of his posing briefs." Her smile had turned nasty. "If I'm going to disappoint Big Mac, you're going to have to make a better offer. Five hundred dollars won't even handle the sales tax on what I need."

"It may have escaped your notice, Melissa, but I'm not doing quite as well as I was last year. I'm under a lot of financial pressure . . . "

He stopped because she had picked up a *Teen People* and was ignoring him, thumbing through the magazine, looking at long-lens pictures of Lindsay Lohan in rehab.

"Melissa, I'm not kidding. Big Mac is not to come to your mother's funeral."

"Then you better call and tell him. His number's on the Post-it next to the phone in the kitchen. But be careful 'cause he already hates your guts and if he thinks he's being dissed, the shit can really jump off with that guy."

There was no dealing with her. A hundred grand wouldn't be enough, so he walked into the bedroom, seething, and looked at the notes he had been making for Evelyn's eulogy. In truth, he was only making this speech to one person. All of Chick's thoughts, all of his remarks were aimed only at Paige Ellis. He had made a list of Chandler's musings to work into his speech—saccharine things he'd said in Hawaii.

Chick sat down at his desk and opened the book on grief he'd just bought. It would be great if he could crib some of this shit and palm it off as his own.

He started to work again on the eulogy, but he was so mad at Melissa he couldn't get into the right mindset.

In the other room the television blared. Springer was orchestrating another bikini strip and the horny college boys were loving every minute of it . . .

"Jer-ree, Jer-ree, Jer-ree . . . "

CHAPTER

3

A FLASH OF LIGHTNING LIT THE DARKENING AFTER-
noon sky. Chick looked small as he stood at graveside in his
black pinstriped suit. When he finally spoke, his voice was
so weak I had to lean forward to hear him.

"As I stand here, looking across this casket, I am shocked
that such a small container could be the final resting place
for somebody so important in my life."

More lightning, this time followed by the distant roar of
thunder. I saw Chick hesitate. His shoulders slumped. Silence
followed the rumbling of the storm. Then he straightened
and seemed to gain enough strength to continue.

"Eighteen years ago, Evelyn and I agreed to be a team,
a partnership. Agreed to share our lives together. She was
the visionary, I was the student. Through the years, that
never changed. As I stand here today, it seems all wrong
that I should be the survivor and she the departed. Why

did God take the teacher and leave the struggling student behind?"

Distant lightning flashed, more thunder, and then the rain started. This weather was uncharacteristic for L.A. in the fall, but the storm had blown in overnight, unannounced. People opened umbrellas and inched in closer around the grave to get under the tent that had been set up to shade five rows of wooden chairs from what the mortuary had assumed would be another sunny California day. The mourners turned up their coat collars and waited, their eyes turned on Evelyn's grieving husband. Chick's daughter, Melissa, stood on the edge of the crowd. She was wearing jeans and didn't seem to be paying any attention to her father.

I stood halfway down the gravesite, on the west side, just under the canvas tent. I felt a gust of wet wind blowing moisture onto my legs. As Chick struggled to get through the eulogy he seemed close to tears.

"Words are not adequate to carry the emotional weight of this day. I know what I want to say, but I find myself struggling to find ways to communicate it to you. My vocabulary just isn't adequate. Words cannot express my horrible sense of loss. But words are all I have so I have been trying to choose the right ones.

"There are five that seem especially relevant. Five words to try and mark the gravity of this moment. The first, of course, is 'loss.' You see, I've lost my best friend. I've lost my rudder. I've lost my teacher. I've lost the meaning for my life. I keep trying to believe it hasn't happened. I keep trying to deny it. You see, I've lost just about everything but my beautiful daughter, Melissa, so 'loss' is the first word."

I saw Melissa look down at her shoes and frown. Chick started to sob. Then with great effort, he pulled himself back together. It was a monumental struggle, which, after almost two minutes, he finally won.

"'Loneliness,'" he began again, "a word that describes an emptiness so desperate that my mind reels above its dark caverns. But then when I least expect it, loneliness is pushed aside and suddenly it's replaced with anger. The anger frightens me because it seems the wrong emotion in the wake of Evelyn's passing, but it's there nonetheless, redefining the way I must now deal with myself. So like it or not, 'anger' is the third word."

He paused and looked very small, very fragile. I remembered having these same feelings of anger at Chandler's funeral. All of this was discussed in the book on grief I had with me. The five stages of grief were denial, anger, bargaining, depression, and finally acceptance. I made a mental note to give the book to Chick.

"'Memory,'" he said softly. "I remember all the things she did, all the examples she set, all the ways she taught me to be stronger. My memory tortures me. It depresses me. It will not release me from this pain I feel."

He started to choke up again and had to wait for almost a minute more before continuing. "As I look across this casket, all I want is to crawl inside and be with her. I want to go where she is going because, from now on, I know my life will be little more than a pale shadow of what it once was. As I stand here I can't even begin to contemplate the horror of going on without her."

And now, for some reason, Chick looked directly at me. "You all loved her as I loved her," he said. "You saw her gentleness and caring. You saw Evelyn the teacher, or Evelyn the leader. You saw her strength, her good deeds. You saw her devotion to life and to her friends. So the last word is 'promise.' You were her dear friends, so as her friends I make this solemn promise to you all."

He stopped and swung his gaze away from me, looking at each face gathered before him. "I promise to be a better man. All of my choices will be nobler, more giving, more aware. I will struggle to do more for others and worry less about myself. I know I am forced to live on, but I will never be the same. Pray for me as I take this path. Pray for both our spirits as we both begin our new separate journeys. Pray for Evelyn Sheridan Best as she goes to a better place, and pray for me as I must find a way to continue on earthbound and alone."

When he finished, he was crying. I felt Chandler in those words. Like Chick, I was unable to fill the hole Chandler had left in my life and in my heart. I had also looked at his coffin and had thought, "He was so much larger than that. How did he fit in there?"

After the funeral the rain cleared and we all followed the mortuary limousine over to the Best's house in Beverly Hills. At least a hundred people from the funeral showed up. Waiters in white coats passed champagne and finger foods. Chick was in one corner of the living room, surrounded by friends.

Later, a short, muscular man in a form-fitting T-shirt and black sport jacket descended on me unannounced. "You look like you work out."

I winced at that overused line. "I'm a marathon runner," I replied, wondering how to get away from him.

"Ever lift?"

"No. Could you excuse me for a minute?" I tried to step around him, but he didn't move. He had me trapped in the corner.

"I used to train Evelyn. I'm Mickey DePolina. Everyone calls me Mickey D." He stuck out his muscular hand and shook mine. "You ever want, we could get together and work up a fitness routine—aerobics, even yoga. I do it all. I train over at Gold's in the Valley."

"I'm not from around here. I live back East. I really need to speak to somebody over there. Could you excuse me?"

I finally managed to get around him and find a more protected backwater where I could observe the party without being hassled. The crowd was attractive and upscale, the mood subdued.

I saw Melissa over by the door, keeping to herself. I couldn't help but think that Melissa Best was heading for a big crash. Looking at her, I could see a lot of danger signs. The body piercings, the purple hair. The constant angry scowl.

Then Chick made his way over to me.

"Your words at the funeral were beautiful," I told him.

He nodded and looked around the room. "These people all mean well. I know they want to help, but it feels like I'm putting on a show here. I have to try and be what they want. It's like an obligation."

"It gets better," I said.

"You know what I'd like?"

"What?"

"After this is over, I'd like us to just sit in the backyard out by the pool and talk. You've been through this. I really need help getting my head around it."

I didn't answer. Something told me staying after the reception would be a mistake, so I was looking for a polite way to duck him.

"And then tomorrow I've got to go up to our mountain cabin and get some of Evelyn's things out of there for her sister," he continued. "I can't tell you how much I'm dreading that project. That was . . . that was the place where . . . where we . . . " and then he put his hand up to his eyes and just stood there.

"Oh Chick, I'm so sorry," I said, feeling a wave of guilt. "Look, if it will help, I'll stay for a little while after your other friends leave. Melissa, you, and I could just sit and talk."

"I think Melissa has some plans for tonight." Then he shook his head. "I feel like such a putz, breaking down, crying all the time. I gotta get a grip on myself. I'm not usually such a weepy guy."

"There's nothing wrong with crying, Chick. Please don't apologize."

He nodded, and then someone was spinning him around—the bodybuilder in the black T-shirt and jacket. He was saying something about wanting to buy gym equipment, so I moved off.

I wandered around for a while but I didn't know any of the other people and basically kept to myself. A little while later I went outside to get some air. I noticed a man looking at a gold Mercedes parked behind the garage. I guessed it was Evelyn's car. The one she was murdered in. It seemed sort of macabre having it parked back here. I walked up and looked over the man's shoulder. He sensed me standing behind him and turned around.

"Hi," he said. He was remarkably handsome, olive skin, square jaw, complete with a deep cleft in his chin. His blue suit fit him perfectly, set off by a yellow shirt and striped blue and yellow tie. His shoes were blood-red Oxfords, buffed to a high shine.

"Hi." I hesitated and then asked him, "Was this the car?"

"Yep."

"Don't the police hold a car where a murder was committed until after the trial?" I said. "Isn't it part of the crime scene or something?"

The man put out his hand. "I'm the detective assigned to the murder. Apollo Demetrius, LAPD."

"Paige Ellis, friend from out of town." I shook his hand.

"Once our forensic and print teams are finished and our chain of evidence is intact, the courts don't need the car. We could have kept it in impound if it was a junker, but with an expensive rig like this, we'll often cut it loose. Chick wanted it back. I think he's going to sell it."

"I heard you got the guy," I said.

"Yep. Delroy Washington. We ought to get that brain-dead banger on America's Dumbest Criminals. He left prints all over the car, all over the murder weapon, left the gun right where he ditched the vehicle after he stripped it. Bunch of car-jack priors, all violent. At worst, it's a special-circumstances, murder-one, death-penalty case. At the very least, life without parole."

"My husband was killed by a hit-and-run driver in Charlotte, North Carolina, earlier this year. They still haven't solved it." It just came out. I didn't even know why I said it.

"You have to get a little lucky sometimes. But this guy Del-roy was so sloppy he might as well have mailed me an invitation to the murder."

"It's really helped Chick, I think, that you caught him."

"Chick seems like a good guy. At first, I wasn't so sure. But I've been around him a lot the past few days and he seems okay."

Then the detective smiled at me. "Since you've just been through the same thing with your husband, maybe you can help him."

"Maybe so," I finally said.

CHAPTER

IT WAS DUSK AND THEY WERE IN THE BACKYARD of Chick's beautiful Beverly Hills house. The pool light was shimmering, the Jacuzzi projecting a promising message. The catering company had just cleared out. Chick changed into his cool, new, blue Versace silk shirt and black Roberto Cavalli stretch jeans. He had a pair of expensive Gucci suedes on his feet. No socks, of course.

They both sat in pool chairs. The name of the game was Get Paige into the Jacuzzi. That was the end zone. But he had to go easy. Keep it simple, keep it sad. And then, if his wood hardened up just a tad, he'd make his move.

Chick worked his neck around in a circle, then stretched it side to side, front and back, making a big deal of it.

"Stiff neck?" Paige asked after a couple of minutes.

"Yeah. Maybe after you leave, I'll pop into the Jacuzzi and see if I can get it loosened up. But right now, all I want to do is talk and relax a little. I'm all wound up. If this ever really hits me full on, I'm afraid I'll go down for the count."

Chick looked over at her, sitting with her feet tucked under her in the pool chair. Adorable. "After the initial shock of it, having to plan the funeral was a Godsend, because it kept me thinking about a zillion details," he said sadly. "I couldn't focus on the loss. Did you ever have that with Chandler?"

"Yes," she said softly. "Yes, I did."

"God, you guys had so much, just like me and Evelyn."

"Y'know, I don't think I ever really understood who Evelyn was," Paige said. "The things you said today at the funeral made me realize it was too bad we didn't have a chance to know each other better."

Chick gave her a thoughtful, sad, penetrating look, while thinking Evelyn and Chandler were at the exact opposite ends of the spectrum. Chandler had stupidly given away his fortune. Evelyn had greedily spent Chick's. If Evelyn had Chandler's money, she wouldn't have set up a center for learning disabled children. She'd have set up a center for the beautification and fashionable excess of Evelyn Sheridan Best. But he didn't say any of this. Instead, he kept working his neck, pretending to loosen the stiff muscles.

"After denial comes a lot of vengeance and anger, Chick. You mentioned that at the funeral. I need to warn you, it stays for a long time and it is very destructive. I'm still seething inside, and I know it's not good for me. After that comes the bargaining. Sort of promising you'll do better in the wake of death. It's the way we say goodbye. There's a great book on grief called *Death of a Loved One*. I'll loan it to you. Although, you surprise me, because you seem so in touch with yourself. You already seem to know most of it."

Chick thought this couldn't be going better. Half the shit he had been saying to her was right out of that silly book, and so far she hadn't picked up on it.

He let his face go blank.

"What is it?" she asked, noticing his expression change.

"Nothing," he said, "nothing, really."

"If I can help . . . "

"Just worried about this horrible task I have ahead of me. Forget it."

"I didn't mean to pry." She sat back, and a minute of silence followed.

"Okay, what I was thinking, really more like dreading, was going up to that damn cabin in Big Bear and sorting through all of Evelyn's things. She had a lot of family mementos up there . . . photo albums from before we were married, paintings, stuff her sick mother wants. I've agreed to go hunt it up and send it to her sister, who's going to give it to her mom, who's in pretty bad shape. She's in assisted living and it seems she doesn't have much longer."

"Was Evelyn's sister at the funeral?"

"No . . . no, Mariah couldn't come. She's taking care of their mom in Michigan. Neither of them could get here. Evelyn's father died two years ago."

"I'm sorry."

"Me, too," Chick said sadly. "He was a great guy." Chick thought Bud Sheridan was a pompous asshole who pumped out useless advice, one horrible suggestion hooked to another like bad sausage. The man had opinions on everything from the stock market to the best way to wash your car. It was hard to take instruction from a guy who got fired every eighteen months and ended up as a nonunion plumber doing illegal work for an unlicensed contractor. But that was another story. Bud was gone. Taking a well-deserved dirt nap. No need to revisit that sack of hopeless memories.

Chick leaned back and worked his neck some more.

"That neck's really bothering you, isn't it?" Paige said. She got up and moved around behind his chair and began to massage the muscles in his shoulders. She worked silently for a few minutes, her long, strong fingers kneading him professionally. Chick actually felt his johnson tingle, then quiver, then begin to rise like a mummy from the tomb. A smile spread to his lips. This was actually about to happen.

"Better?" She stopped without preamble, shook out her hands, and moved back to her chair.

Fuck, he thought. *What kind of a massage is that?* But what he said was, "Much. Thank you."

He stood up and turned on the Jacuzzi, making a big deal out of setting the temperature. "After you leave, I'll just soak in this thing for a while. I'm sure I'll be fine."

Then he sat back down and, while the Jacuzzi bubbled sexual innuendos beside them, got back to business. "Anyway, I have to go up to the cabin and sort through all her stuff, and honestly, Paige, I don't think I'm up to it. I think, if I try, I'll crack up."

"Then don't go," she said. "At least not for a while."

"I wish it was that easy, but I don't know how long Evelyn's mom has. The death was very hard on her. Mariah says she's been crying all day, asking for the photo albums, pictures of Evelyn from when she was a kid. There are also some of Evelyn's personal effects, her journals. She was a great writer and kept wonderful journals. Anyway, Mariah thinks getting this stuff will help. She made me a list, so I really have to go. Besides, like I said at the funeral, I'm in my bargaining stage, trying to be a better Chick. This is something worthwhile that I can do for Evelyn's mom, so I'll just gut it out . . . just go up there and do it."

"I still haven't cleaned out Chandler's office," she said. "It's too painful to go through it all by myself right now."

Yes, that's the whole point, Chick thought. *Are you really going to let me go up there and do this morbid task alone?* He worked his neck again and waited to see what would happen.

She got up and moved around the chair and again started working on his neck.

"I thought you were through," he said.

"I used to do this for Chandler. You work for about five minutes, let the blood come back in, then do it again." She flashed a smile. "You're gonna have to sit still for three of these, my friend."

He could feel her fingers working themselves deep into his shoulder muscles while his johnson began to unwind like a snake under a porch.

"I don't feel any knots," she said after a minute.

"Probably psychosomatic," he replied, "but it sure feels much better. Ahh, ahh, there, there . . . that's the spot . . . perfect."

She kept kneading for a few minutes longer, then sat down again.

"Look, Chick, cleaning out that cabin might be an emotional mistake right now. You should call Evelyn's sister and see how long you could put this off. Even a few weeks would help."

Chick appeared to be giving this some thought. Then he shook his head. "God, I wish I could just run from this, but I promised Mariah, so tomorrow I'm gonna drive up there and give it a shot. Wish me luck." *Come on*, he thought, *don't just sit there.*

But she sat quietly in her chair. He could see indecision flicker. "Would it help if I went with you?" she finally asked.

"Oh Paige, that is sweet of you but, my God, you've flown all the way out here. You barely knew Evelyn. You've made these days bearable just by showing up." He stopped and shook his head. "I can't ask you to do that. I'll be okay. I'll get through it somehow."

"Okay, if you think you can manage."

"It will only take a few hours," he said. "Three painful hours and it will be over."

He watched indecision play on her face.

"I don't really have anything to do tomorrow," she finally said. "It's only a few hours, and if it would help you, then I'd be happy to go. It's the first time in months that I feel like I can actually pitch in and do something worthwhile."

"You'd really drive up there with me?" he said, hardly believing he'd pulled this off. Once he got her up there, he would figure a way to make it last for days.

"I've got to go see Chandler's parents in the morning for breakfast, but after that I'm free."

She stood up. "I'd better get going. It's late, and you should jump in that Jacuzzi and get your neck loosened. I'll see you mañana." She gathered up her things and headed toward the house.

He got up and followed. At the door, he gave her a quick hug, remembering to keep it sexless. He watched her drive away. But after she was gone, he beamed.

Man, he was good. *You just can't teach this shit*, he thought.

PAIGE

DRIVING BACK TO THE LANGHAM HUNTINGTON IN
Pasadena I wondered how I could have allowed myself to get
talked into this. What on earth had I been thinking?

At the hotel, I gave the Mustang to the valet and took
the elevator up to my room. When I walked in the telephone
message light was on. I picked up the receiver, punched the
right button, and listened to a recorded message from Peter
Ellis notifying me that breakfast tomorrow was at 10 A.M. at
the family offices on Wilshire Boulevard.

Then I played my second message. It was from Bob Butler.

"Mrs. Ellis, it's Detective Butler. I've been trying to reach
you, but your cell phone must be off 'cause I'm going
straight to voice-mail. Anyway, here's my update: The body
and fender guy in Virginia remembers the car had New York
plates and a Hertz sticker on the mirror. He helped me refine
the sketch, which I'll be sending to you once the artist is
done. I'm flying to New York to recheck the Hertz agencies

there. I think I'm on the verge of solving this. Please call ASAP. God bless you."

I cursed myself that I'd left the damn cell-phone charger at home. I tried Bob's number, but he was either out of range or already on the plane. I finally stripped off my clothes and fell into bed. But, as tired as I was, I couldn't go to sleep.

The more I thought about my trip to the mountains with Chick, the more second thoughts I had.

I knew that impulsive decision was tied up with Chandler's death and a sense that I no longer fit in. I was trying to feel needed.

I tossed and turned and began to look for a way out. A way to renege. I got up, pulled some Evian out of the minibar, then turned on the TV and plopped back down on the bed and started absently roaming through the channels looking for something to take my mind off it. I stopped at *The Late News on Channel Five,* just as the blonde anchorwoman was saying:

"Evelyn Best, the slain wife of Internet exec Charles Best, was buried today at Forest Lawn Cemetery. While that event was taking place in front of several hundred family members and friends, across town the key suspect in her murder, Delroy Washington, was arraigned before the Superior Court Magistrate."

The picture switched to a shot of Delroy being led into the courthouse in handcuffs. The insolent teenager glared at the camera.

"Assistant District Attorney Brent Briggs had these words for our KTLA camera outside the courthouse."

The shot switched to a young D.A. with a serious expression. He was standing in front of the mahogany door to Superior Court Six.

"The physical evidence here is pretty overwhelming, and pending an arraignment on capital murder, we are going to ask that Mr. Washington be held without bail."

The shot switched to a black woman in her mid-forties wearing a print dress. She was with a heavyset man, who turned out to be her attorney. The anchorwoman's voice continued over the shot.

"Delroy Washington's attorney, David Atwater, had this to say . . . "

I was now sitting up straight in bed. I turned up the volume as the attorney spoke.

"Delroy Washington was at home with his mother when Mrs. Best's Mercedes was carjacked. This is just another example of police scapegoating. Because my client had a history of carjacking, they're trying to pin this crime on him, despite his alibi. This case is shortly going to be exposed for the rail job it actually is."

I thought of Chick and what he'd said at the funeral, how he had pledged himself to live a better life—use Evelyn's death to improve his life. I was suddenly ashamed about wanting to duck out. I decided anew to help him through this task in Big Bear. It was only going to take a few hours. I could certainly get through that.

I shut off the light and turned over on my side. Just before sleep took me, the same subconscious voice I'd heard earlier delivered another warning.

"*Don't go,*" it whispered softly.

CHAPTER

34

THE NEXT MORNING CHANDLER'S PARENTS AND I
sat in the handsome wood-paneled dining room in their corporate offices at a beautifully appointed table and picked at our food. Chandler's death was still a wall none of us could get over. After the meal was cleared away, we finally talked about what Peter Ellis called my next life option.

What it came down to was I had to get off my ass and start moving forward again.

The real reason the Ellis's had invited me to breakfast was to propose that I become managing director of Chandler's learning foundation. Peter said he and Sophia would continue to sit on the board as advisers without compensation. I would have full discretion on how to spend the foundation's capital distributions. I could manage the fiscal resources, decide what research equipment to buy, what new projects we would fund and develop.

There was important research being conducted on dyslexia at Yale by Drs. Sally and Bennett Shaywitz using MRIs to determine what part of the brain was activated when reading. Chandler had been excited with Sally and Bennett's work and had invested foundation money to speed their research. Peter said that I was the natural choice to run Chandler's foundation.

I was exhilarated by the challenge but scared to death of the responsibility. I also knew this was just what I needed to kick-start my life.

I was definitely interested but wanted the rest of the weekend to think it over. I told them that I had promised to go to Big Bear with Chick Best to help him clear Evelyn's things out of their cabin and would give them my decision when I returned.

It was noon by the time I left. I got caught in bumper-to-bumper traffic and didn't arrive back at the Langham until after one. I valeted the rental car and walked into the lobby. The concierge stopped me and handed me a fax in a sealed envelope. I was starting to open it when I heard my name.

"Paige?"

I turned, and standing there, dressed in black steel-toed cowboy boots, a blazer, and stretch designer jeans, was Chick.

"Hi . . . " I said. "Have you been waiting long?"

"Just half an hour, but it's no sweat. I love this place. Evelyn and I used to come here and go dancing when the old Ship Room was still open. That was back at the beginning of time when this was still a Sheraton Hotel." He smiled.

"I'm sorry I kept you waiting. I got caught in traffic."

"It's okay. You ready to go?"

"Guess so," I answered hesitantly. He took my arm and led me out to the parking lot, where Evelyn's gold Mercedes SL600 was parked.

I stared at the damn car.

"Everything all right?" he asked.

"Isn't this Evelyn's car?"

"Yes . . . " He seemed confused.

"The car she was killed in?"

"It's been detailed and cleaned out. I'm getting set to sell it."

I didn't want to ride in a car that, only a week ago, had hosted Evelyn's death.

"It's just . . . she was killed in this car. I mean, come on, Chick," I stammered.

"Oh yeah, right." Realization finally dawned. "I decided to drive it because the trunk's bigger than the Porsche and we'll be bringing quite a few of Evelyn's things back."

Your wife was murdered in this damn car, I thought. *How can you even stand to be in it?*

"Another reason I brought it was it has chains in the trunk that fit these tires and the Porsche doesn't. It could be snowing up there and we may need them."

I couldn't think of anything to say.

"Would you rather we rented something?" he asked, a perplexed look on his face because I was still standing there, glaring at the damn car.

It was a logical explanation, I guess, but I was struggling to understand how Chick could be so insensitive.

What I said, dumb-ass that I am, was, "No, it's okay. This car's fine."

"Ready?" he asked. "We'll be back by eight or nine tonight."

I didn't answer, so he came around and opened the door, and I reluctantly got in. Once the door was closed, I was engulfed by the sweet, lilac scent of car shampoo.

Chick got behind the wheel. When he looked over at me he had a wide smile on his face. He started the car and pulled out of the hotel entry.

As we turned onto Oak Knoll Avenue I looked down and saw a dark maroon speck. It was just above the carpet, on the lower kick panel. I didn't have to look long to know what it was. A piece of Evelyn's brains that the car cleaners had somehow missed was stuck in a tiny crack below the radio speaker. A little speck of Chick's dead wife. A little piece of her DNA was going on this mountain trip with us. I grimaced and pulled my eyes away.

"Paige, this is so amazing of you." Chick was still smiling at me. "I can't tell you what it means."

I nodded but didn't answer.

"You'll love Big Bear. It's beautiful up there. I always feel so close to nature in that cabin. The air is like pine perfume."

I nodded again. I was thinking that events had piled up on me too fast and had produced this situation. My own quest to get moving again, the parallel deaths of Chandler and Evelyn. This damn Girl Scout thing that I've been doing since I was nine. All of it had conspired to produce a terrible decision.

I already wanted out of the car, but I couldn't think of a graceful way to accomplish it. So instead of demanding that Chick stop and turn around right then, I started telling myself to calm down and not overreact.

But for the next five miles, I couldn't take my eyes off the little speck of Evelyn's brains that rode the door panel by my right foot.

CHAPTER 35

THE AFTERNOON SKY WAS DARKENING, THREATEN-
ing another storm. Chick was chatting about his house up
in Big Bear, bragging about what a great real-estate deal it
was and how smart he'd been to buy it. I was just trying to
keep my eyes off Evelyn's brain spatter. Somewhere past San
Bernardino, he moved on to his land speculation and real-
estate philosophy.

"When the property market crashed with the junk
mortgages last year, all the ribbon clerks panicked and
started selling. There was more dirt for sale at low prices in
Big Bear than in fucking Baja. All that action drove land
prices down even further. Of course, I never even considered
selling. I plan a strategy, think things out carefully in advance. When I buy something, I'm making a long-term investment. It's not about short-term profit or loss, like with
these other hit-and-run, get-rich-quick guys. For me, it's

about looking for a market opportunity and capitalizing on it. Real estate is where the really great long-term fortunes are made, but you have to have an approach and a long-term philosophy."

I was getting very put off by all this, especially while we were taking this grisly mission to clean out his just-murdered wife's mementos.

Where was the abject grief from yesterday, the terror at the looming prospect of having to sort through Evelyn's belongings? I'd only come along to help him through that trauma, but here he was chatting me up on his long-term business goals.

"The Internet, where I work, has redesigned everything, all aspects of commerce," he was saying. "I predict, for instance, that there won't even be real-estate agents in the future. Everything, all property, will be listed and sold online. Virtual property tours, deals, negotiations in secure chat rooms, all final transactions subject to an actual viewing of the property, set up on the Web by the buyer and the seller. The ten-percenters will all be dust."

He was giving me a headache.

We had left the 210 and were on Highway 18, climbing up toward Running Springs. There were patches of fresh snow on the side of the road, and long mounds of it lay in the center of the highway where the snow plows had left it. Chick kept talking endlessly about money and how good he was at making it. The further out of L.A. we got, the more animated he became. Suddenly, he jerked his thumb at the passing scenery.

"All of the property up here is gonna be for sale soon. It's mostly parkland now but we're gonna be seeing the Fed cutting loose big parcels of this stuff. All the CC&Rs are going to vanish." He looked over at me. "That's Covenants, Conditions, and Restrictions. It's why I wanted you to see how beautiful it is, 'cause once that happens, I'm set to pounce."

I was seriously beginning to wonder what on earth this trip up here was really all about.

Then he actually said it. "I'm planning on taking my considerable assets from the sale of bestmarket.com and sticking them in a long-term, high-growth project, like this raw land here. I know just about everybody who's anybody in L.A. Got a bunch of state contacts to help with zoning changes. All the serious insiders are watching me, because they want to take a ride on the Chick Best Express. Lotta people, right now, are waiting to see which way I'm gonna jump. The people who end up with me are gonna make a fortune. The people close to me, my 'investment family' so to speak, they're gonna do very well."

Then he looked over and gave me what I'm sure he thought was a sexy smile and added, "That could be you if you want it to be, Paige."

My heart sank, because in that instant, I pretty much knew I'd been played. In that moment, only twenty miles or so from his cabin in Big Bear, I was absolutely convinced Chick had invited me up here to see if he could get something started. I sat there, looking at that tiny speck of Evelyn's brains, and tried to choke down my anger.

As we kept winding up Highway 18, my mind focused on how to get the hell out of this car and down off this mountain.

How could I have been such an idiot? I had ignored the warning voice in my head. I had projected my own feelings onto him. Not the first time in my life I've made that mistake.

Shortly after we turned onto the highway, huge snowflakes began to fall. They stuck on the glass and drifted like large pieces of white confetti past the windows. The heavy sky was gunmetal gray, and dropping ever lower. As an army brat, I'd lived in enough cold climates growing up to know that this was the beginning of a big storm, a heavy dump.

During the next half-hour, we slowed because it was hard to see through the falling curtain of white. Soon the road was covered with snow. Chick stopped at a gas station in Fawnskin and paid the attendant twenty bucks to put the rear chains on the car for us.

I asked to use the phone, but the attendant told me that the storm yesterday had taken down the lines and cellpod communications. The phone crews were working on it, but it wasn't back in service yet. I was now feeling very cut off and uneasy.

We got the chains on and pulled out. The cold air was freezing the snowflakes on the side window. The landscape was quickly becoming a Christmas card of white jagged mountain peaks and snow-covered pines. I could hear the chains crunching and ringing on the concrete under us as we cut through the wet, drifting snow, always moving further up toward the mountain summit.

The cabin wasn't in Big Bear proper, but in a smaller, more remote area called Sugarloaf, a few miles off Highway 18 on I-38.

Finally, around three-thirty, we turned left off the interstate and pulled up a long drive.

"Where are we?" I asked.

"Casa Best," he grinned. "This is my driveway. The
cabin's about two miles up ahead. It's nice up here. No neighbors, real peaceful . . . "

Great, I thought, *no neighbors, what a break.*

I finally saw the outline of his cabin in a shard of afternoon light that was streaming through a hole in the clouds,
lighting the curtain of fast-falling snow. It was an A-frame
at the end of a line of snow-covered pine trees facing back
toward the narrow road.

"There she blows," he said with hearty good cheer.

He pulled up in front of the cabin and turned off the engine. Then while I sat in the car, not wanting to get out, he
hurried up the walkway to the porch, opened the front door,
and went into the house.

My next thought chilled me. *Now I'm stuck with this asshole in the middle of a blizzard.*

CHAPTER

36

THE PASSENGER DOOR WAS YANKED OPEN. I ALMOST shrieked, but managed to choke it back.

"What's wrong?" Chick was saying, standing over me.

"I, uh . . . look, Chick, I think it's a little remote up here with all this weather coming in. Maybe we should go back to L.A. and tackle this another time."

"We'll never make it down the mountain. That road will be closed soon."

"Then we should go back to the Bear Mountain Lodge in town."

"Never get in during ski season. It'll be booked solid. Come on inside."

"It didn't look too full to me, when we passed. Almost no cars. Why don't you call? Maybe the lines are back up now."

"Look, Paige, if you're feeling funny about being here alone with me, I'll try and get us some rooms in town. In the meantime, come on in. I'll get a fire going. You look like you're freezing, sitting there. At least you can get warm." He was holding the door open, as the cold, snowy air whipped around my shoulders.

Reluctantly, I grabbed my sweater and purse, got out of the car, and followed him into the cabin.

The house was impressive. Chick turned on the gas fire in the huge stone fireplace. The flames crackled, licking the edges of some preset pine logs. The living room was decorated Southwestern style with rough-hewn furnishings and lots of Navajo rugs. A few stuffed heads of mountain lions, deer, and Kodiak bears hung on the walls, their sightless glass eyes flickering in the reflected firelight. Chick saw me looking at the animal heads.

"Shot most of those puppies myself," he bragged.

Great, I thought.

"Close the door there. I'll see if I can get through to the lodge." He crossed to the phone and picked it up. "Good deal, I got a dial tone." Then he punched in a number he seemed to know by heart, and waited for an answer. "Yes, may I speak to the front desk?" He smiled at me while he was waiting. "Reservations, please." Then: "Yes, this is Charles Best. I live up on Sugarloaf. It's a little blizzardy up here right now and a lady friend of mine and I were wondering if you have any space in the lodge?" Then he looked right at me to emphasize his next point. "Since the road just got closed I guess we'll need *two* rooms for tonight."

He listened, frowning before he spoke again. "I see. Well, when will you know, exactly?" Another long pause. "Can I give you my number so you can call me if they don't get up the mountain? Okay, good . . . I'm at 555-3769. In an hour then." He hung up and turned to me.

"They're sold out. They have two rooms reserved for a family of four coming up from L.A., but they said the county plow team just lost the road, so those people probably won't make it. If they don't show up in an hour, the rooms are ours."

I sat there trying to figure out what else I should do. I was getting so many mixed messages I still didn't have a real sense of how much jeopardy I might be in.

I decided that the best way to get through this was to turn to the job at hand. Find the things that Evelyn's sister wanted for her mother, get them out of storage as fast as possible, and then get the hell out of here. If the storm lightened, or the roads cleared, we might still be able to drive back to Los Angeles tonight using the chains. Failing that, we could stay at the lodge and drive down tomorrow.

"Why don't we go get a look at the storage room, see how big a project this is going to be?" I suggested.

"Wouldn't you rather have a glass of wine first?" Chick countered.

"If we get this done now, maybe we can still drive out of here tonight. I really have things to do in L.A. If we drive slowly, I'm sure we can make it back to Fawnskin. The roads are probably still okay from there on down."

"Good idea," he said, but he was frowning slightly. "I have a nice red Bordeaux . . . My wine broker is the same guy who sells to Jack Nicholson. This Château Gruaud-Larose is very rare. Supposedly only five cases in L.A. I got three bottles at two thousand apiece. It's a once-in-a-lifetime experience. Not too oakie . . . Got a nice little smoky quality to it. What do y'think? Or, I have two bottles of 1997 Screaming Eagle Cabernet Sauvignon. Right now, it's some of the hottest wine on Planet Earth. Cost about three grand a bottle."

"Whatever you want, if we can drink while we work."

"Deal."

He went to the bar and started looking around in his built-in wine cooler for the bottles. Then he pulled one out and uncorked the Screaming Eagle Cab. "You're supposed to let it breathe for half an hour first, but let's cheat and have a glass now." He poured some into two wine goblets, then picked his up and swirled it around, watching it hang on the side of the glass, doing the whole wine connoisseur thing. "Good consistency." He sniffed the glass. "Great nose, not too sweet or acidic . . . A great little wine for three grand a pop."

He handed me a glass and clinked against mine. "To new beginnings."

Shit, I thought. *New beginnings? What the hell does that mean?* We'd both just lost our spouses. For me, it was hardly a beginning. It was a vast, unacceptable ending. But I held myself in check, didn't respond, and took a small sip of the wine, which was remarkable. Then I looked up at him. "Let's see the list."

"I'm sorry?"

"The list. Let me have a look."

He seemed puzzled.

"The list of things your sister-in-law wanted you to find for Evelyn's mother."

He reached into his pockets and started pulling things out. "I know I have that damn list someplace." He grinned and started patting his pockets like a guy trying to dodge a dinner check. Then he looked at me sheepishly and shrugged.

No list, I thought. *Great.*

My panic alarms were all blaring. If there was no list, then the whole trip up here was bullshit.

I was now beginning to think I might actually be in some physical jeopardy, when he suddenly snapped his fingers and crossed the room, picked up the car keys on the hall table, and opened the door.

"Left it in the car," he said as he walked outside.

I stood there wondering what I should do next. The elk and bears hanging on the walls glared down at me. Since they were former victims, they offered no sympathy.

After a few minutes he returned, list in hand. "Got it," he smiled. "I forgot, I stuck it up under the visor while I was driving over to the hotel to pick you up. Come on, most of this stuff is out in the garage."

He picked up the wine bottle, then led the way through the house into a large game room, where more stuffed animal heads hung on the walls.

"Bagged that big guy over the fireplace in Oregon last year," he said conversationally, gesturing toward a huge dusty-looking elk head.

"Mmm . . . " I answered.

He continued through the kitchen, opened the door to the garage, and turned on the light.

The garage was almost floor-to-ceiling junk. I'd rarely seen a space with so much discarded stuff piled randomly. There were boxes jammed up on the rafters, stacked in precarious disarray. The shelves contained more labeled boxes: old linens, tools, and household goods. Discarded furniture and scraps of broken lumber were stacked in both parking stalls.

"I told you it was going to be a big project," he said brightly.

"My God, Chick, what *is* all this stuff?"

"We redecorated last year. This is what we didn't keep. I wanted to just throw it all away, but Evelyn wanted to clean it up and donate it to the homeless shelter down in Longview. That was Evelyn, always looking out for the less fortunate." He sipped his wine and smiled. "Boy, this really is smooth. Hard to believe it's a California red. I bet it's almost decanted by now. Let me pour you another and see if we can spot any difference."

"I'm fine. Let's get started."

He looked down at his list. "A box of her baby and high school pictures from the summer house in Michigan. Should be up there, somewhere."

He pointed to a shelf full of boxes, then found a stepladder, carried it over, and climbed up. "We brought a lot of this stuff up here when we ran out of storage space in town," he said, starting to pull out cartons and hand them down.

As I took the first box, I glanced out the window and noticed a shed of some kind behind the garage, which I hoped wasn't full of more junk. I placed the box on the floor behind me.

We worked steadily for an hour. Chick had opened the second bottle and kept topping off my glass. Even though I was trying hard not to drink, I have to admit it was a great wine, and after a glass or so, I was feeling much better. The more we worked, the more harmless it all seemed.

When we had taken quite a few boxes down, we started going through them and pulling out the things he wanted to load into the trunk to take back to L.A. Then we carried those items out of the garage and stacked them on the kitchen counter. Once we got organized, it went quicker than either of us had imagined. After an hour and a half, we were almost finished.

Chick was up on the ladder, pulling out a big box of Evelyn's journals. I picked up the list that he had left next to the wine bottle. I read the last item: "E's paintings."

"I didn't know Evelyn was a painter," I said to Chick, who was up on the ladder with his back to me.

"Yeah, she wasn't real accomplished, like you are, but she used to like working with watercolors. Still lifes mostly. She said painting relaxed her. There's a slew of them up here somewhere."

I glanced down at the list, and then turned it over to make sure there were no more items on the reverse side. That's when my heart froze. The list was written on the back of an invoice from the Fawnskin gas station. The date on the top was today's. It was the receipt he'd just gotten for putting the chains on the Mercedes.

The list was less than three hours old.

I SET THE PAPER DOWN AND TOOK A STEP BACK-
ward, trying not to let my voice convey anything. "Find the
paintings yet?" I asked.

"Yep, right here. Got 'em." He pulled a box out and
climbed down the ladder backward, then turned and carried
it into the kitchen, setting it down with the others.

"That's all of it. Come on in and we'll uncork the French
Bordeaux to compare and celebrate. This is thirsty work."

I moved into the kitchen and stood as far away from him
as I could.

He must have noticed my stiff posture because he asked,
"Something wrong?"

"I forgot to tell you, but I need to call Peter Ellis. We're
redoing some things with the learning foundation. Peter's attorneys need to know where I am. They're working through
the weekend because we have to file all this stuff with the

Corporations Commission on Monday. I'm supposed to check over some of the redrafts this evening. Since the phones are working now, I'd better give them your number."

"First, let's crack another bottle," he persisted, blocking my way to the phone in the living room as he opened the bottle of Bordeaux. He refilled my glass without asking me.

"To a job well done," he said, clicking rims.

I pressed the glass to my mouth and let the wine run up to my lips, but didn't swallow. I didn't want any more alcohol. I was now in a full panic.

"So what was the deal with you and Chandler anyway?" Chick suddenly said, leaning back and studying me, a sly smile playing at the corner of his mouth. "I've been meaning to ask you about that."

"What was the deal?" I said, puzzled. "What do you mean?"

"Well, you guys seemed so different is all. I could never quite figure what that was all about—how it worked with you two. He didn't seem to have your ambition, your sense of adventure."

The statement was so out of line I didn't answer.

Chick smiled. I'd had about a glass and a half of wine, but he'd had at least five. I was standing there, calculating my odds, preparing for battle.

"Yeah. Guys like Chandler really baffle me," he went on, obliviously. "Kind of like a John Kennedy Jr. type, if you ask me. Money, nice to look at, but you gotta admit, these guys pretty much had life handed to them on a platter. John Jr. knew he was hot looking, and the press called him an American prince. But he crashes his plane in a whiteout, which was just plain stupid. I was always thinking why is everybody bawling? What it boiled down to was the guy didn't know what he was doing and he killed himself."

Then he gave me a little smile. "*People* magazine puts out a special edition. *Entertainment Tonight* couldn't run enough profiles. If I killed myself flying in zero visibility with no instrument rating, they wouldn't sing my praises; they'd open up a fucking accident investigation. See what I'm saying? Totally outta whack."

"Why are we talking about JFK Jr.? And what the hell does his death have to do with Chandler's?"

He took another sip of wine, then turned and focused his gaze out the window. It was now dark outside and I could hear the wind howling. He was quiet for about thirty seconds before he said, "*People* magazine was going to do a profile story on me when bestmarket.com made the *Forbes* list. But the fucking entertainment editor killed it. Not newsworthy enough." He turned back to me. "I popularized a whole new form of Internet commerce and they say it's not newsworthy. Instead, we get a story on Cher's plastic surgery. See what I'm saying?"

"Chick, we've cleared out this stuff. I think you've had enough to drink. Let's get it in the car and go."

Chick's eyes were shining. There was sweat on his upper lip. He cleared his throat and then said something so inappropriate it actually staggered me.

"I know you loved Chandler, and hey, there was a lot to love about the guy, I'll grant you that, but giving away his fortune to help L.D. kids? If he'd earned that money himself, I could maybe respect the gesture. But he didn't earn it, he inherited it. Unlike Chandler, I know what it means to earn a dollar. Chandler never had to go out there and struggle to survive."

"Let's check on those lodge reservations again," I said, a surge of adrenaline hitting my bloodstream.

"They'll call if the rooms are available." He drained his wineglass in two long swallows and immediately poured himself another. Then, apropos of nothing, he said, "You ever notice that everything in America seems be about nothing or about just getting laid? We don't have dipshit royalty to fawn over like the Brits. We've got Gwyneth Paltrow and Johnny Depp. Who cares if Rosie is gay or who these celebrity airheads are cheating on each other with? Yet there are forests being cut down so we can read this shit."

My back was flaring up from the long ride in the car and from moving boxes. I figured I'd better do something about it because I wanted to be in top form and pain-free if this got any loonier. I moved away from him. "May I have some water? I need to take a pill for my back."

He crossed to the refrigerator, talking over his shoulder all the way. "Americans are focused on all the wrong things, Paige. We've made celebrity more important than accomplishment. It's better to be Kevin Federline than Charles Best Jr. You can't get any respect in America if you don't own the right stuff. What kind of car do you drive? Is your house on North Elm? We don't read about the guys who invest in the future—guys like me, who pioneer whole new areas of

Internet commerce. Instead, it's all about the lucky sperm club. Guys who were born looking like Calvin Klein models, or who inherited their position and wealth."

"And you're saying Chandler was in that category?" My voice was shaking with anger.

"Chandler?" He stopped and looked at me, then came over and handed me the water.

"No," he replied. "No . . . " Then the condescending smile appeared again. "Okay, maybe. That's what I was saying about not getting you two as a couple. You don't seem like a woman who would just give it up to some great-looking guy with perfect teeth who never did anything but clip stock coupons. You deserve so much more than that, Paige. It's why I'm glad we finally got a chance to get away and be together."

I was praying he was drunk, because if he wasn't, then he had to be insane.

CHAPTER 38

I TOOK MY PAIN PILL, WASHED IT DOWN WITH water, then turned toward him, subtly giving him my right side and settling into a open-legged, karate-ready stance. A *soto-hachiji-dachi*. I was trying not to telegraph it, but if Chick went to the next level, if he tried to even so much as lay a finger on me, then I was going to unleash some dojo whup-ass on him. Or at least try.

". . . Life should be about more than good times and a great backhand, don't you think?" he rambled on.

"We should get this stuff loaded into the car and get out of here," I repeated firmly.

"I was hoping we could sit and talk."

"Why don't we talk in the car on the ride back to L.A.?"

"There's things I really need to discuss with you," he pressed. "Things we need to sort out. A few conditions for our relationship."

My heart was now slamming inside my chest. Conditions for our relationship? This was totally nuts.

And then, he took a step toward me. I flinched and dropped the bottle of pills. It rolled across the floor and settled between his feet.

He stooped and picked it up. Then he squinted at the label. "Percocet?" he said, reading it. "I thought you took Darvocet for your back."

"I need to pee," I said and picked up my purse. I had to get to the bathroom and collect my thoughts. "Where's the loo?"

"Right through there, off the living room. Or you can use the one upstairs in the master bedroom."

"This one's fine." I crossed to the guest bathroom, and carrying my wineglass, went inside, closed the door, then locked it.

The first thing I did was dump out the wine. Then I looked at myself in the mirror. The eyes staring back at me were frightened and tense.

Of course the new big question was: *How had Chick known about the Darvocet?* It had only been prescribed once—the night Chandler had gone out to the drugstore to get it for me, the night he was killed. I had never told anybody but Bob Butler about having changed medications. *So how did Chick know? How had he found out?*

Then a chilling thought hit me. *Had Chick been there the night Chandler went to the store to pick up my prescription? Was it Chick who had run my husband down?*

Then another thought. Seven months after Chandler was murdered, Evelyn was shot to death in her car. Could Chick have . . . ?

I stopped in mid-thought as the enormity of that possibility overpowered everything else. Was I trapped in this house with a monster? A serial murderer?

I stood in front of the mirror hyperventilating. *If you don't calm down, you'll never be able to deal with this.* I began to pull myself back together. So far, all of it was just conjecture.

Maybe Detective Butler told Chick about the Darvocet. He said he'd talked to Chick at Chandler's funeral. But would a seasoned cop like Detective Butler reveal information like that to a stranger?

I didn't think so.

Suddenly, I remembered the envelope given to me by the concierge. I'd been so upset by the Mercedes with Evelyn's brains on the kick panel that I'd completely forgotten about it. I put my purse on the counter and frantically searched through it.

"Everything okay in there?" Chick called through the door, jolting me.

"Just fine. Be out in a minute. Pour me another wine, will you?" I said, trying to make my voice sound light and friendly. I found the envelope, tore it open, and sat down on the commode to read. The fax was printed neatly in Bob's hand on a piece of New York hotel stationery dated this morning.

Dear Mrs. Ellis:
I have tried desperately to reach you. I've left message after message at your hotel and on your cell voice-mail, but for some reason I have not been able to get through, so I am putting this in a fax in the hope that it might reach you. I think I have finally solved your husband's hit-and-run. As I wrote earlier,

Top Hat Auto in New Jersey is where the Taurus was repaired. The owner remembered the guy who was driving and I've enclosed a much better drawing. This morning I rechecked all the Hertz agencies in New York and eventually found the car. It was rented by your friend Charles Best on April 12th and returned on the 13th. On my instructions, Hertz reexamined the car. It had severe right front fender damage that had been Bondoed up and repainted. I just found out from one of your friends yesterday that you went to Mr. Best's wife's funeral in L.A. That really has me worried. You must get in touch with me immediately, and Mrs. Ellis, please stay away from that man. I have notified the L.A. police and am on my way out there. In the meantime, be extremely careful.

Chick Best is a cold-blooded killer.

Very sincerely yours,
Detective Robert Butler

Then I dug into the envelope and pulled out a folded fax picture and opened it up. The drawing depicted a dark-haired, middle-aged man.

It was Chick.

I sat on the toilet as my whole body went numb. Sweat started beading on my forehead and under my arms. I sat motionless trying to decide what to do next.

"Hey, Paige, what the hell're you doing in there?" Chick's voice came through the locked door again, shattering my thoughts and jangling my nerves. "Are you going to the bathroom or redecorating?"

"Be out in a minute," I sang out brightly. Then I took the wineglass, wrapped it in a towel, and held it over the sink.

I tapped it lightly on the gold faucet fixture. It shattered, leaving me with the rounded pedestal base and a good shaft with a sharp, jagged point. I took this weapon, such as it was, and carefully fit it into my purse with the bottom up, so I could draw it quickly. I decided to keep humoring Chick. Stall. Delay. Find a way to make a phone call out. That was the gist of my feeble plan.

I knew Bob Butler was, if nothing else, a bulldog. His letter said he was on his way to L.A. and had already notified the LAPD. Maybe they could figure this out in time. He would probably start with the Langham Hotel, where he knew I was staying. Since Peter Ellis had left a message for me there earlier, it would be on their computer. He would get to Chandler's parents. I'd told them I was coming up here. However, I'd only mentioned it in passing. I prayed they would remember.

Stall . . . Delay . . . Humor . . . Try and get a call out. That was my mantra.

I looked out the bathroom window. The snow was coming down even harder than before. We would soon be snowed in—maybe already were.

I had to assume, for the time being, that no help would be coming. This was going to be completely up to me. I was going to have to save myself. The Japanese meaning of *karate* suddenly flipped into my mind: *Way of the empty hand . . . How appropriate.*

I took a deep breath, opened the door, and stepped out of the guest bathroom to face my husband's killer. It was . . .

GAME ON

39

CHICK

I STOOD IN THE KITCHEN WAITING FOR HER TO from the can. I felt my tool tingling—filling with blood, threatening to rise. On the other hand, it was more than a little off-putting that Paige kept wanting to load up the car and head down the mountain, as if I hadn't gone to a helluva lot of trouble to plan this romantic weekend. If I wasn't so in love with her I might have actually been a little pissed off about the way she was behaving.

To get my mind off my irritation with Paige, I started to rate my presale performance. I gave myself a 7 for account research, an 8 for account prep, and a blistering 9.5 for account management. I was now at the really important moment. The Client Close.

I'd made only one little mistake so far. The rant about JFK had definitely put a bone in her nose. It seemed to really tick her off. It obviously wasn't smart running down Chandler like that, trying to make myself look better by making him look small. Like one of those African birds that stands in a crocodile's mouth picking food from its teeth, I'd been taking a huge chance with that. If I wasn't careful, Paige would lose patience with me and all that would be left of my plan would be blood and feathers.

That aside, I was still trying to feel good. The red wine warmed me, and the old tube steak was threatening to become a full-fledged changeling for the first time in months. As I waited for her to reappear from her overnight camping trip to the can, a few things started to tug at my memory and make me wonder if, instead of being on the verge of victory, this whole thing might actually be going bad instead.

What the fuck was that look she gave me when I mentioned the Darvocet? Sometimes Paige could act damned weird. Now that I was closer to her, spending more time in her orbit, I could see there were things about her personality that I definitely had to work on. Things I needed to change if we were going to have a long-term relationship.

I poured the last of the French Bordeaux into my glass, held it up to the light, and swirled it. I'd taken a class at Wolfgang Puck's in Hollywood on how to evaluate great wines. Actually, if you want to know the truth, all this shit tastes like Ripple to me. I've never been good at sorting out the complex tastes and textures I'm supposed to experience. Some of these wine reviews can be pretty obscure, like saying a wine tastes like wood ash with a trace of pencil lead, for God's sake. Who the hell knows what pencil lead tastes like?

There is also a complex protocol that goes with drinking this stuff. The entire cork-sniffing, glass-swirling, lip-smacking extravaganza. You learn the right words and always try to act faintly above it all, pretend to be constantly evaluating, add a skeptical frown, and you've got it.

I buy and drink this stuff mostly because it impresses the hell out of women. The idea that they're consuming something worth thousands of dollars, which overnight their body is going to process into bright yellow piss, really gets them off. It's such a totally unacceptable depreciation of value, they start fantasizing about all kinds of obscene bedroom calisthenics. Overpowering excess makes women want to fuck. Something I discovered in the eighth grade when I gave that fifty-dollar ring I couldn't afford to the thirteen-year-old girl I couldn't get a feel from and got laid.

These ruminations were interrupted as the bathroom door opened and Paige emerged, clutching her purse.

"Everything come out alright?" I grinned, trying not to project the irritation I was beginning to feel toward her. "How's your back?"

"It takes a minute for these pills to work," she said.

"I think all that lifting may have thrown my neck out as well," I told her as I proceeded to go through an elaborate neck flex, back and forth, right and left, hoping I could get her back into massage mode again.

"Chick, I need to get home. We need to pack the car and leave now."

"Nonsense," I smiled. "Look, all that stuff I said about JFK Jr. and Chandler, I could see that bothered you, okay? I didn't mean that Chandler was anything like JFK Jr. Maybe you misunderstood me there. All I was saying is, I didn't quite understand him."

"It's okay. Shall we get this stuff out to the car?"

"I'm not gonna risk that road at night," I said. "It's iced over—dangerous as hell."

"It wasn't iced over an hour ago," she countered defiantly.

Okay, let me say right here and now, that female defiance ranks right up there on the irritation scale with female credit-card excess, female menopause, and females who interrupt me when I'm telling a cool story. Maybe I'm overly sensitive because I spent sixteen loathsome years living with Evelyn and Melissa, but I've sort of had it with defiant women.

"You don't know how dangerous icy roads can be," I told her, struggling to contain my anger.

"I live in North Carolina, Chick. I drive icy roads all winter. Let's get this stuff into the car. I want to leave."

She picked up a box and I had to block her from walking out the door with it.

"Leave it," I said. "You're not going."

"An order?" Her eyes turned instantly hard. She stepped back, still holding the box, but turned sideways and spread her feet like she was settling into some kind of corny Bruce Lee fighting stance.

After more years of Evelyn's bullshit than I care to remember, you'd think I would have developed a few calluses for this kind of horseshit—an attitude shield. But I obviously hadn't, because right then all I wanted to do was smack her in the mouth.

Here's the deal. I invite a girl up to the mountains. I treat her to a beautiful Christmas card setting. I light a fire, turn on music, make every damn effort to be charming. I even pour three fucking bottles of expensive wine, which, believe me, shouldn't get uncorked unless I do. And what do I get? I get a lot of nutty shit about wanting to go home. She was standing in my kitchen, her mouth pulled down, looking way-the-hell-too-much like Evelyn.

Suddenly, blind, white anger flashed through me. But it passed quickly. I looked at her carefully over the rim of the wineglass, calmed myself down, and smiled.

"Let me lay out a few ground rules, just so we'll both know what's going on."

"Before you do that, Chick, here."

Paige handed me the box she'd been holding, then without warning, turned and sprinted into the living room, heading toward the telephone.

I dropped the box and took off after her, but she was quick, and by the time I got into the main room she already had the handset to her ear and was trying to get a dial tone. There wasn't one. I already knew that. It didn't matter if the phone company had fixed the lines because the first thing I did when we got here, while she sat in the car refusing to get out, was disconnect the phone at the junction box.

"What's going on, Chick? Am I a hostage?"

"Bad choice of words. You're a houseguest who I will not permit to make a dangerous trip down the mountain on icy roads at night. I have your safety to protect."

"The phone is dead."

"Lines are down again because of the storm."

"Then how did you call the lodge? Were you faking that call?"

"I don't take well to being quizzed, Paige. I'm not some country club pussy like Chandler. I'm a man who is used to being in charge—used to controlling his space."

Of course, the minute I said that, I knew it was wrong but this wasn't turning out the way I envisioned it.

Her teeth were bared, her feet spread. In that moment, she looked like she was getting ready to kick my ass.

I had another rush of anger. I was beginning to hate her guts.

CHAPTER

 40

PAIGE

ANGER COLORED CHICK'S FACE AS I STOOD
there with the dead phone in my hand. Apparently, I wasn't
cooperating with his twisted fantasy. I watched as he made a
huge effort to compose himself, taking half a dozen deep
breaths.

"I need to tell you something," he finally said. "I've been
waiting for just the right moment, and now that we're alone
with no distractions, I think you need to understand a few
things. It's important because it affects everything between us."

"There is no 'us,' Chick."

"When I first saw you in Hawaii almost a year ago, I had
never seen anyone so breathtakingly beautiful . . . "

"Please, Chick . . . "

"Stop arguing and interrupting! Listen to me, for chris-
sake!" He took several more breaths, then calmed himself
again and continued.

"Y'see, Paige, I've never been a man with a big emotional component. I don't know why that is. Maybe it was my dad dying so early in my adolescence. Maybe it was because my mother and grandmother were such hovering crones. I don't know what caused it. But then, in Hawaii last January, I saw you. You were my definition of human perfection. Right then a floodgate of emotion just opened. All these feelings I'd never felt before, they just swamped me."

"Chick, please! Don't do this. You don't have a clue who I am."

He cocked his head like an animal scoping prey. The look was chilling.

"But I was married, so it was one of those impossible things," he continued, as if he hadn't heard me. "You had Chandler. I had Evelyn. So you went home; I went home. That should have been the end of it. But Paige, I couldn't get you out of my mind—couldn't erase the memory of you from my thoughts. Little things, adorable things about you haunted my every waking moment. The birthmark on your calf, I love that birthmark. The way you like to sit with your legs tucked under you, the giggly laugh you have. The little hairs on your arms, so fine, so perfect."

Jesus Christ, I thought. *This guy is out of his fucking mind.*

"Chick, you've had quite a bit of wine, so let's stop this right now, before either of us says something we don't mean."

"I've been planning to tell you this for months, Paige. I've thought about nothing else for almost a year. From the second I first saw you getting out of the pool at the Four Seasons, it was love at first sight."

He took another sip of the Bordeaux and set down the glass. "I have plans for us. Dreams."

I thought, *I've had enough. This asshole murdered my husband. If I'm going down, then it might as well be swinging.* So I shouted my next words right in his smug face.

"Plans for us? I'm not interested in you, you silly son-of-a-bitch. I still love Chandler!"

"Chandler is dead!" he shouted back. "He's gone. Evelyn's gone. It's just us now."

I could see where this was headed. He would convince himself that I wanted him, despite my protests. First rape, then maybe even murder.

Suddenly, Chick lunged toward me and grabbed my purse. "What've you got in there?" I was clutching the bag so tightly he must have sensed I had something inside. He jerked the bag open and pulled out the broken wineglass stem, waving it between us. "What's this for?"

I didn't answer.

His eyes fell on Bob Butler's letter and the drawing. He reached into the purse and plucked them out. He opened the letter first, took one step back, and scanned it quickly. Then he glanced at the picture.

The truth of Bob's accusation was immediately all over his face.

He dropped the letter to the floor. His eyes went dead, like the flickering glass eyes on the wall-hung animals.

He whispered something. At first I didn't understand him, but then he said it louder. "You complete me."

The insanity of that remark rocked me.

"You killed them both, didn't you? First Chandler, then Evelyn. All of it because of this twisted fantasy that you and I would one day be together."

I had to get out of here now or die trying. "Give me the keys to the car, Chick."

"I can't let you leave, Paige."

"You gonna kill me, too?"

He stepped forward. Both his hands were extended toward me, a strange look of frustration clouding his face.

It was time to make my move, so right then, when he wasn't expecting it, I gave him a *kin-geri*, which is a polite Japanese term for a kick to the balls. My foot strike caught him squarely in the bulge of those tight, Roberto Cavalli stretchies. He grabbed his crotch, doubled over, and then dropped to his knees in pain.

I exploded through the house and out the front door into the night. The fresh snow was almost a foot high on the porch. I ran down the steps, slipping once and going down, but I rolled immediately up to my feet and sprinted toward the gold Mercedes, running my fingers under the front bumper, looking for the hide-a-key. Nothing.

"Paige, come back here! Don't make me do this!"

I turned and saw Chick standing on the front porch holding a scoped deer rifle. I spun and ran as fast as I could, into the trees at the side of the drive. I had carelessly left my sweater inside and the cold, wind-whipped snow swirled around me. Then I heard a rifle's report, heard a limb snap nearby. I kept running, heading up the steep bank into the forest by the side of his driveway, my short choppy sprinter's stride churning in the deep drifting snow.

CHAPTER 41

CHICK

I'VE PRETTY MUCH SPENT MY ENTIRE LIFE BEING
what other people wanted. First, it was my loser father. Then
I was forced to endure that hen party with my mother and
grandmother. I've tried to fit in. Tried to belong. I've joined
clubs full of people who bored me, brown-nosed people
who, if they weren't socially or corporately important, I
probably wouldn't have wasted a bullet on. My life was ordered by the stringent guidelines and demands of others.

And what had come of all this endless ass-kissing? Disaster, that's what. I had a personal balance-sheet that resembled the crater on Mount St. Helens and a dead wife who
mocked me from the grave, the memory of her coarse in-
sults bubbling relentlessly in my subconscious. I had an
angry daughter I'd come to hate, and a business career that
was like nine miles of dirt road.

The only thing I'd asked for in my crummy life, the
only perk, if you will, that I had applied for, was just a little

happiness in the arms of this one woman. I had fantasized over her. I had even killed for her. And what did this contribution to my own madness produce? Nothing. It produced not one damn useful thing, except an ever-widening circle of rage.

So here she was, standing before me like a crazed kamikazi, armed with the broken stem of a fucking hundred-dollar Venetian crystal goblet, ready to unzip my ass with its jagged point. You see what I'm saying? When the hell is Chick Best gonna catch a fucking break? When's the Chickster gonna get a little TLC?

And then, next comes this bullshit letter from Bob Butler, accusing me of murder. My instincts on that toothpick-chewing Carolina hayseed had been right on target. He'd sniffed around until he'd finally found the auto body shop, and then written Paige that I was the one who'd run Chandler down.

I had lusted after this silly woman, my nose filled with her scent from the first moment I'd seen her. Then just when I was on the one-yard line, I lost everything.

She was my fantasy. But if I let her get out of here now, knowing what she knew, she would destroy me. I needed to finish this and make a run for Mexico before Bob Butler caught up to me.

My new absurd reality was I'd become a hostage to events. To this woman who was too fucking stupid to realize what she was throwing away.

I tried one last time. I stood there while she screamed at me. I tried to make her understand that she completed me.

But to be perfectly truthful, I don't know if she really did or not. Maybe I just needed to possess her, like every other damn thing I'd ever lusted after, then collected, and eventually thrown away. She was the ultimate trophy, but now I had to destroy her before she could destroy me.

Then while I was evaluating this fucked-up dilemma, she kicked me right in the balls. That was it. That was the last straw. There's only so much shit I'm prepared to take.

She bolted out the door, and without thinking, I grabbed the deer rifle and took off after her.

"Get your ass back in here!" I screamed.

I blundered out onto the porch, saw her clambering up the hill through a foot of fresh snow. I put the deer rifle to my shoulder and fired a warning shot, intentionally aiming high and snapping off a tree limb. You see, despite my rage, I didn't want to kill her. At least, not yet.

Somewhere back in the reptilian part of my brain that services my need to reproduce, I still thought I might be able to talk sense into her and put this mess back together. Am I so repulsive that there was no set of conditions that would cause her to reconsider? I still had a shred of hope. It fluttered bravely, a torn fragment of my Hawaiian fantasy.

"Come back! We can work this out!" I shouted.

But she kept scrambling up the hill, her snow-wet shirt sticking to her back.

"You fucking bitch! Come back here, now!" I roared and fired again, this time trying to wound her. But the second shot was rushed. I heard the bullet snapping limbs before it thunked into a tree trunk. She was fifty yards away, disappearing in a blizzard of snowflakes. I had to stop her. Had to keep her from getting to a neighbor for help.

I could still make a run for it, but if she called 911 and the sheriff came after me, with only one road down the mountain, I'd never get away.

If she went north she might get to the Mitchells' place, so I fired again, aiming blindly, because I had now completely lost sight of her in the snowstorm.

"You come back here!" I screamed again.

But she was gone. Somewhere up on the hill by the side of the house. She was running for her life with my destruction her only goal.

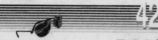

42

PAIGE

THE SECOND BULLET CLIPPED A BRANCH RIGHT over my head.

I could barely see—my eyes watered with melting snow. A branch scratched me badly under my right eye, spinning me around. I ignored the pain and kept going. I was in great shape from hours of marathon training, but the air was thin up here and as I ran uphill in the heavy snow my lungs were beginning to heave.

Chick was out of shape and I didn't think he could keep up. However, I was wearing only a light shirt, cotton slacks, and flats. The snow was already coming in over the tops of my shoes, and I knew that once I stopped running and my body started cooling, I stood a good chance of getting hypothermia.

I paused and turned to look back. When I did, I saw I had another, much more immediate problem than just freezing to death . . . I was leaving a trail of easy-to-follow footprints in the fresh snow. Chick didn't have to run very fast to catch me. He could simply follow my tracks and stalk me with that deer rifle until I fell or froze. Unless I could find help fast, I was going to lose.

I paused every so often, holding my breath to listen. I could hear him somewhere down the hill, kicking an occasional boulder with those steel-toed cowboy boots. How far back was he? I didn't know. How far does sound carry in a snow-filled night? You got me . . . All I knew was he was hunting me with a rifle, and if I didn't keep moving, I was dead.

I started off again, climbing higher up the slope. The wind whipped my wet shirt, my jaw clamped against the cold. My body was beginning to shiver.

Then I heard him. "Paige! I don't want to kill you, but I will if I have to. If you come back, we can work something out."

Right. All we have to get past is two fucking murders.

His voice sounded like he was further away than I'd first thought. Even so, I knew I couldn't rest, I had to keep going. I finally realized that my best chance wasn't to keep climbing, but to double back and head down to the road. Maybe I could try and flag down a passing car or find another house. If I got to the road I could move away from here faster on the flat grade than I could by climbing this thirty-degree slope.

I traversed several hundred yards to my left before beginning my descent. I was trying to maintain a parallel course to the one I'd used on the climb up. I went slower, trying to be very quiet, because I knew that somewhere along the way I would pass Chick coming up. However, each time

I stopped to listen, I heard nothing but the rustling of falling snow in the treetops. I had no idea where he might be.

Finally the rate of descent lessened and I was back at Chick's driveway about a quarter of a mile from his house. I crouched low, my own breath and heartbeat thundering in my ears. My teeth were chattering so badly that I couldn't hear anything else. I couldn't just wait here. I would freeze to death. I stood, and hugging the tree line next to the drive, headed down toward Interstate 38.

The snow was in my hair, falling in giant flakes on my face, melting and running down my back, chilling me to the bone. My shoes and feet felt like blocks of ice. Every hundred paces, I started running again to get my circulation and body temperature up.

Finally, I arrived at the highway and saw that it was a perfect field of snow. No tire tracks marked the surface. No cars had passed by in hours. I turned right and headed toward town. I couldn't see the road but followed the plow markers.

I wasn't going to last much longer. My body was so cold I was already beginning to lose coordination. A half-moon was now peeking through, lighting the undersides of the storm clouds, throwing a soft, silver light on the drifting snow. Every time I looked back, I saw my telltale tracks stretching out behind me, traitorously pointing the way. If Chick figured out my plan, he would have no trouble finding me.

And then I heard it.

A high distant whine that sounded like a buzz saw cutting down trees. I paused and listened, then backed away from the road. It was getting louder, coming toward me. I finally identified the high-pitched sound as a gas engine, changing pitch as the throttle changed. I crouched down in the snow and then saw a lone headlight, about half a mile away, moving fast. *A snowmobile.*

I prayed it was a neighbor trying to get into town, or perhaps a road crew checking the highway for cars in the ditch.

The vehicle veered and started coming right at me, following my tracks in the snow. Panicked, I turned and started to run, but there was no way I could outrun a snowmobile. I stumbled and fell, going down face-first in a snowbank.

Then the headlight was on me. I rolled over, dripping wet, blinded by its glare. As the vehicle pulled to a stop ten feet away, all I could see was the manufacturer's name vibrating on the front bumper: YAMAHA.

A man climbed off the idling red machine and came around the front. He was dressed in a three-quarter-length gray parka. The hood was up and he had on yellow-lensed goggles to protect his eyes from the swirling snow. I prayed I was going to be rescued. Then the man kneeled down, crouching over me.

"Look what you've gone and done," Chick snarled.

CHICK

I FOLLOWED PAIGE'S TRACKS UP THE HILL, SAW that she had made her way over and was coming back down. She was heading toward the main road, trying to get into town.

I had two Yamaha snowmobiles in the shed by my garage, one red, one yellow. I stripped off the covers, grabbed some snow goggles and a parka, and then checked the gas tanks. I tried to start each one, but both the batteries were dead. I had to jump the red one with a wall plug to get the damn thing going. Then I got on and raced it down the drive, the treads throwing a white rooster tail high in the air behind me.

She'd left an easy trail in the snow, her footprints pointing the way. I turned left at the driveway entrance and headed in the direction of town, roaring after her.

I felt at loose ends, out of control, frightened.

As I roared down that snow-covered highway, with the undercarriage of the Yamaha eating up Paige's footprints like a deranged Pac-Man, I knew I had to come up with a plan to end this. It was already a disaster, but before committing a third murder, I had to chart a course. I had to take stock of my options.

I'd killed Evelyn and Chandler, but how much could the cops really prove? Could they *prove* I'd run Chandler down? Even though they'd found the Bondoed fender on the Hertz Taurus, would the story about hitting the deer still hold up? It might. And Evelyn's murder wasn't exactly a prosecution slam dunk either. I'd certainly framed the shit out of Delroy Washington. His fingerprints were on the murder weapon and in the car. He had half a dozen priors. I still had Melissa as an alibi.

I was pretty sure Delroy would go down for Evelyn, which meant Paige was my only real problem. I had all but confessed to her. I had to take care of her first and then assess the damages. L.A. juries were notoriously thickheaded. If O.J. Simpson and Robert Blake could walk, why not Chick Best?

As I zapped along in the darkness, these thoughts swirled, sticking in my head like the snow on my windshield. If I was going to kill Paige Ellis, I knew one thing. It had to look like an accident.

Then I saw something moving in my headlights up ahead. I slowed and steered the Yamaha in that direction. It was Paige. Her hair was soaked. Dripping ringlets hung in her face. Her blouse clung to her like a second skin. She didn't look like a goddess anymore. She looked like a half-drowned cat—cold, wet, and totally at my mercy.

I pulled the snowmobile to a stop a few yards away, then walked up and crouched over her. She looked up, fear and supplication finally where they belonged, right there on that bitch's snow-wet face. Chick Best was the victor. The Chickster was finally back in control.

PAIGE

HE GRABBED THE DEER RIFLE OFF THE YAMAHA
and pointed it at me. "Get up. Start walking."

"What are you going to do?" I stammered through chattering teeth.

He poked me in the back with the barrel, so I got to my feet and started to walk.

He followed on the snowmobile, ranting as we went. I could only hear snatches of what he was saying over the whining engine.

". . . hard to find . . . no way she could have . . . The bitch . . . Chandler . . . " He was rambling. Occasionally he would stop and shout directions.

"Right, dammit! You have to go right!"

We were way off the highway. I was trudging through almost two feet of fresh snow while the Yamaha's headlamp lit the terrain in front of me. I couldn't feel my feet. My clothes were sopped, my body shivering uncontrollably. My fingers and toes had gone mercifully numb.

I didn't know where Chick was taking me. I stumbled along in front of the snowmobile until he finally yelled for me to stop. Then he climbed off the Yamaha carrying the rifle. He pushed me forward. I stumbled, unable to even feel my legs now. My jaw was clenched so tightly against the cold that I wondered if I would even be able to open it to beg for my life.

"That's far enough," he growled.

I stopped and wiped my eyes with a wet sleeve. I glanced around and saw that he had brought me to the edge of a cliff. I was standing on the lip of a deep ravine.

"You see my problem?" he said, his voice harsh and accusing.

I dragged my sluggish brain back and tried to focus on what he was saying. I felt like I was in the early stages of hypothermic ataxia.

"You ruined it. Now I have no choice but to do this."

I tried to say something, but my jaw was locked, clamped shut.

"You . . . you were everything, y'know? Everything. I would have given it all to you. Evelyn just took, but I would have gladly given everything to you."

At that moment, I was wishing he'd go ahead and push me over this cliff or put a bullet in me, whatever his plan was. I was so bone-freezing cold that anything was better than standing here listening to this lovesick drivel while my body and brain were going dead, inch by paralyzing inch.

Then as I stood waiting to die, I heard the same voice that had warned me not to go when I was back at the Langham Hotel in Pasadena. It was close to my ear, or even inside my head this time. The strange thing was, this voice wasn't a memory or a thought, it was a clear voice and it was speaking directly to me.

"Paige, you can take this guy," it said.

It was so real that I actually glanced behind me. There was nothing there but a snow-filled ravine that dropped down hundreds of feet.

"You can take him, Paige. Forget the pain. Just do it."

I know it's crazy. But that's what it said. And then, with the next sentence, I knew the voice was Chandler's.

"It's not your time yet," he whispered. *"You can take him, babe. You're at the twenty-mile mark, just like last year. Do it! You can make this finish line, too."*

It sounds nuts, I know, but it was him. He was talking about the Boston Marathon last year. By the twenty-mile mark, I was so spent I didn't think I could take another step. But I had. I had pushed myself beyond my endurance and had finished the race with my best time ever. Chandler was telling me to do the same thing now. Only this time my life depended on it.

"I loved you," Chick was saying, "but I can't go to jail. I can't pay for all this."

He raised the rifle and pointed it at me.

Without thinking, I lunged and grabbed for the gun with numb fingers. We struggled on the edge of the cliff. I yanked on the barrel, pulling the rifle toward me. The muzzle ended up buried in my stomach. Call it luck or fate, but for some reason the gun didn't fire. I shoved it aside. Chick and I fought on silently, two or three feet from the lip of the ravine.

With no feeling in my arms and legs, I wasn't doing much damage. But I managed to hang onto the gun, trying without luck to pull it out of his hands. I could smell his hot, sour breath on my cheek as we fought for control. But I was weakening rapidly. I was losing.

He finally wrested the rifle from my grasp and pushed me down at his feet. It was finally over. I had nothing left.

Then I heard the gun cock . . . the sharp ringing sound of steel against steel. Time slowed. I waited for him to fire. Waited for the end.

But Chandler wasn't finished. He wouldn't leave me alone. *"You can still win! Do it now, Paige. Do it!"*

Somehow, with strength I didn't know I had, I lunged at Chick, rolling and twisting as I dove, trying desperately to take his legs out from under him. At first it was like crashing up against two solid tree trunks. He didn't move at all. But then I sensed him tipping. His knees buckled and he fell forward over my body, landing on my ribcage. Pain shot through me.

Suddenly, Chick let out a panicked shriek and I felt him roll over my back. He hit the ground on the far side of me and I heard the snow crunch as he began to tumble. I was too spent to get to my feet or even look, but I heard him scream—loudly at first—but slowly the sound fell away from me until it stopped abruptly with a distant thud.

I struggled to get my arms under me, but nothing would work. Total numbness. I couldn't feel any of my extremities.

I finally managed to get into a sitting position and pulled myself to the edge of the cliff. There, fifty feet below, lit by a sliver of intermittent moonlight, I saw him. His arms and legs were sprawled out at bizarre angles. Chick had landed on a small ledge that stopped his fall halfway to the bottom. I couldn't tell if he was alive or dead.

"Chick?" I called out.

He didn't answer.

I knew I had to get on that snowmobile and get the hell out of there before hypothermia shut me down completely. I dragged myself over to the red Yamaha and tried to climb on. At first, I couldn't even pull myself up onto the seat, but I finally managed to roll onto the saddle and fumbled for the key, which was thankfully still in the ignition. Just then, I thought I heard a faint voice calling to me from far away.

I hesitated for a moment, wondering if it was really him, or the wind, or just my imagination. Should I go back? As it was, I'd be lucky to get to the cabin before I froze to death. If he was alive, the only way I could help him was to call mountain rescue, get somebody out here who could rappel down with a stretcher and get him off that cliff.

Then I heard him again. His plaintive wail was clear in the still night. "Paige! Paige, please don't leave me! I still love you!"

Right. I struggled to turn the ignition key. The snowmobile coughed to life. I pressed the hand throttle slowly, afraid my numb fingers would not work properly and I'd shoot the Yamaha out over the edge and fall to my own death. But it finally started moving. I managed a U-turn and headed back the way I'd come, leaving Chick behind.

Half a mile down Highway 38 I saw a snowplow approaching, its headlights cutting holes in the curtain of snow. I pulled alongside and told the man behind the wheel my problem. He helped me into the cab where it was warm. Then he bundled a blanket around me and radioed for help. I knew it was going to be up to me to lead the rescue team back to the spot where Chick was stranded.

An hour later, Emergency Services hoisted that sorry son-of-a-bitch up off the ledge where he had landed. Two broken legs, a broken right arm, a crushed elbow, and two fractured ribs. As they rushed him to the hospital he was howling in pain.

Not long after that I was sitting at the Bear Mountain Lodge in front of a fire, with my hands and feet wrapped in bandages. The paramedics assured me I wouldn't lose any fingers or toes.

I was celebrating that fact with a blended scotch when Bob Butler walked in along with LAPD detective Apollo Demetrius. When he wasn't able to reach me, Bob had called Chandler's parents, who told him where I was. He had arrived only four hours late. Not bad. If I'd played my hand more carefully and not foolishly let Chick see his letter, Bob might have actually made it up there in time to save me.

My sad, dogged detective just looked at me with those friendly gray eyes and carefully held my bandaged hand. He was my real hero in all this. He never gave up. He had finally proven that Chick Best killed Chandler. It had taken him more than half a year working weekends and nights, but Bob Butler solved my husband's murder, just like he promised he would. Between the two of us, we now had enough evidence to prove it.

A few days later in L.A., Chick confessed to Evelyn's murder as well. His status-heavy Cavalli jeans had been trumped by an orange prison jumpsuit.

The story went wide. All the national news outlets picked it up. "Killer of Chandler Heir Arrested."

Two weeks later Chick finally got his feature story in *People* magazine.

He made the cover.

CHICK

WHAT IS IT THEY ALWAYS SAY ABOUT REAL ESTATE?
It's Location—Location—Location.

That fact has come crashing home as I sit in my new residence, an eighteen-by-eighteen-foot square box on Death Row at California's Pelican Bay Prison.

The house on Elm had status. It had views of my perfectly landscaped yard. This little box I'm currently residing in has almost no view. The corridor that runs by my cell is less than inspiring. Concrete walls and two colored lines on the floor. The red line leads to the exercise yard, where I rarely go. The green marks what is known around here as The Last Mile. It's not a mile, however; it's more like fifty feet, but you get the idea. It leads to the execution chamber.

While the vistas in this place are far from great, the status attached to being a condemned man is a fucking head trip.

They treat you like a celebrity, which I guess I finally am. My time is short now. I have only a few days.

This morning I went for my last physical, because for some reason, the state of California doesn't want to kill me and then find out I have a toenail infection or bleeding hemorrhoids. All the way to my physical and back, the guards called out, "Dead man walking," which is a hell of a lot more respect than I got at bestmarket.com, where I actually was a dead man walking, but nobody had the decency to tell me until it was too late.

I'm sure after reading this, you fully realize that women have always been a huge problem for me, and the events of this journal plainly attest to that fact. I wouldn't be here in the first place if it weren't for a woman. Or two women, if you count Evelyn. Three, if you want to add in Melissa, who, by the way, is no longer a Best. She's a Sheridan now, taking her mother's maiden name.

I always wanted to impress women, and for most of my life, that need only produced a lot of disappointments, along with an occasional head slap.

But now that I can't do anything about it, I'm finally a big deal on the cock market. I get tons of mail from lonely, half-crazed females who want to talk to me. They want to hold my hand. They fantasize about having sex with me. Last week I got two proposals of marriage.

Who are these women? Are they hopeless losers, or is there perhaps a Twinkie cupcake or two in the mix? I've been writing them all back asking for pictures. Most, as you might expect, look like basketballs with ears, but some are what could be loosely described as normal-looking women. They write that they are lonely and want to add some excitement to their otherwise dull lives. The fantasy of screwing a serial killer seems to be just what they're after.

Oh yeah, that's what they call me now. According to the press I'm a serial killer. I looked that term up on the FBI website from the prison library. Technically, in order to qualify for that designation you have to kill three people. I only killed two, with a failed attempt on Paige, but the press, never ones to stand on technicalities, has dubbed me with the label anyway. Status and respect being my Achilles' heel, I've gone along with it because, as I said, being a serial killer makes me pretty damn special around here.

I'm trying to get ready to walk that last mile. Trying to get my courage up. But I really don't want to die. I still think there ought to be a way to cut a deal here. After all, looking at the two deaths I'm responsible for proportionally is almost nothing when compared with the ten people who died yesterday in California traffic accidents, or the hundreds last year in Iraq. Do I really need to shed blood over Chandler Ellis, who was a Boy Scout and a twit, or Evelyn, who was an adulterous whore?

I'm still praying for a reprieve from the governor, but if you saw our governor greasing off carloads of assholes without a second thought in those *Terminator* movies, you know there probably isn't much hope.

After coming to the end of this journal you may be wondering how I currently feel about Paige Ellis.

The truth is, I no longer feel anything. As a matter of fact, since the trial, I can barely remember what she looks like. I called her my goddess. I said she was put on earth to complete me, but now I think she was just a phase I went through to stifle my endless bouts with self-loathing and boredom.

So here I sit on my metal bunk with my asshole puckered, waiting for my final stroll. I've been told that my execution viewing chamber is sold out. Standing-room only. So, in death, I'm finally a hit. I'm going to try to go out like a starker, live up to my new bad-ass "serial killer" label. But something tells me when they roll up my sleeves and insert the needle, I'm going to snivel and whine, just like always.

We'll find out in two more days. I guess that's it. That's the whole enchilada. I've written my last page and it's time for my afternoon meeting with the prison chaplain, because, strange as it sounds, I've at long last found Jesus. I know, I know, pretty transparent and pathetic. I'm sure St. Peter won't be standing at the pearly gates with my white robe, wings, and a map of the celestial grounds.

But you never know. As P. T. Barnum said, "There's a sucker born every minute." A sentiment my bullshitting father certainly always endorsed.

And who knows? Maybe I'll get a few points for chutzpa.

CHAPTER

PAIGE

THE DAY CHICK WAS SCHEDULED TO DIE IT WAS
rainy and cold in Los Angeles. I'd moved here four years ago
to run Chandler's foundation. I had fifteen people working
for me and was well into my new life. I was happy, or at least
as happy as I allowed myself to be.

I woke up that morning feeling angry. I was angry because Chick's death was the final chapter of the worst event
of my life, and I knew that no matter how hard I tried to deny
it, this would be a day of vengeance for me. I wanted Chick
to die for what he did. I hated myself for it, but I had lost so
much, it was hard for me not to be vengeful.

I tried not to watch television, but I was drawn to it.
Finally, I was sitting in front of the tube, channel surfing,
hunting for stories about Chick's upcoming execution. On
several of the newscasts, there was B-roll of him being led

down a prison corridor. He had lost weight. He looked stoic. His eyes never came up toward the camera.

All day, I listened for Chandler's voice. Maybe he would reach out and find a way to talk to me today, the way he had at the hotel or on the cliff in Big Bear. Maybe he could ease all of this, take away my thirst for revenge, cut through all this self-destructive anger. I waited patiently, but his voice never came. He never whispered in my ear, never told me what to do.

I heard from Robert Butler instead. It was a card. On the front there was a yellow bird sitting on a tree limb with an olive branch in its mouth. Inside, it said:

GET WELL

Under that, he had written in his neat, careful hand:

> *Avenge not yourselves,*
> *but rather give place unto wrath:*
> *for it is written, Vengeance is mine;*
> *I will repay, saith the Lord.*
> *Romans 12:19*

THE PALLBEARERS
A Shane Scully Novel

By
Stephen J. Cannell

THEN

CHAPTER 1

IN 1976 AMERICA WAS JUST COMING OUT OF A depression called the Vietnam War, but back then I was still deep in the middle of mine. I was twelve years old, and boy, was I pissed.

It was early in May on that particular spring morning and I was huddled with some other children on Sunset Beach around 25th Street. We were staring out through a pre-dawn mist at the gray Pacific Ocean while consulting Walter Dix's old surf watch to time the AWP—the Average Wave Period of the incoming swells. Walt called swells "the Steeps."

The beach we were on was about fifteen miles from the Huntington House Group Home, which was in a rundown neighborhood in Harbor City a few minutes southeast of Carson. Excluding Walt, there were four of us, all gathered around him wearing beaver-tail wetsuits with the '70s-style long flap that wrapped around under your crotch and left your legs uncovered. We were his lifers. The yo-yos. The kids who kept getting thrown back. We all knew we would probably never get another chance at a foster family or adoption because we were too ugly or too flawed, or we had lousy county packages, having already been chosen too many times and then returned with bad write-ups.

But there were other reasons we didn't make it. We were an angry group. I held the Huntington House catch and release record, having just been sent back for the fifth time. My last foster family had called me incorrigible, unmanageable, and a liar. Probably all pretty accurate classifications.

The four of us had been specifically chosen for different reasons by Walter Dix for that morning's sunrise surf patrol. Of course we had all desperately wanted to be picked, but it wasn't lost on any of us that we'd earned the selection because of a variety of recent setbacks. Walt, who everyone called Pop, understood that even though we'd failed, it didn't mean we were failures. He also understood our anger, even if nobody else did. Pop was the executive director of Huntington House and was the closest thing to a father I'd ever known.

"Okay, Cowabungas. Good stuff. We're gonna bus 'em out big time," he said, glancing up from the watch to observe the incoming sets, speaking in that strange-sounding Hawaiian Pidgin that he sometimes used when we were surfing.

"We pack large dis morning. Catch us one big homaliah wave, stay out of de tumbler and it be all tits and gravy, bruddah."

He grinned, kneeling in the sand wearing board shorts, displaying the surfer knots on the top of his feet and knees—

little calcium deposits caused by a lifetime of paddling to catch up to what he called the Wall of Glass.

Pop was a tall, stringy, blue-eyed guy with long blonde hair that was just beginning to streak with gray. He was about fifty then, but he seemed much younger.

There was an Igloo cooler with juice and rolls in the sand before us, packed by Walt's wife, Elizabeth, for after surfing. We'd take our clean-up set at around seven thirty, come in and shower by the lifeguard station, eat, and change clothes in the van. Then we would pack up and Pop would drop us at school by eight thirty.

Walt had been born on the North Shore of Hawaii, which he said made him "Kamaaina to da max." His parents had taught school there, and he'd ended up in L.A. after the army. That was pretty much all I knew about him. I was too caught up with my own problems to worry about much else.

Because he'd been raised on the North Shore, Pop was a throwback surfer, what the Hawaiians called a logger. His stick was a nine-foot-long board with no fins and a square tail—very old school. On the nose, he had painted his own crescent symbol, an inch-high breaking curl with the words "Tap the Source" in script underneath. He said the source was that place in the center of the ocean where Kahuna, the god of the waves, made da big poundahs—double overhead haymakers with sphincter factor.

Other than a couple of Hawaiians and one or two Aussies, Walt was one of the few surfers left who could ride a rhino board. It was heavy in the nose and a bitch to stay up on. The rest of us had new polyurethane shorties with multiple skegs for stability. The boards and wetsuits belonged to the Huntington House group home and were only used for special occasions like this.

We were sad children whose dark records were cryptically defined in the terse, cold files kept by Child Protective Services. But our nicknames were much crueler than our histories because we bestowed them on each other.

Nine-year-old Theresa Rodriguez knelt beside me, holding her short board. She had been set on fire by her mother shortly after birth, but had miraculously survived. Terry was damaged goods, with an ugly, scarred face that looked like melted wax. Everyone knew Theresa was a lifer from the time County Welfare had first put her in Huntington House at the age of five. She was chosen for this morning's field trip because she had no friends and never got much of anything, except from Pop. We called her Scary Terry.

Also kneeling in the sand that morning was Leroy Corlet. Black, age eleven. Leroy's dad was in prison, his mother was dead—a heroin overdose. He had been sexually molested by the uncle he'd been sent to live with until a neighbor called child services and they took him away. We called him Boy Toy behind his back, but never to his face because Leroy wasn't right in the head anymore. He was a violent nut case who held grudges, and if you pissed him off, he'd sneak into your room in the middle of the night while you slept and beat you in the face with his shoe. He couldn't stand to be touched.

Pop had picked him that morning because he had just failed a special evaluation test at elementary school and was being held back for the second time in four years. He'd been sulking in his room for the last two days. Nobody wanted him either.

Next to Leroy was Khan Kashadarian, age fifteen, half-Armenian, half-Arab or Lebanese. He'd been abandoned at age ten and was living in an alley in West Hollywood when he was picked up and shoved into the welfare system. Khan was fat, and a bully. We had given him two nicknames: Sand Nigger and Five Finger Khan, because he stole anything you didn't keep locked up. I didn't know why Pop picked him to be with us. As far as I was concerned, we'd have all been better off if he was dead. Even though he was three years older and a hundred pounds heavier, I'd had six or seven violent fights with Khan and lost them all.

I was small back then, but I didn't take any shit. I was willing to step off with anybody at the slightest hint of insult. I didn't get along with anybody and had convinced myself that my five ex-foster families were a bunch of welfare crooks who were milking the system.

"No floatwalling," Pop said, his blue eyes twinkling.

Floatwalling was paddling out beyond the surf but never going for a wave, not to be confused with backwalling, which was acceptable behavior because you were treading water, waiting for the big one.

The sun peeked above the horizon, signaling that it was time for us to go out.

"Let's go catch some bruddahs!" Pop said.

We picked up our boards and started down toward the early morning break. I was fuming inside. I couldn't believe nobody wanted me, despite the fact that I insisted I didn't want or need anybody. Before we got to the water, Pop put out a hand and turned me toward him, as the others moved ahead. He lowered his voice and dropped the Hawaiian Pidgin.

"Get your chin up, guy. There's a place for you, Shane," he said softly. "Sometimes we have to wait to find out where we belong. Be patient."

I nodded, but said nothing.

"Until you get picked again, you've always got a place with me."

Then he flashed his big, warm smile and switched back to Pidgin, trying to get me to smile. "I always want you braddah. What's a matta you? Your face go all jam up. You no laugh no more haole boy?"

I glanced down at the sand and shuffled my feet. But I still didn't smile. I was too miserable.

"Come on then." Pop put a hand on my shoulder and led me toward the water.

I was Shane Scully, a name picked for me by strangers. No mom, no dad. No chance. I had nobody, but nobody messed with me either. My nickname around the group home was Duncan because I was the ultimate yo-yo.

All any of us had was Pop Dix. He was the only one who cared, the only one who ever noticed what we were going through and tried to make it better.

And yet we were all so self-involved and angry that, to the best of my knowledge, none of us had ever bothered to say thank you.

NOW

CHAPTER 2

"THIS HOTEL IS GONNA COST US A FORTUNE," I said, looking at the brochure of the beautiful Waikiki Hilton. The photo showed a huge structure right on the beach in Honolulu. "You sure you got us the full off-season discount?"

I called this question inside to my wife, Alexa, while sitting out in our backyard in Venice, holding a beer and warming my spot on one of our painted metal porch chairs. Our adopted marmalade cat, Franco, was curled up nearby. He looked like he was asleep, but he was faking. I could tell because he was subtly working his ears with every sound. Cat radar.

The colorful evening sky reflected an orange sunset in the flat, mirrored surface of the Venice Grand Canal. It was peaceful. I was feeling mellow.

Alexa came out of the sliding glass door wearing a skimpy string bikini. She looked unbelievably hot—beautiful figure, long legs, coal-black hair, with a model's high cheekbones under piercing aqua-blue eyes.

"Ta-da," she said, announcing herself with her own chord. She stood before me, modeling the bathing suit. "You like, mister? Want kissy-kissy?"

I grabbed her arm and pulled her down onto my lap.

"You are not wearing that in public. But get thee to the bedroom, wench." I grinned and nuzzled her behind the ear, as I picked her up to carry her inside.

"Put me down," she laughed. "We'll get to that later. I'm trying to pack."

We were leaving tomorrow for Hawaii. It was our annual two week LAPD-mandated vacation. I could hardly wait to get away. As usual, we'd timed our vacation periods to coincide and for fourteen glorious days, I'd have no homicides to investigate, no gruesome crime scene photos or forensic reports to study, no grieving families to console. Only acres of white sand and surf with my gorgeous wife in paradise.

Alexa had worked twelve-hour days for a week to get her office squared away so she could afford the time off. Alexa is a lieutenant and the acting commander of the Detective Division of the LAPD. She's about to make captain, and the job will be made permanent. That makes her technically my boss. I'm a D-3 working out of the elite homicide squad known as Homicide Special where we handle all of L.A.'s media-worthy, high-profile murders. It's a good gig, but I was feeling burned out and needed some time away.

"Put me down. That's a direct order," she said, faking her LAPD command voice.

"You can give the orders in that squirrel cage downtown, but at home it's best two out of three falls, and in that outfit, you're about to get pinned."

"You brute. Stop making promises and get to it, then." She kissed me.

I was trying to get the sliding glass door opened without dropping her. I barely made it, and lugged her across the carpet into the bedroom, which was littered with Alexa's resort outfits. It looked like a bomb had gone off in a clothing store. Bathing suits, shorts, and tops scattered everywhere.

"What the fuck happened in here?" I grinned and dropped her on the bed, then dove on top of her.

Sometimes I can't believe how lucky I am to have won her. I'm a scarred, scabrous piece of work with a nose that's been broken too many times and dark hair that never quite lays down. Alexa is so beautiful she takes my breath away. How I ended up with her is one of my life's major mysteries.

I reached for the string tie on her bikini, and she rolled right, laughing as I grabbed her arm to pull her back. Just then, the phone rang.

"If that's your office again, I'm gonna load up and clean out that entire floor of pussies you work with," I said, only half in jest.

The phone kept blasting us with electronic urgency. It was quickly ruining the moment. Alexa rolled off the bed and snatched it up.

"Yes?" Then she paused. "Who is this?" She hesitated. "Just a minute."

She turned toward me, covering the receiver with her palm. "You know somebody named Diamond Peterson?"

"No, but if she's related to Diamond Cutter, tell her she's killing her little brother."

"Stop bragging about your wood and take this," Alexa grinned, handing me the phone.

I sat on the side of the bed and put the receiver to my ear.

"Yes? This is Detective Scully."

"You're a police detective?" a female voice said with a slight ghetto accent. She sounded surprised.

"Who is this again?"

"Diamond Peterson. I'm calling from Huntington House Group Home."

The mention of the group home shot darkness through me. Memories of that part of my life were negative and confusing. I now only visit them occasionally in dreams.

"How can I help you, Miss Peterson?" I asked cautiously.

"It's about Walter Dix. Since you're in the police, I assume you've heard."

"Heard what? Is Pop okay?"

"Not hardly." She hesitated, let out a breath which sounded like a sigh, then plunged ahead. "Pop's dead."

A wave of overlapping feelings began cascading. When they settled, the emotion on top was guilt. I had left Walt and the group home in my rearview mirror decades ago. I had been studiously ignoring the man who had injected the only bit of positive energy into my life growing up—the man to whom I probably owed a large portion of my survival. Pop provided a thread of hope that had been all that was left when I hit rock bottom eight years ago.

Even during my lowest days, because of Pop, I clung to the belief that there was still some good in the world, despite the fact that by the time I reached my mid-thirties, I'd managed to find almost none.

It was hard to know the complete mixture of events that had finally led to my salvation. The easy ones to spot were Alexa and my now grown son, Chooch, who is attending USC on a football ride. But Pop was also there in a big way. He had somehow convinced me that it was possible to survive the horrible start where I was left unattended in a hospital waiting room, a nameless baby with no parents, and then shuffled off to a county infant orphanage.

Child Services had finally placed me at Huntington House at the age of five, but by then I was already starting to rot from the inside. It marked the beginning of a life of loneliness, which was only occasionally interrupted by a parade of strangers.

Once or twice a year I was forced to put on my best clothes and stand like a slave waiting to be purchased. "*This is Shane, he's seven years old. This is Shane, he's nine. This is Shane, he's twelve.*"

All the rejection, all the rage, Pop had seen me through it—the crinkly smile, the weird '70s surfer lingo, the sunrise surf patrols. "*Shane, there's a place for you. You have to be patient.*" All these years later, it turned out he'd been right.

But once I'd survived it, I'd turned my back on him. I'd moved on. It was too painful to go back there and revisit that part of my life, so I hadn't. I'd left Pop behind as surely as if I'd thrown him from a moving car.

The memory made me feel small as I stood in our bedroom scattered with Alexa's colorful clothing. I'd been getting ready to run off to paradise, but had just been pulled back with one sentence from a woman I didn't know.

"Dead?" I finally managed to say.

"Suicide. He went into his backyard yesterday and blew his head off with a shotgun."

Diamond Peterson was talking softly, trying to mute the devastating news with gentle tonality. It wasn't working. I knew from years of police work in homicide that there is no good way to deliver this kind of information.

My stomach did a turn. I felt my spirits plunge.

"I've been meaning to stop by and see him," I said. It was, of course, completely off the point and pretty much a huge lie.

"He left a note," she continued. "He wanted you to be one of his pallbearers."